NOTHING TO LOSE

'SUMMARY JUSTICE' SERIES - BOOK 5

THEO HARRIS

ALEMAR
PUBLICATIONS

Nothing to Lose
Book 5 of the 'Summary Justice' series

Edited by Linda Nagle
Cover art by Keith Johnston (Keith Draws Cover Art)

CONTENTS

PROLOGUE

Cathay Pacific CX251 from Hong Kong landed at Heathrow at 5.40am with fifteen Ghost Dragon triad gang members onboard. Three more Cathay Pacific flights followed later that day, along with two British Airways flights at Terminal 5. Each of the six flights carried a minimum of fifteen gangsters, one hundred in total. Their arrival did not go unnoticed by Border Force staff, who were diligent in checking their passports, visas, and other documentation.

'What is the nature of your visit?'

'Business.' The stock answer.

'What business is that?'

'We are here for the international security event at the ExCel Centre, at the request of our employers, Hurricane Security Solutions,' came the standard reply. The paperwork was in order and was also sponsored by judges, members of Parliament, senior police officers or other prominent businesses. All legitimate, all as it should be.

'Who am I to question a judge?' one of the Border Force assessors asked her supervisor.

'I checked online, and the security event is a large one and very popular, with hundreds of international exhibitors. I guess this company is doing something big this year, and as you pointed out, they all have the correct paperwork and sponsor letters from some impressive people. There's nothing for us here, let them pass through,' the supervisor said.

The men were all allowed through the Border Force controls and went straight_to arrivals, every one of them having travelled with one small carry-on case with just their essentials. A man with a placard waited for them. *Hurricane Security Solutions*, the sign read. The men were all directed to waiting coaches where they were whisked away to a yet-unknown location. They knew better than to ask questions and did what they were told.

The following day, a hundred more followed on similar flights, all with legitimate documentation, sponsorship and permissions. A small army of two hundred gangsters was now in place in London.

'That company must be doing well for them to bring so many staff over,' the Border Force supervisor murmured to her colleague.

'There's not much we can do if they've been given permission to be here, is there?' came the reply.

'I make that a couple of hundred that we're aware of,' the supervisor added. 'It's only a security convention, what the hell do they need so many for?'

'I wouldn't worry about it, boss, I'm sure there's a perfectly legitimate explanation.'

∾

THE COACHES TOOK the men to a huge warehouse next to the Ford Dagenham assembly site, which had seen many of its factories and buildings closed over the past decade, some having been demolished. The loss of jobs had been devastating to the local population. One particular warehouse, once used to store engines before they were exported, was now a food-and-drink distribution wholesaler to the Chinese community, supplying many of the restaurants, takeaway outlets, and supermarkets. It was a hugely prosperous business that was controlled strictly by the Ghost Dragons, who had maintained a stranglehold in the area for many years. Their share for keeping this and many other Chinese-owned businesses safe–by way of extortion–was very lucrative and they had expanded their operations over the years. Their operations were about to be taken to the next level, with their ambitious plans now going into overdrive. For those plans to work, they needed their newly arrived army.

Having planned for this day, the legitimate wing of the organisation had purchased a large number of new properties in the area, which had been built on the ashes of some of the demolished Ford buildings. They had secured a row of twelve houses in one new development along with a ten-storey block of flats in the same complex, with four three-bed flats on every floor, and which would now house the two-hundred-strong army that had arrived from Hong Kong.

They disembarked at the rear of the distribution warehouse, out of sight, and were ushered into a marquee that had been erected specifically for their visit. Once inside they were given refreshments and sent to a row of tables at the far end where they were greeted by ten seated men, each of whom had a list of twenty names that would make up their squad. From big boxes next to their chairs, the team leaders retrieved a small backpack for each of their men, containing a Glock G17 handgun loaded with seventeen rounds, two spare magazines containing a further seventeen rounds apiece, a wicked looking fourteen-inch watermelon knife— or *chopper,* as they liked to call it—and a basic mobile phone that had numbers pre-installed. Additionally, one member per squad was given an MP40 submachine gun and hundreds of spare rounds. The gun, a design originally used in the Second World War, was a trusted triad weapon and would prove devastating in the right hands. Catastrophic in the wrong ones.

The team leaders then took their teams to one side to introduce themselves and impart the instructions they had been told to give. The order was a very simple one.

'We have been waiting a long time for this. We are to prepare for war.'

1

'Honestly, I don't know what you were thinking of. It's a stupid name for a boat,' Trevor told Andy, as they continued with their long-overdue trip along the Thames.

'I think it's a great name. It's fun and it's relevant,' Andy replied defensively. 'What do you think, Kendra?'

'I think I should throw you both overboard, it's like listening to a couple of bickering school kids. When are we going to get to a pub, like you promised?'

'We can stop at the Isle of Dogs if you want something soon, otherwise it'll be a while until we pass through central London,' said Andy.

Kendra looked at him and started giggling–again.

'Seriously, why can't you just accept that I look the part?' he said, adjusting his new white captain's hat to a less jaunty angle.

'It looks silly, Andy, that's why I'm laughing.'

Having spent a couple of weeks on an intensive course, Andy was proficient enough to pilot the forty-six-foot motor cruiser with its powerful twin diesel engines. A gift from a grateful hacker who had made millions thanks to Andy's tip-off, the boat had been a source of amusement for Trevor and Kendra, especially when Andy hadn't a clue how to pilot her.

'You don't sail her,' he had found out, and had corrected them, 'you pilot her.'

'You think the boat is *she*?' Kendra had said, 'with an insulting name like *Soggy Bottom*? I think she'll drown you the first chance *she* gets.'

Taking them both out for the first time was supposed to have been an enjoyable, stress-free experience, but it was turning out to be yet another humorous adventure for the trio.

'Well, as long as you're laughing, I'll take that as a win,' Andy said, puffing his chest out proudly.

'I'm just pleased we're still afloat,' Trevor added, winking at his daughter conspiratorially.

'Keep it up and you can swim back,' Andy retorted. 'Now pass me a sandwich and keep an eye out for the pub.'

They snacked on cheese-and-cucumber sandwiches, accompanied with ginger beer, all provided by Andy, as they went along at a steady twelve knots, as required by law. The past few weeks had been more relaxing than they had been used to, so despite the banter, they were enjoying each other's company along with the lack of excitement that had prevailed recently.

'It's so much more relaxed on the river,' Trevor mused, 'as opposed to the hell that is London traffic, just a few hundred feet from here. I never really took notice, you know?'

'I think we take London for granted. Yes, there is a lot of nasty crap that goes on, and yes, there is too much traffic and too many rude people. But when you take a closer look there is so much more to this city, so much good that we don't appreciate as much as we should.'

'We complain a lot about it, but I bet we'd miss it like crazy if we were away for any length of time,' Andy said.

'Well, we're here and we're doing our little bit to try and keep it crap-free, so I for one will try not to complain as much,' Trevor replied.

'Hello, what's going on here then?' Andy said suddenly.

They were approaching the famous s-bend at the Isle of Dogs, with City Airport on their right and the huge ExCel Conference Centre just past it.

'That's a lot of security,' Trevor said, as they slowed down for the approaching yellow-and-blue liveried police boat, its blue light making it clear who they were. They noticed several other similar craft within a short distance, all seemingly keeping closer to the north side than the south, along with armed police officers patrolling on foot and in vehicles on the adjacent road.

'There must be something going on either at the airport or the conference centre,' Kendra added.

'Oh, I saw something about this on the news. It's an International Security conference, they have a pretty good turnout,' Andy said.

'I've been to a couple of those but I've never seen security like that,' Kendra replied, looking up at the police helicopter that was circling the conference hall high above.

'Apparently,' said Andy, 'the UK is signing a huge trade deal with Taiwan, not just for normal trade goods but also for the newest military and cyber tech that we've developed recently. The Chinese are really pissed off about it, hence the extra security.'

'That's understandable,' Kendra said, 'many of the

companies exhibiting there are Chinese, trying to garner more deals with the west, so they can't be too happy.'

'Like I said, hence the extra security.'

The patrol boat eyed them up for a few minutes before moving on to the next craft behind, seemingly happy with *Soggy Bottom.*

'How long 'til we get to the pub, Andy? I'm parched,' Trevor said, uninterested in the activity.

'It'll be a while yet, remember we can only do twelve knots and once we get to Wandsworth Bridge we have to slow down even more, to eight.'

'So tomorrow, then,' Trevor said, shaking his head.

'No, not tomorrow, it's not that bad. Maybe a couple more hours?'

'It may as well be tomorrow.'

'It's just as well that I brought some beer, then, isn't it?' Kendra announced, pulling out two bottles from a cool bag. She handed one to her dad and kept the other for herself.

'Sorry, Andy, you're not allowed,' she said, taking a long swig.

'Damned speed limit,' he replied, licking his lips. As tempted as he was, the training was fresh in his mind, and topmost in his thoughts were the fines dished out to those who broke the law.

'You should've bought a helicopter instead,' Trevor said, smiling and raising his bottle in a toast.

'Actually, that's not a bad idea,' Andy mused.

'No!' Kendra and Trevor both exclaimed.

~

Security inside the ExCel Centre was even more visible, with pairs of armed police officers stationed every fifty metres alongside hundreds of extra security staff. The Taiwanese delegation were accompanied by their own plain-clothed security personnel and shadowed by specialist police protection officers from the Metropolitan Police, who were employed to protect visiting heads of states or those clearly at risk of attack. The Taiwanese President rarely visited the UK, but such was the importance of the trade deal that her presence was necessary.

As the President and the Prime Minister sat facing the hundreds of press cameras arrayed in the vast room, surrounded by both delegations, the extensive leather-bound trade agreement was placed in front of each of them and the ceremonial signing commenced.

Hundreds of cameras clicked as the delegates signed the documents in front of them, before they were swapped over for them to do the same again. The camera flashes and clicks continued for several minutes as the signings were concluded, the pair standing and shaking hands warmly in front of the world's press.

One of the cameramen stood staring as his neighbours jostled amongst themselves to get the best possible shot. He wasn't there to take pictures but to witness the signing of the agreement, before reporting back to his handlers in Beijing.

And so it begins, he thought, continuing to stare at the show ahead.

'See? Aren't you glad you came now?' Andy said as they sat on the wooden benches in the pub garden, the parasols shading them from the midday sun. They had found a mooring alongside The Swan in Walton-on-Thames and were soon enjoying their gourmet meals with a bottle of chilled Pinot Grigio.

'I must admit, it took a long time to get here but I'm enjoying it very much,' Trevor replied, 'so thank you, Captain.' He raised his glass to Andy, who responded in kind.

'Thank you, Trevor, the pleasure is mine.'

'We've come a long way in the past year or so, haven't we?' Kendra added, raising her glass too. 'When you consider what we've gone through and what we've achieved, having this break to recharge our batteries is the very least we should be doing.'

'Hear, hear,' Trevor said, clinking her glass.

'Luckily for us, and for the criminal fraternity,' said Andy, 'things are nice and quiet at the moment. There's nothing we can get involved in at this time, so we may as well enjoy it while we can.'

As if on cue, Kendra's phone rang.

'You had to go and say that, didn't you?' Trevor scolded.

'It's Jill, I'd better take it,' Kendra said. 'How's it going, Jill? You know I'm not back for another three days, don't you?'

Andy and Trevor watched the colour drain from Kendra's face.

'What? When?' she said, her shock clear for all to see.

'What is it, love?' Trevor asked, sensing her growing discomfort.

'Jill, we're miles from home and will be back late tonight. I'll be in the office first thing tomorrow but if you hear anything in the meantime please call me, okay?'

She ended the call and sat staring at Andy.

'What is it?' he asked gently.

'Rick Watts has been kidnapped.'

Kendra was in the office early the following morning, having asked Jill to meet her there before the rest of the Special Crimes Unit came in. Jill was waiting as Kendra walked into the office, and a quick nod confirmed that they would be alone.

Jill stood as Kendra reached her desk and she could see that her colleague had been crying recently, her eyes still red and her mascara smudged. They hugged, with no words exchanged until they sat facing each other.

'What happened?' Kendra asked, holding Jill's hand.

'We're not quite sure yet, but we think Rick was grabbed off the street when he was on the way back from the gym.'

'Rick went to the gym?'

'He was training for that stupid annual fitness check that we all have to do, remember?'

'Damn thing, they're threatening to move people now if they don't pass, so it doesn't surprise me.'

'He loves this unit, K, he would have done anything to stay on it, so I'm not surprised. What I am surprised about is why they would take him.'

'Are there any clues as to why? Has he pissed anyone off recently?'

'He's pissed off a lot of people recently, or should I say *we've* pissed them off with the successes we've had,' Jill said, rubbing her temple to ease the headache she hadn't been able to get rid of.

'Yeah, but most of those bastards are inside, there must be a way to narrow it down somehow,' Kendra said. 'Can you think of anyone that would use Rick as leverage for anything? They must have kidnapped him for a reason.'

'It could be any number of things, K. It may be to distract us from a current case or to stop us from closing in. Or it could be a past case they want revenge for. Or it could be they want someone sprung from prison. I could go on.'

'What was the last confirmed location, do we have that, at least? Maybe we can check CCTV or canvas the locals to find out if they saw anything,' Kendra added.

'His wife told me about the gym, which is in Chigwell, ironically near the Metropolitan Police sports club. Other than that, we haven't received anything back by pinging his phone and we can't find his car, either.'

'Who's running the investigation?'

'That in itself is a concern: it's the NCA,' Jill said.

The team had recently had a run-in with a pair of detectives from the National Crime Agency who had resigned before they were sacked for gross misconduct. It had not been a good experience for any of them.

'At least the douchebag and his sidekick aren't there anymore, maybe it will be a more pleasant experience,' Kendra said. 'Who's running it?'

'A Detective Sergeant Jim Adair and his colleague, Detective Sergeant Jon Sisterson. They seemed like a decent pair, just doing their jobs but telling us to stay out of it for now.'

'Why would they say that?'

'In case it's something to do with a current investigation,

they don't want anything to mess it up,' Jill replied. 'We have to do something, Kendra, it's Rick!'

'I know, Jill, and I agree. But we need to keep this very quiet otherwise we could end up in the shit, okay? Let me have a think on what we can do to help.'

'Thanks, Kendra. You can count Pablo in, too, if we need help.'

'I wouldn't have it any other way, you guys are inseparable now.' Kendra smiled.

'This is messed up, nothing like this has ever happened before. Something tells me that we've stepped on some very dangerous toes, Kendra.'

'You may be right. I'm going to make a quick phone call and I'll be back in a few minutes,' Kendra said, leaving her colleague. She had to go and update Andy, as every second counted.

≈

'What are they saying?' Andy asked.

'They don't even know where he was taken from, let alone why,' Kendra replied, clearly frustrated.

'What can I do?'

'If I send you his phone number and car registration, will you be able to pinpoint his last known locations?'

'I'll certainly give it a go. If he was anywhere near a CCTV camera then Cyclops will find him pretty quickly.'

Cyclops had proven a very useful–albeit illegal—way of tracking vehicles or people on CCTV by hacking the systems and utilising the existing software. Andy had used it to great effect in most of the cases they had dealt with recently, and it had proven invaluable so far.

'Great, I'll text you the info. Can you update Dad? I need to go back to work, and I'll probably be here for a while.'

'Sure thing, K. Let me know if there's anything else I can do.'

'The NCA are involved and they've tied our hands, so we need to find ways to help without them knowing it was us. If you can think of anything please let me know. I'll call you later.'

'Bye, Kendra. Take care,' Andy said, ending the call.

Trevor had told them both that he'd be at the boxing club all day, helping the twins, Mo and Amir, get things back to some semblance of normality since the death of his great friend and mentor, Charlie, at the hands of the Albanian gang leader. The youngsters had been badly affected by his death, and the twins had volunteered to help get the place going again.

When Andy called, he could hear that Trevor was out of breath.

'Have you been running, old man?' he asked, knowing he'd get a reaction.

'Less of the *old*, peg-leg. You should try it some time, you won't get out of breath running a hundred feet like you did last time.'

'I don't need to run, I have you to do that. But that's not why I'm calling, I wanted to update you on what's happening at the police station.'

'Come on, out with it, I have another couple of pounds I want to lose.'

Andy repeated what Kendra had told him. Trevor had surprised him with his tactical knowledge and then when it was revealed that he had once been an undercover operative in the British army it had all become clear. He was good at strategy because he'd had the very best training and experience.

'Alright, thanks for that. Let me know if your checks come up with anything. Are you working from home or the factory?'

'I'll be at home. I don't like the smell of fresh paint, so I want to wait a bit until I go back. There's not a lot going on there, other than the redecorating, anyway.'

'Okay, I may pop over later this evening, we can have a brainstorming session when Kendra gets off work.'

'That would be great. I'll make us a nice chilli con carne.'

'As long as it doesn't burn like the last one, we'll be good,' Trevor said. 'I'll see you later.'

As soon as Trevor ended the call, Andy was at the computer logging on to Cyclops. Kendra's text had come through with Rick's car registration number, so Andy started by gaining illegal access to the London Borough of Redbridge CCTV control room, using the trusted method of back-door entry via the weakest part of the system, the older existing cameras. The David Lloyd gym was in Chigwell and Andy started with cameras around the area of the gym that was council-run. On a separate computer, he accessed the CCTV covering the gym grounds themselves, via the gym's security office. Both systems had been upgraded in the past two years, now utilising programmes that allowed for a historic search capability.

Once Andy had input the car registration number, the search took less than a minute to give results on both systems.

'That's my girl,' Andy said out loud, patting his computer. He printed the results and called Kendra.

'Can you talk?'

'Hang on,' she said, 'let me go outside.'

When she was in the yard downstairs and free to speak, she said, 'Go ahead, what did you find?'

'He was at the gym yesterday, like his wife said. I have the car arriving at six-forty-five and him entering the gym. He was there until eight-twenty, which was when he got back in his car and left.'

'So, there's nothing untoward at the gym?'

'No. I wanted you to know that I'll now start searching the route back to his house. It will take a while but at least you know it didn't happen at the gym. Can you get me his home address?'

'Yes, I know where he lives. I'll send a text. Thanks, Andy.'

The text arrived within thirty seconds, so Andy mapped the route to Rick's house and resumed tapping away at the keyboard with Cyclops.

'That's strange,' he mumbled, 'why did he turn right instead of left?'

It took thirty minutes, but he finally found where Rick had driven to. He called Kendra back.

'Andy, that was quick. Tell me you found something.'

'I checked the route to his house, but he didn't go that way, he went somewhere completely different,' Andy said.

'Where?'

'He lives near Fairlop Waters, which would be a left turn out of the gym, but for some reason he turned right and drove to Chingford, in the opposite direction.'

'Where in Chingford?' Kendra asked.

'He drove into the car park of Chingford Golf Course,

which is where I lost sight because there are no cameras there. He didn't leave the car park so whatever happened must have done so there.'

'Shit, so someone must have called him to meet there knowing there were no cameras, knowing it's an ideal place to grab someone at night when it's empty,' she said.

'Well, they're not as clever as they think, K, because I hacked into the surrounding systems and I have a good idea about what happened.'

'Go on.'

'Thirty-five minutes before Rick drove into the car park, a white Transit van drove in there. Again, nobody walked out so I can only assume they stayed there to wait for Rick. Four minutes after Rick drove in, the van drove back out and turned right towards Waltham Abbey. I think Rick was in that van, Kendra.'

'I have to find a way of leading the investigator to the car park first, to see if Rick's car is still there,' she told him. 'What else did you find?'

'I have the van number which I need you to do a PNC check on, but I have a feeling it will come back to a hire company. Once I have the details I can dig deeper. Also, I checked the footage back at the gym and saw that the van had been there, parked up, when Rick turned up for his session.'

'So, they knew his routine and waited for him, knowing he would be coming from there to the meeting,' she added.

'Correct. And that's what's deeply worrying, K. Rick must have either known who called him, or trusted them. Is there any way you can get his phone records?'

'I don't know, Andy, the NCA are playing it tough and

telling us to stay clear, like I said. We're gonna struggle to get anything out of them.'

'Are they based at the station?' he asked.

'Yes, they've set up an incident room especially for the investigation, but nobody from the team will be allowed anywhere near the paperwork without arousing suspicion,' she said.

'Don't you have anyone who can help you?'

'Actually, I do,' she said, 'I'll call you later. Thanks again, honey bunch.' She ended the call quickly.

'That's ok... *honey bunch?*' Andy said to himself, bemused. 'Is that a good thing?'

～

2

A t the rear of the Chinese wholesaler premises, the activity had started early in the morning as the triad army gathered, ready to be briefed. The ten teams lined up behind their team leaders and waited patiently, with each team having been assigned two vans to transport them to their destinations. The men were all disciplined and ready, knowing that some of them would not be coming back. It was what they had trained for, what they were waiting for, and exactly what they wanted. The quiet murmur of their talking stopped immediately as a group of five men walked into the warehouse. Three of the men were senior triad leaders and the other two were of western appearance.

The men stopped in front of the small army and looked at the men, nodding appreciatively at their demeanour.

'You are ready,' one of the triad leaders said. 'As the Dragon Head I have gathered you here to tell you that from this moment you will listen to the men that stand beside me. Deputy Dragon Head and Assistant Dragon Head are in charge of this operation on my behalf. The two westerners are allies, you will refer to them as Red Master and Blue Master. If anyone disobeys any order, you will be killed on the spot. Is that clear?'

'*Shi!*' was the immediate response from the soldiers.

'Red Master will tell you your orders. Listen carefully, for we are here to change this country and make our enemies pay. Do I make myself clear?'

'*Shi!*'

The leader turned and nodded to the closest westerner, the one he had referred to as the Red Master. He wore a smart navy-blue suit, a crisp white shirt with no tie, and well-polished black designer shoes. His slicked-back hair hid the growing bald patch at the crown. The man stepped forward and paused as he regarded the men before speaking.

'You have been selected for your skills, not only as soldiers but because you have mastered the English language. This will be very important in your roles here, for not only will you be required to vanquish your foes, but you will also be required to extract information from them. It is vital we know everything about their operations before we dispatch them, nothing must be left to chance. Do I make myself clear?'

'*Shi!*'

'Wonderful. If only everyone obeyed orders like you. Your orders for tonight are very simple. We will give each team leader an address and you will go to that address, quietly and covertly, where you will crush your enemies. But not before you find out everything that we need. I have provided each team leader with a list of questions that need answering, such as names, contact numbers, bank information, that kind of thing. Do not come back without that information. Am I clear?'

'*Shi!*'

The Red Master turned to his colleague, now known as the Blue Master, and smiled, nodding in appreciation.

'These guys are exactly what we need, Dave, how can we possibly fail?' he said.

'You'll get no argument from me, Eddie, they're fricking amazing.'

The Red Master turned to the Dragon Head.

'Sir, this is a very impressive group of men you have. I think we will have very few problems tonight,' he told the man.

'As long as you meet your end of the bargain and keep the police and the authorities off our backs then you will be very rich men,' the triad leader replied.

'Sir, as much as we love money, this is not what we are after. It's the cherry on the cake that is made of power and vengeance,' Red Master said.

'Then order the men to do your bidding, Red Master.'

The westerner turned back to the men, pausing for a few seconds to enjoy the sensation that came with being in charge of a powerful group.

'You have your orders, men. Now go and cause havoc, just do it discreetly,' he said, smiling.

'*Shi!*'

The team leaders turned to their men and shouted orders. Seconds later the men turned in unison and trotted to their respected vans. Within two minutes all twenty vans were loaded and had driven from the rear of the complex, unseen. East London would never be the same again.

Eddie Duckmore turned to Dave Critchley, his loyal part-

ner, both ex-detectives in the National Crime Unit, both
enemies of Rick Watts and the SCU—and of Kendra March.

'It's good to be back, Dave. It's good to be back,' Duckmore said, rubbing his hands together. 'Now, let's go and
speak to our old friend, Rick Watts.'

Rick Watts was in bad shape. The bruising to his ribs was
bad enough but the lump on his head was giving him a
permanent headache that was making him grimace every few
seconds. He had known something was wrong as soon as
he'd stepped out of his car and walked over to the waiting
van. He had answered the earlier phone call, despite it
coming from an unknown number, because it was common
in most police units to withhold numbers. When he had
answered, he'd spoken to a known source at the NCA, so he'd
had no reason to distrust the man. As he approached the van,
he could not see his source, just a smiling Asian man in the
driver's seat. He stopped, alarm bells ringing.

The two men that had sneaked up from behind had
wasted no time and before he even knew of their presence it
was too late for Rick to put up much of a fight. He was struck
viciously on the head by a lump of wood before being kicked
repeatedly whilst he was on the ground, curled up and trying
to fend off the blows.

It took a few minutes, but his attackers were soon drag-
ging him into the back of the van, where he received more
blows to his head and body. The attackers forced him down
and tied his hands behind his back, one of them eventually

sitting on him to keep him from thrashing any more. A final kick to the head stopped his struggles as he blacked out.

'Enough!' the team leader told his men, 'Red Master wants him alive, so if you also want to live then stop kicking him and let's go.'

When Rick eventually woke, he was tied to a chair in a small, dark, windowless room, like a police cell from a hundred years ago. It was cold and damp and he knew he was in big trouble. His captors had used handcuffs to secure him to the chair, so as much as he tried to get free it was to no avail. The pain was incessant, and he was exhausted, so his struggles did not last long. He sat in silence, his head slumped, his eyes closed, as he tried to think of a reason why he was in this predicament.

I guess I pissed off one person too many, he thought.

The door suddenly opened wide, and light streamed into his cell and temporarily blinded him. When his eyes adjusted, he looked up and saw three men standing before him, one unknown Asian man and two familiar faces he had hoped never to see again.

'Well, if it isn't my old mates Duckmore and Critchley, or should I say Dumb and Dumber,' he said, his dry mouth making his voice sound raspy and faint. 'Have you come to rescue me? Oh, wait, you're not good cops anymore, are you?'

'Still smug, even when you're tied up like a hog waiting for us to decide your fate. I'll give you that, Watts, you're a brave son of a bitch,' Duckmore said, laughing.

'What do you want, Duckmore? Are you still pissed at me for what I said? Did it upset you?' Watts asked.

'What, you think that threatening to punch my lights out upset me? You have it all wrong, mate. Tell you the truth, you did us both a favour by grassing us up. We quit before we were kicked out, yes, but we've landed on our feet in a very big way, and it's all thanks to you.'

'You mean that being a bent ex-cop has made you a bunch of money? Good for you, but that just makes you a bigger piece of shit than you were before,' Watts replied.

Critchley, who hadn't spoken yet, stepped forward and punched Watts in the ribs, the same ones he'd been kicked in earlier and which were probably cracked. He grunted in pain.

'That's for all the shit you put us through, Watts,' his attacker hissed.

'Easy, tiger,' Duckmore said, 'we need him alive, remember?'

It took a minute before Watts could recover from the blow.

'I'll ask again, what the hell do you want?' he asked, gritting his teeth.

'What we want is information, Detective Sergeant. We want to know what you can tell us about our old friend Brodie Dabbs, and we want to know about your team and how the hell you managed to find out about the Albanian gang and those other arseholes you've been putting away so successfully. Nobody else has had that much success, and I want to know how,' Duckmore said, leaning forward to look Watts in the eye.

'Seriously? You think I'll just tell you everything you want to know because you haven't got a bloody clue how good police detectives work? What, are you worried we know something about you and your mates at Hurricane Solutions? Oops, I've said too much already.' Watts remembered that the two ex-detectives had been recruited by the company after they had quit, and had mentioned it in the hope that it would stall them from doing whatever they were planning to do to him.

Duckmore and Critchley exchanged a look, their faces grim, surprised Watts had that information.

Critchley punched him again, this time in the face, striking the right side of his already aching jaw. He stared back at his captors, despite the pain.

'What else do you know?' Duckmore asked.

'I know that whatever you're planning isn't going to work out for you. You won't get away with it,' Watts growled, spitting out blood.

'Well, we'll see about that, won't we? Let's see what a few days without food or drink will do to a man like you, shall we?'

Watts laughed out as loudly as his raspy voice would allow.

'You're still as stupid as ever. The weaker I get, the less likely I'll be able to talk. Didn't they teach you anything at detective training school?'

'This is a waste of time,' said Duckworth, 'let him rot in here, we have better things to do. Let's go, Dave, the docks await us with an abundance of wealth.'

Giving Rick a contemptuous gaze, he turned and stormed out, quickly followed by Critchley, who gave one last menacing look before slamming the door shut.

'Wankers,' Watts said, his head slumping back down to his chest as the pain continued.

$\approx$

'It must be important if you're buying me a coffee and a doughnut,' Gerrardo Salla told Kendra as they sat in the canteen.

Gerrardo had always been very fond of Kendra and had even asked her out once. Despite the anticipated rebuttal, they had become good friends and regularly confided in each other, particularly when it came to office politics.

'I need a favour, Gerrardo. We've been told to back off from the investigation into Rick's kidnapping, but I think I have found a possible lead to finding his captors. Can you help me out by doing a PNC check? I don't want any trace of me on the system if they decide to check later.'

'Is it a genuine lead?' he asked, looking around and lowering his voice.

'Yes, it is. I know you're all scared of him, but Rick is a good friend and looks after us all, so if there's anything we can do to help find him then I'll take the chance and try and find out what I can. What do you reckon, can you help?'

Gerrardo smiled and nodded.

'Of course I'll help. What's the number?'

Kendra handed him a piece of paper with the registration number on it.

'I'm guessing it's a rental van, but anything you can get to me will be useful,' she said.

'No problem, leave it to me. Now, do you want to share this delicious doughnut?'

'Does a bear shit in the woods? Carve it up, and don't be tight about it,' she said.

~

'Kendra, did you manage to find anything?' Andy asked.

Gerrardo had been true to his word and had conducted the check on the van's registration.

'I have,' she said. 'The van comes back to a rental company in Barking: Besthire Vans.'

'That's original. Okay, leave it with me. Hopefully their computer systems are as uninspiring as their name,' Andy said.

'Let me know if you get anything and I'll catch up with you later,' Kendra replied.

'Will do, catch you later, honey... oh, she's gone. Okay, then.'

Andy set aside his embarrassment and searched the internet for anything he could find on Besthire Vans. When he had saved the information he'd found, including owner-ship details, office address, contact information and their website, he prepared an email to send to them requesting a quote, coming from a bogus company that he had created and which was untraceable. The email included a virus that would be triggered once opened by the recipient, which would then infect their computer systems and allow Andy to have access–without anyone ever knowing.

It took several hours to receive the expected response, and a further thirty minutes for Andy to gain access.

'Yep, I was right. A shambles, just like their name,' he said out loud.

He spent the next hour trawling through the folders on their computers, searching for the van and any clues that would lead them to the hirer.

'Well, that was both interesting and illuminating,' he said, when he called Kendra.

'What are you talking about? Come on, Andy, we don't have time to mess around, what did you find?' she asked tersely.

'Okay, okay, don't bite my head off. What I found was that the van was hired by a company based in Dagenham. What was interesting was that it was one of twenty similar vans that they hired on the same day a week ago.'

'That's a lot of vans,' said Kendra. 'What is the company and what do they do?'

'That was the interesting part. There is no such company that exists physically, no premises or staff or anything I could find. They're registered with Companies House and their accounts are all seemingly in order, but they don't actually seem to do a lot. It's like a legitimate holding company with the purpose to deflect attention from others, whether domestic or overseas,' he said.

'What does that even mean?'

'It's like they exist simply to facilitate third party transactions that look like legitimate transactions with other companies but which are actually a smoke screen to something dodgy, like allowing overseas companies to move funds more easily and pay less tax. Whether it's a tax scam or more, I don't know yet, but I'll keep looking.'

'So, we have nothing, no address or any people to check on?' she asked, disappointed.

'I didn't say that. I told you what they've put in place to make it hard for the real owners to be traced, but I didn't say I hadn't found them.' He smirked.

'Seriously?'

'Alright, sorry. Okay, when they hired the vans, they went to great lengths to hide who the vans were really for, hence this weird set-up. What they didn't account for was that those vans need refuelling regularly, and that's where they've been less clever.'

'Go on.'

'I checked local council CCTV and found that three of the vans fuelled up within the last couple of days, and they all used the same company's debit card.'

'That's great, Andy! Which company and what have you found?'

'The bank cards are registered to a company in Dagenham, a Chinese wholesaler called Golden Dragon Foods. They supply food products and drinks to the Chinese restaurants around the southeast of England. It's a very successful and lucrative company.'

'How the hell are they involved in Rick's kidnapping? None of this makes any sense,' Kendra said. 'Andy, can you please brief my dad and I'll catch up with you both later. We need to make some plans, so if you can have a think in the meantime and maybe do some more research, that would be great.'

'Will do, I'll see you later,' he replied. Seconds later his hands were dancing over the keyboard as he searched deeper for anything about Golden Dragon Foods.

'I know you're hiding something, so out with it, time is short,' he said out loud.

～

3

The vans arrived at their assigned destinations; the signal would not be given until all vans were in place, allowing them to attack simultaneously and prevent any warnings being sent. Duckmore and Critchley had researched Brodie Dabbs' organisation well and still had access to confidential records that well-connected ex-police officers could get, however corrupt they were.

Brodie Dabbs was an ally—of sorts—of Trevor's, and had helped provide manpower when they had taken on their first mission, the removal of the vicious Qupi gang. As a result, Dabbs had benefitted by gaining the operations that had been abandoned by Qupi, including brothels and money-laundering operations. His organisation was now the biggest in east London and there were few opponents to challenge him.

Duckmore's plan was simple but ambitious. His stint for the National Crime Agency had given him plenty of intelligence when it came to the main criminal gangs in the country, including the likes of Brodie Dabbs' operations and the secretive Ghost Dragons. Knowing he would eventually be kicked out of the police, he had put a plan in place, with the help of his sidekick Dave Critchley, to ensure their futures. He aimed high and saw very quickly that taking the one main gang out of action in east London would allow him to take control of their lucrative operations. In order to achieve his goals, he also realised that he needed an ally, which was when he had contacted the triads.

What Duckmore didn't know was that the Ghost Dragons had another partner, one he would never find out about–the Ministry of State Security, the official name of Chinese intelligence. MSS were informed of the officer's approach and immediately saw opportunities to take care of a major concern involving the UK and also expand their growing operation there, an operation that had brought them great success from an intelligence perspective.

MSS, under the guise of the Ghost Dragons, had made a deal with Duckmore to help pave the way for him to take over Brodie Dabbs' operations, in return for helping them expand their own operations in south-east England. This would involve partnering with Duckmore–once he'd taken over—in increased criminal activities. It was a simple but effective plan that would allow MSS to grow their operations significantly, increase their intelligence capabilities, and as a bonus make a ton of money with their criminal activities. It was a win-win scenario for them with the added bonus of anonymity, as Duckmore would be the one attracting attention. The extra special bonus was the disruption it would cause to the country, something that MSS were very keen on, as payback for the UK collaborating with Taiwan the way they were doing.

As a result there were now twenty vans parked at twenty

different locations, including business premises, home addresses, and the cornerstone of Dabbs' operations: the brothels and the money exchange bureaus. They didn't have to wait long before the signal was given by the Red Master, who had received messages from all ten team leaders that they were in position and ready. Each location had been carefully reconnoitred; it was important that the attackers were in and out quickly at locations where they would be seen by the public and other witnesses. At those locations they were ordered to bring one person back with them, due to the lack of time on scene to retrieve everything they wanted. At the more remote locations where it was unlikely they'd be seen, they would have more time to interrogate Dabbs' staff and take what they needed.

'Go, go, go!' was the order from the team leaders as the triads disembarked from the rear of the vans. The soldiers, happy to be free from their confines, quickly approached and then expertly forced entry into the premises they'd been assigned. The brothels gave no resistance as they had no meaningful protection. The money exchange bureaus were more difficult and had to be threatened with guns to prevent staff pressing the alarm. The security doors were quickly opened, again upon the threat of being shot through the obligatory gap in the security screen. All available money, bank cards, and other useful financial information was taken from the safe and the person in charge was frog-marched to the waiting van. They were in and out in less than five minutes.

Staff at two private gambling clubs resisted, where armed guards were on scene and exchanged fire with the attackers. They had none of the experience or training of the triads, though, and were quickly overcome. Three of the guards were shot dead and two badly wounded, along with seven gamblers who couldn't get out of the firing line quickly enough, two of whom were killed instantly. Money, cards, and anything else useful were taken quickly and the person in charge taken from each club.

Five private homes were also attacked, including Brodie Dabbs'. Shots were exchanged at Dabbs' house and one other, where one of his deputies was injured. Dabbs himself resisted hard, exchanging fire for several minutes before he was attacked from behind and clubbed unconscious. He was taken away and dragged down the staircase as his wife screamed for help. One of the triads, holding his arm where a bullet had grazed it, slapped her in the face hard enough for her to fall to the ground, silent. She whimpered but avoided eye contact, knowing it could mean her death.

Within the space of just twenty-five minutes, Brodie Dabbs' empire, which had taken decades to grow, was in tatters and rudderless—much like a head taken from a snake. The prisoners were taken back to Dagenham where secure rooms had been set aside for their interrogation. Duckmore wanted to bleed the organisation dry and demanded every drop of information needed for the absolute control of the gang.

It would not be long before he was in complete control.

Dabbs was woken again by a bucket of water thrown in

his face, now heavily bruised courtesy of the beating he'd taken. He had chosen to resist, which had been a big mistake, as his captors were ruthless, patient, and very effective at garnering information.

'Wakey, wakey, Brodie,' Duckmore said, leaning down to show his face to the gang leader.

'Who the hell are you?' Dabbs asked, confused.

'Never mind that. Sorry about the beatings; I told him to be respectful, but he chose to ignore me. Bad torturer!' He wagged his finger mockingly at the smiling torturer, his leather apron covered in splotches of blood and other fluids, left on purpose, much as pilots marked their kills on their fuselage during the war.

'Why am I here?' Dabbs asked.

'Well, seeing as we're being respectful, I'll come straight to the point. This is a ceremonial handover, of sorts,' said Duckmore.

'What the hell are you talking about?'

'What I'm talking about, Mister Dabbs, is that your reign as king of east London has come to an end. You are clearly no longer in charge and your organisation is in chaos. Now, you can choose to abdicate and help me take over nice and smoothly, or you can continue to resist and endure more pain than you have ever felt in your long and fruitful life. It is entirely up to you, respectfully,' Duckmore said, placing a hand on his chest mockingly.

Brodie Dabbs looked into the cold eyes of a man who was clearly a psychopath. Duckmore held his gaze, challenging his prisoner, almost wanting him to resist. Dabbs spat a mouthful of blood at the floor, his ears ringing, his head hurting, and his resistance draining away.

'You'll kill me whatever happens, so why should I help you?' he eventually asked.

'You can take my word that one of two things may or may not happen if you agree to help. I will either let you live, or I will kill you quickly. Either way, you'll be free,' Duckmore replied.

'I may as well resist then, eh? If I'm gonna die anyway, I may as well have some of that pain you're promising so I can live longer. What do you say?' Dabbs laughed.

'What I say is this. If you choose to resist, then yes, you will endure a world of pain. What I didn't mention is that you will not be alone. I will bring all your people, one at a time, and have them tortured and eventually killed in front of you. I have more than a dozen here, all ready to go. It'll take weeks if not months, which is a lot of torture and pain. And I will leave your lovely wife for last. What do you say now?'

Dabbs knew he was beaten.

'Bastard,' he said, spitting out more blood. 'I want assurances that my wife will not be hurt.'

'On that, you have my word. I'll allow you a call so that she can pack and disappear somewhere nice and safe. Do we have a deal?'

Dabbs' resistance was broken. It was time to hand over the reins.

'We have a deal.'

'Wow!' Duckmore said, 'I expected a lot more resistance, Mister Dabbs. I guess it really is time for change, eh? I tell you what, I'm in a generous mood so I'm not going to kill you just yet. Call your wife and tell her to get out of town today and I'll send you to one of our nicer establishments to serve out your sentence, maybe get you to do some consultancy work for us as we take over other territories. It'd be a shame to get rid of someone with so many contacts and so much knowledge of the London underworld, wouldn't it?'

Dabbs could only nod his head in agreement. Duckmore was going to have his pound of flesh.

4

Iris Aviation, a leading manufacturer of military drones, supplied the British Army, Navy, and Air Force along with a dozen approved overseas partner countries. Their cutting-edge technology allowed the drones to fly stealthily and deploy advanced munitions remotely with no risk to personnel, with devastating effects. They were particularly lethal against ships and land-based vehicles, where the victims would only learn they were under attack in the split seconds they had to live after the munitions had struck them.Their state-of-the-art factory in Rainham, Essex, not too far from Dagenham, had been completed just the year before on the strength of their recent orders from overseas customers, including Taiwan, who had ordered one hundred of their newest and most advanced models, an order worth more than two billion pounds. It was a huge order designed to send a clear message to China that Taiwan was more than ready to meet their current and future threats.

Security at the factory was excellent; tall fences with razor-wire surrounded the ten-acre property. Advanced

CCTV cameras and sensors covered the entire grounds. Security personnel were present twenty-four hours a day, most of them monitoring the camera feeds and other detection systems from the new and advanced security office next to the factory.

Unfortunately, they had elected to install Chinese-made CCTV cameras and sensors and software, which the Chinese intelligence services were easily able to access, monitor, and disrupt the feeds. The company had elected to use the systems in place based on their advanced software and easily upgradeable cameras, not heeding warnings from government agencies that overseas technology was subject to tampering. They simply hadn't believed the rumours and remained unconcerned. And tonight, they would pay a heavy price.

At precisely two o'clock in the morning, when the factory was in darkness and a skeleton crew of just four security officers were playing gin rummy in their office instead of monitoring the feeds, the tampering kicked in. They were fully engrossed in their game and did not notice the faint glitch in the feeds that lasted just half a second. It was at this precise moment that the Chinese intelligence agents clambered effortlessly over the fencing, using a rubber car mat to protect themselves from the razor wiring. Within seconds the four agents, each carrying a backpack, were lost in the shadows as they went to carry out the pre-planned tasks. A fifth agent stood watch at the other side of the fence from the comfort of his van, ready to give warning at a second's notice.

Fifteen minutes later, the four agents were back over the fence and in the van with their colleague, who used his mobile phone to call his handler in Beijing.

'Phase one is complete,' he said, and ended the call.

Fifteen minutes later the CCTV camera feeds returned to the control of the security office where the guards continued with their game, oblivious to any wrongdoing.

Two hours later, the explosions started.

By the time the fire brigade arrived, the damage was done. By the time they put out the fire, there was nothing left.

$\sim$

Trevor, Andy and Kendra sat in the small factory canteen enjoying an early morning cup of coffee as they discussed the recent developments.

'Any news since last night?' Trevor asked.

'Not really. The wholesaler is a legitimate business that rakes in millions of pounds in profit each year. There's only a handful of similar companies that supply all the Chinese takeaways and restaurants, it's like they have a shared monopoly,' Andy replied.

'I'm guessing the triads have something to do with that,' Kendra added. 'I've dealt with them before and they are very protective of their own, trust me. They don't mix well with others, so we don't get to hear much because it's all kept in-house.'

'So we have no idea why they'd want to kidnap Rick?' Trevor asked.

'Nope. I'll be checking through Rick's old cases to see if he's had any dealings with them in the past, but honestly, I can't remember a thing in all the years I've known him,' Kendra replied.

'Well, I guess we'll have to do some digging around

ourselves, then,' Trevor said. 'Maybe we should go and take a look at this place for ourselves.'

'We need to be careful, Dad, they have eyes everywhere so if we're going to do anything then we need to be ultra cautious.'

'We have some toys we can use, remember?' Andy added. 'Mabel and Tim are more than up for the job.'

Mabel and Tim were Andy's drones, which the team had used to great effect recently. Tim was the smallest available military-grade drone used for spying and intelligence gathering. Not much longer than Andy's index finger, it could fly silently and undetected into places no other drone could, and was equipped with an infra-red camera as well as the regular high-resolution version.

'Every time you mention your toys, I can't help but thank the criminals that paid for them so generously,' Trevor said, laughing. 'It's like a ritual for me and cleanses my soul.'

'In their defence, they paid far more than that for their crimes,' said Kendra, with a smile.

'Well, both drones are ready for their next mission, so we need to find somewhere close enough to deploy one of them without being seen,' Andy said. 'I'll do some digging when I'm in front of a computer and we can have a look tonight.'

'I'll warn the twins, they can take you and look after you while you're flying the drone,' Kendra added.

'Thanks, but make sure to get them some snacks, otherwise Amir won't stop whining,' he replied.

'How are the repairs coming along?' Trevor asked, changing the subject. He was referring to the factory, which had needed plenty of fixing since the attack by the Albanian gang.

'They're almost done, just finishing up with some painting. The blast-proof doors are both installed now, they look just like any normal doors but are bomb- and bullet-proof. The CCTV system and servers have been moved to a secure room, with access restricted at reception. I've also had a few new cameras installed to cover the blind spots we found during the attack, and hidden a couple more on the approaches. It'll be a lot harder to get in, next time,' Andy replied.

'Great, that was a tough lesson or two. The factory held up well, but these changes are a big improvement and we've learned those lessons well.'

'Hopefully there won't be a next time,' Kendra said, 'one attack in our lifetime is more than enough.'

'Best not take any chances though, eh?' Trevor said, 'and thanks to our friends, we have more than enough money to spend on improvements.'

'Agreed,' Andy said, 'and from what I've seen with the Sherwood Solutions accounts, the company has started making decent money now, which is great for the team.'

Sherwood Solutions was now a fully functioning security consultancy that employed the youngsters from Trevor's boxing clubs, along with their colleagues from Walsall, who they were training in various security-related roles. Trevor's ambitious plans to rehabilitate some of the youngsters with boxing training was now extended to what was fast becoming a lucrative business with excellent career prospects for them all. They had even purchased properties for them to live in, which made working for the company a very attractive long-term career path.

'Yeah, I'm well chuffed with how well it's going. Mo has turned out to be a natural salesman, he recently signed up one of the tech companies to work with their cyber-security division. It's worth almost a million quid to us. I might buy him an ice cream as a thank you,' Trevor said.

'That's very generous of you,' Andy said, nodding exag-geratedly. 'I must work harder so that I too will earn such a reward.'

'Stop taking the piss and start planning for tonight, Andy, or I'll make sure Amir has no snacks. You know what'll happen then, don't you?' Kendra said mischievously.

'Yes, ma'am, I'm on my way,' Andy replied, taking his coffee as he left.

'You've got him wrapped around your finger, haven't you, love?' Trevor said, nodding approvingly.

'It's a game we're playing, Dad. You know nothing is happening between us, but at least we can have some banter. Otherwise, we'd go nuts.'

'Yeah, well, don't forget that you have a life, too; you weren't put on this planet to spend all your time going after bad people. Go and have some fun sometimes, take Andy with you, otherwise you may regret it later.'

'We'll see,' she said, standing. 'I'm going to head back to work. I need to find a way of getting some of the information we've managed to find to the right people, see if we can speed things up a little.'

'Drive safe, love. And remember, we'll be taking a look at that place tonight, so don't give too much away too soon, okay?'

'Trust me, Dad, I know what I'm doing.' Kendra waved as she walked away.

Trevor sat in the canteen alone, looking around and nodding to himself.

'It's a good thing, what we're doing.'

When Kendra arrived for her shift, she made a cup of coffee and greeted her colleagues as she made her way to her desk, where she worked alongside Jillian Petrou.

'How's it going, Jill? What have I missed?'

'Not a lot, K. We've hit a bit of a roadblock. Nobody saw Rick leave the gym and there's only CCTV footage from the gym security office of him arriving and leaving–alone. Nobody saw him anywhere near his home address, and his wife didn't mention any other meeting he may have had. His car is still missing, so where the hell did he go when he left the bloody gym?'

'You've got contacts at the local council, haven't you? You should check with them to see if there's any CCTV footage from the roads surrounding the gym. He may have been distracted or received a call. Did you check his phone records?' Kendra tried to guide her friend into some decisions that would help track Rick down.

'There's nothing that stands out in his phone records. He received a call from an unknown number, but we have no idea if it's connected,' Jill said, clearly frustrated with the lack of progress.

'Jill, if I were you, and there's nothing to work with, then maybe you should assume that the call was involved. Getting some council CCTV footage would be a start, you never know what they may have picked up.'

'Yeah, maybe you're right. I'm not happy with all this, K, doing things on the quiet like this. I'll call my mate at the council and ask a favour. Thing is, what do I do if I find something?'

'You'll find a way of getting it in front of those NCA investigators, that's what. I know you're more than sneaky enough to do that.' Kendra smiled at her friend.

Jill's expression changed to one more mischievous.

'You know who's sneakier than me?' she asked, looking around to make sure nobody was watching.

'Who?'

'Pablo, that's who! He may come across as shy and retiring and butter-wouldn't-melt, but I tell you that man is as sneaky and fiendish as they come—in a bloody marvellous way,' she whispered.

Kendra laughed.

'Seriously, I don't want to know what games you two are up to. If you think Pablo can pull it off, then you should recruit him on the double. I need to go and wash my face now, and hope I can get the image of the two of you out of my head.'

Two hours later, Jill returned to her desk looking very pleased with herself.

'You look like the cat who got all the milk and all the cream!' Kendra laughed.

'Ssh, we're not supposed to be doing anything, remember?' Jill replied, sitting at her desk.

'Go on, then, don't keep me in suspense,' Kendra urged.

'I did what you suggested and called my friend at the local council. I lied a little and told her I was looking for a driver who had left the gym after assaulting a woman. She hates wife beaters, so she agreed to help. I know where Rick's car is, Kendra. It's at the Chingford Golf Course car park. It got there shortly after he left the gym so he must have gone straight there.'

'That's great, Jill, great job!' Kendra said, 'did you get Pablo to do his thing?'

'I did. He went to the NCA officers and told them he'd received an anonymous tip from one of his dodgy informants, who told him he'd seen Rick go into his golf club. Pablo told the NCA that the informant had phoned him about something unrelated and because he knew Rick, he had a go at Pablo, thinking he'd sent Rick there to spy on him.'

'And they bought it?'

'They did. They've dispatched a local unit to secure the vehicle for forensic testing,' said Jill.

'Well, it's a start, isn't it?' Kendra said. 'Hopefully it will lead to something else.'

'There's more! When she told me about Rick's car, I asked her to check the feed to see if he'd walked out of the car park. But he hadn't, which means someone must have taken him from there, where there were no cameras to record it. I asked her to go back and see if there were any vehicles that went in before and after him, and there was only one–a white Transit van.'

'Bloody hell, you have a registration number?'

'I do,' said Jill. 'Thing is, we haven't passed this to the NCA otherwise they'd know we were looking into it. All they have is the location of the car. I'm hoping they're switched on enough to check the council CCTV covering the car park.'

'I'm sure they will, Jill. If not, then find a way to give a gentle nudge. In the meantime, is there anything else we can do? It feels wrong just sitting here doing nothing, doesn't it?'

'It does, but I can't make those investigators out, K. One of
them is trying, to be fair to him. Jim Adair has tried
conversing with the team, bringing biscuits, trying small talk,
that sort of thing. He even came in wearing a Norwich City
football shirt one day, which was a little odd. He seems the
nicer of the two. The other bloke, Jon Sisterson, is the quiet,
moody type, and doesn't seem as approachable. He hasn't
made much of an effort with anyone yet. I don't know either
of them well enough to take a chance and piss them off, not
yet anyway.'

'Ah, the ol' good cop/bad cop routine. Fair enough. I'll
have a think on how we can help without helping, if that
makes sense. There's not a lot else going on, so they can't
expect us to sit on our arses doing nothing, surely.'

'Let's have a scrum down later. In the meantime, I'm going
to go and tease Pablo a little. He surprises me more and more
each day, that man.' Jill walked off with a flourish, leaving
Kendra behind, laughing.

Whist alone, Kendra quickly sent a message to Andy and
Trevor, giving them a heads-up.

'*They know where the car is but nothing about the van yet.
Should be ok for tonight.*'

'*Good work, K. See ya later,*' Andy replied.

'*I'll be there too, love,*' said Trevor.

She smiled, thinking of Andy's face when he saw Trevor's
text, which was clearly designed to spoil his evening.

Like a couple of thirteen-year-olds, honestly, she thought.

∽

5

It had been another long but fruitful day for Christine Marlowe. As the Minister for International Trade, she had successfully overseen several international trade deals in the past few months, leading to billions of pounds worth of business for the UK. The deal she had been most proud of was the one with Taiwan. It wasn't the biggest deal she had signed, but it was the most satisfying.

Christine Marlowe was a staunch feminist, fiercely protective of women's rights. She despised any form of bullying or misogyny, something she felt was very apparent with the tensions in the South China sea. Signing the deals with Taiwan had given the island a better chance of defending itself against attack, which she was immensely proud of.

Upon leaving her office at the Old Admiralty Building, she entered the taxi that was waiting to take her to her big, terraced house in Islington, where her husband and two teenage girls would be waiting for her so they could cook dinner together, a weekly ritual she always looked forward to.

'Driver, please drop me at the end of Chapel Market, I need to pop into Marks and Spencer. If you can wait a few minutes, I won't be long,' she said.

'Yes, ma'am. I may be moved along by traffic wardens, so if I'm not here when you get back, I'll be just a minute getting back to you,' the driver said.

'That's fine, thank you,' she replied. The taxi firm used by the department was vetted and trusted, so she knew she was in good hands.

The food hall in Marks and Spencer was a favourite of hers, and she knew the ingredients would be fresh and of good quality. It took just a few minutes to pick them out and pay for them, filling two plastic carrier bags. She made her way to the exit and saw the taxi had indeed been moved on. She stood by the edge of the kerb, the shopping bags now on the ground, and waited for the car to return. She looked for it and saw only one vehicle, a white van, driving at speed from the junction of Liverpool Road.

She shook her head disapprovingly at the Asian driver who was smiling as he approached her. Christine did not notice the man behind her and could not stop herself from falling forward when that man had given her a gentle nudge in the back. The van struck her at forty-three miles per hour, flinging her into the air like a rag doll. She struck the windscreen on her way up, the screen cracking from the blow. The impact threw her up and to the edge of the pavement, where she landed heavily on her back, her head striking the tarmac hard. The last thing she heard before she lost consciousness was a woman screaming and the van revving its engine as it sped away from the scene.

DUCKMORE'S 'GUESTS' were escorted into the warehouse by the triads and shown towards a long table where their personal possessions were. They stood by the table, looking around fearfully and waiting for the inevitable lethal attack. Duckmore laughed and spread his arms out wide in a strangely welcoming gesture.

'Please, don't worry. And yes, they are your personal things. I've switched off your phones for now, for obvious reasons, but everything we took from your person is still there, I promise,' he said, crossing his heart theatrically.

'So... you're letting us go?' one brave man asked.

'I don't see why not. It was never my intention to harm any of you,' Duckmore replied genially.

Half the prisoners looked down, not wanting to challenge his comment by showing their cuts and bruises. It didn't go unnoticed.

'Oh, come on, if I wanted to kill you, I would have done so straight away. A few bruises were necessary for me to make sure you got here in one piece; don't you see that?'

'What about the guards at the club?' another brave soul asked, 'and the two guests that were shot?'

'Listen, I don't have time to argue with you. My people had strict instructions, not to shoot unless they were being shot at. Your people started firing first, simple. Now, do you want to hear my proposal or not? Because I'm losing my patience.'

The silence was accompanied by several prisoners nodding.

'Good. This is my offer, it is non-negotiable, so I suggest that you consider your responses very carefully. Brodie Dabbs is no longer your boss, I am. You can either stay and carry on working for me, or you can take your chances against my soldiers. For staying and working for me, I will double whatever Dabbs has been paying you and I will make sure you benefit greatly from what we are about to do. How does that sound?' The arms spread out again and the smile returned.

'Double?' the first man said.

'Yes, sir, double. And there will be much, much more to come later, I assure you,' Duckmore replied.

The prisoners looked at each other and started smiling and nodding, surprised by the sudden turn of events.

'So, do we have a deal?' Duckmore asked.

'Yes!' came the emphatic response.

Brodie Dabbs' head slumped to his chest when he heard the response. Duckmore had placed him behind a screen so that he could hear everything. So that he could hear his empire finally taken from him. So that he could hear his people, the people that had stood by him for so long, now turn their backs on him—for money.

Duckmore hadn't finished.

'I'm very happy to hear that, we have much to do and not a lot of time to do it in. When you go back, it is likely that the police will want to ask you lots of questions as to your where-abouts and your health. Anyone who tells them what we are doing will be considered traitorous scum and a bounty placed on their head. You will tell the police that it was a case of mistaken identity and that you were not kidnapped or harmed in any way, that you went voluntarily. Think of some-thing else, if you want, but stop any investigation from happening, do we understand each other? They can't do anything without victims or witnesses.'

The nods were unanimous.

They were now Duckmore's people, his gang, and

London was in big trouble. Brodie Dabbs knew this more than anyone as he was escorted out of the warehouse to a waiting car, where he would be taken somewhere more comfortable and put to work.

Andy drove his cherished camper van, which he had lovingly nicknamed Marge, whenever he could. He did not trust anyone else to drive her, especially after the damage caused when Mo used her as a battering ram to break through metal shutters to rescue Kendra. Andy would have done the same but was left feeling sorry for his much-loved van and had made sure she'd been repaired well.

'Honestly, you're never gonna forgive me, are you?' Mo asked as they neared the destination, 'even though you told me to do it.'

'I do forgive you, Mo, of course I do. I just don't want anyone else hurting my baby again, that's all,' he said, smiling.

'Well, that's pretty shitty of you. She was a lot of fun to drive, and you should share the love,' Mo replied.

'I think you're both nuts,' Amir piped up, in between chewing on his favourite toffees. 'Give me a car any day, or a pickup, that'll do me. Not a house on wheels, how can you see any fun in driving this thing?' he asked his brother.

'It wasn't the driving, bro, it was the ramming. It was awesome!' Mo replied.

'You can ram something with a car, too, you know,' Amir added.

'Yeah, but this beauty is a beast, and it was the most fun I've ever had in a motor... ever.'

'Alright, we're here,' Andy suddenly said, glad to cut the conversation short. He parked in a quiet side road amongst other vehicles, far enough away from the warehouse they had come to check over. It was late enough that there were no passing pedestrians or traffic and the road they were in was not likely to see much of either until the morning. They were close to the river Thames, close enough to hear the water lapping against the sea defences.

Andy prepared Mabel, the palm-sized drone, for its mission to fly over the warehouse with its infra-red camera. It would highlight how many people were there at this time of the evening and so give the team something to work with when it came to planning future operations.

'Okay, same as before, guys. When I put my headset on, I won't be able to see where I'm walking, so make sure you hold on to me and put me back inside the van, okay?' Andy said.

'No problem, Andy, Amir will hold on nice and tight, won't you, bro?' Mo said, smiling at his brother.

'I'll try not to give you a wedgie, Andy,' Amir replied.

'Please do try. Now, if you're both ready, here we go,' Andy said. He had placed Mabel on the landing pad where it would take off and then land after its mission was complete. He started the motors and Mabel flew upwards silently, reaching the three hundred feet that Andy had selected as its optimum ceiling. As it hovered, he lowered the VR headset into place, giving him an immersive experience as the drone flew into position. Towards the warehouse.

'Okay, you can move me now,' he said, as he was in control and comfortable with the approach.

'Here we go,' Amir said, grabbing Andy's belt and guiding him slowly towards Marge. 'You're by the steps, lift your foot,' he added.

'Hang on, Amir,' Andy suddenly exclaimed, 'something's wrong. Something is interfering with the signal to the drone. Shit!'

'What is it?' Mo asked, confused.

'They must be using counter-drone technology to jam the signal. I'm bringing her back before the jammer works completely,' he replied.

It took only a minute before Mabel landed safely on the landing pad. Andy removed the headset and breathed a sigh of relief.

'That was close,' he said, sitting on the step, 'another ten metres and we would've lost her.'

'What do you mean? What just happened?' Amir asked, just as confused as his brother.

'I think they're using a jammer that prevents the signal from the remote control from reaching the drone. If that signal is lost then the drone will either drop down vertically, potentially crashing, or, as programmed in this case, it would return to where it took off. Because I caught it in time I could bring her back safely, I didn't want to take any chances,' Andy replied.

'Well, that's a bummer. What do we do now?' Amir asked.

'I know exactly what we're going to do,' Andy said, determined, 'we're going to send Tim to do the job instead.'

Tim was the much smaller, finger-sized military drone that was Andy's pride and joy.

'But you just said they're using a jammer, aren't you worried that Tim will crash instead?' Mo asked.

'No, because I'm going to pre-programme his route. That

way it will fly autonomously and there won't be a signal to jam. It will fly a pre-programmed route and then return.'

'You can do that?' Amir asked.

'Yes, I can, Amir. It takes longer but if it means my little friend will return safely then I'm happy to do the work,' Andy replied.

'Okay, then. We'll just chill out for a bit while you do that,' Mo said, shrugging his shoulders. Andy laughed.

'Relax, guys. It'll take me literally ten minutes,' he said. He sat down at one of the terminals in the rear of the van and started typing away.

Almost six minutes later, he was done.

'Right,' he said, bringing the tiny drone with him and placing it on the landing pad, 'let's try that again, shall we?'

As the flight path was pre-programmed, Andy didn't need to use the headset. He started the motors and pressed the button that activated the flight path. Tim rose silently to two hundred feet, which Andy believed was ideal for the tiny drone and this mission. It was quickly out of sight and earshot and the three men sat in the back of the van, watching the monitor.

'He'll be there in thirty seconds,' Andy said, pointing to the monitor as Tim approached its destination.

'It's not very clear,' Amir said, 'is it supposed to be that blurry?'

'That's the infra-red camera. We need to check and see how many people are in there and their heat signatures will show up clearly,' Andy replied.

'Ah, okay. And will it just fly over the warehouse and come back?'

'I've programmed it so that it flies a zig-zag pattern that will cover the entire plot, just in case they have any other outbuildings. Once it has completed that pattern it will return to us.'

'There's some people now,' Mo said, pointing, as Tim started his zig-zagging. The drone was over the main warehouse, which was now closed to the public. They could clearly see five strong heat signatures moving around inside, workers restocking shelves or preparing the next day's orders. There were also two other signatures of people in static positions covering the front entrance and the rear shutters.

'Those two are probably the security guards,' Amir said.

Tim was covering the ground quickly, so they were able to see more within a few moments.

'They look like very lazy workers or someone that doesn't belong there,' Andy said, pointing to four men sitting around a table in an adjoining warehouse space not accessible to the public.

'What are they doing, do you think? Could they be security staff?' Mo asked.

'Maybe, why would you need more than two guards to cover a food supplier? It doesn't add up,' Andy said.

'Maybe they're guarding that person there,' Amir suddenly exclaimed, pointing to a solitary and stationary heat signature in a small room close to where the four men were sitting. The heat signature suggested it was a person sitting in a chair and slumped over, probably tied to the chair and either sleeping or unconscious.

'Shit, that could be Rick,' Andy said. He hadn't expected this, so he was unprepared.

'That's gonna be a tough ask, getting him out of there,' Amir said, shaking his head.

'I'll call Kendra,' Andy said, unlocking his phone and dialling.

'How's my favourite bionic man?' Kendra replied, referring to Andy's prosthetic foot that had allowed him to be
more mobile.

'As much as I'd like to answer that, I have something more
important. I think we've found Rick, Kendra. The drone
picked up a single heat signature in a small room that looks
like a cell being guarded by four bad men,' he replied.

'Shit, does he look like he's okay?'

'Not really, he's likely tied to a chair and unconscious. We
need a plan to get him out so I thought I'd ring you to see if
you or Trevor could assist. I've got the twins here, but I think
we need more, it's a well-guarded building.'

'Okay, let me speak with Dad. Send me some info and I'll
call back as soon as I have something.' Kendra ended the call.

'So, what do we do now?' Mo asked.

'We sit and wait, and hope they come up with something
clever enough to lure eleven potential baddies away from that
room so that we can go in and rescue Rick.'

Kendra met Trevor and the rest of the team at the factory.
As soon as she'd put the phone down on Andy, she called
everyone and told them of the urgency. Within thirty minutes
they were all there.

'Andy and the twins are parked close by and think that
Rick is being held captive in the Chinese distributor's warehouse. It appears he is being guarded by six security
personnel and there are also five members of staff on the
adjoining premises,' she told them all.

'So, we need to deal with six security men, there's no need to involve the staff next door,' Trevor added.

'Can't we just gas them or taser them like we normally do?' Darren asked. He and his five colleagues from Walsall were now nicely settled in flats provided by the team. Along with their adventures against criminals, the team were also being trained as security specialists for the thriving business Trevor had set up there.

'I'm not sure that'll work as effectively this time, Darren,' Trevor said. 'I reckon the four security personnel guarding Rick may be armed, so we need to plan for that, just in case.'

'The first thing we have to do is make sure our plan is a quick one, in and out in minutes so that they won't have time to react and get more help,' Kendra said. 'Which will mean a really good diversion, followed by really quick entry at the rear, which will also be our exit point.'

'So, we'll need to take care of the single guard at the rear shutters, right?' Charmaine asked.

'Yes. According to Andy the place is fenced all around, but it isn't anything we can't climb easily. Getting Rick out will be a problem, though, he could be in bad shape,' Kendra said.

'Can I make a suggestion?' Jimmy looked to his Walsall mates for support.

'Go ahead, Jimmy,' said Trevor.

'If one person can climb the fence and take care of that single guard, the rest can then join up and go for Rick; if we left two or three behind to sort the exit point, maybe they can cut the fence while Rick is being rescued. What do you think?'

'Simple but effective,' Trevor said, 'I like your style, young man.'

'It's a gift, what can I say? I learned from the best.'

'Why, thank you,' said Trevor.

'I meant Frazer, but you're cool, too,' Jimmy replied, to much laughter.

'I guess I asked for that,' Trevor said, laughing along with the others.

'Okay, so who's doing what?' Charmaine asked.

'Well, I can't think of anyone better to deal with the security guard at the rear than you, Charmaine,' Trevor said. 'Fancy the job?'

'Hell, yes!' she replied.

'Darren, can you take your group in to deal with the four men inside?' Trevor continued.

'Consider it done.'

'I'll stay behind and sort the fence out with Zoe, Greg and Danny. We'll take some bolt cutters with us for that.' Trevor regarded his small team, who nodded back.

'Remember, guys and gals, these people are likely armed, so make sure you take your vests and other gear, okay? Stay safe, whatever happens,' Kendra added.

'Let's go, people!' Trevor shouted, rousing the team into action.

Kendra and Trevor stayed behind for a few minutes.

'You know what this means, don't you, love?' he said, once the team had dispersed.

'I do. It means that by rescuing Rick, we reveal ourselves and risk the entire operation.'

'Are you okay with that?'

'It's not ideal, Dad, but his life is important so I'm willing to risk it.'

Trevor nodded and gave her a hug.

'Then let's go and rescue your friend.'

'I'll stay here,' she said, 'I don't think it will be a good idea for him to see me too soon. I'll call with updates as and when they come in.'

'Okay, love, see you later.'

Five minutes later, three cars left the factory, en route to Dagenham and potentially the most dangerous armed criminals they would ever encounter.

6

'What are we supposed to do while they're rescuing Rick?' Mo asked, when they had been briefed by Kendra, who was already halfway through the twenty-minute journey to the warehouse.

'We'll keep an eye out in case there's more of them,' Andy added, 'just in case. We're their backup.'

'Typical, missing out on all the fun,' Amir added.

'You have more than enough fun for all of us, Amir, so stop pouting and put your protective gear on, just in case,' Andy replied.

'I know, but it would be boring if I didn't complain every now and again, wouldn't it?' the young twin said, smiling, as he put his protective vest on. 'So how do you want to do this?'

'I think I'll stay here and send Tim up again. I can programme him to hover while the team do their thing,' Andy said, 'but you two can go on foot and check the area out, it may help later.'

'Consider it done,' Amir said, quickly making his way out of the van before Andy changed his mind.

'I'll call when things start happening,' Andy told Mo as he left.

'Lock the door behind us,' Mo said, 'it's a bit rough around here.'

'Yep, so it is,' Andy said out loud as he settled down to programme his little drone again.

$\sim$

Rayburn Technologies was one of the leading defence companies in Britain. Having supplied a variety of missile systems to the British Army and other friendly countries including Australia, Canada, Poland and Sweden, they were a leading candidate to fulfil the procurement of advanced anti-aircraft defence systems for Taiwan.

The *Steel Defender* system that had eventually been chosen was comparable to any leading system in the world, defending the skies against missile and aircraft attack with an unmatched success rate. The three-billion-pound contract that was awarded was a boost for the company and the promises of more sales later encouraged a close relationship.

It was for this reason that they were targeted by the Chinese agents that had destroyed Iris Aviation's factory recently. The same crew parked close to the Rayburn factory that had been working through the nights to fulfil its bursting order books. At two in the morning the whirring of machinery could still be heard, albeit faintly, by the menacing agents who were hell-bent on destroying another factory responsible for making their enemies stronger.

As with Iris Aviation and most advanced CCTV systems, they were manufactured in China and susceptible to covert hacking by the intelligence agency that had sent its agents to disrupt the trade deal. It was a simple task to show no changes on the monitors that were currently being looked at by two security guards in the purpose-built control room. As soon as the feeds were disrupted the Chinese agents were given the signal to move in.

The three agents that had climbed the wall at Iris Aviation did so again, making easy work of the twelve-foot fence, despite its razor wire. Within seconds they had disappeared into the shadows, their bulging backpacks holding the explosives that would destroy their target.

They were confident of success.

They had not researched the factory as well as they thought and so missed Tom and Jerry, the two very well-trained Alsatians that had heard and smelled the intruders as they went over the fence. Luckily for the Chinese infiltrators, their handler was fast asleep in the control room. Unluckily for the intruders it meant that when Tom and Jerry attacked, they did so very quickly, only barking ferociously as they approached within thirty feet of the two unfortunate agents they first encountered. Both dogs snapped at the intruders, who, well-trained as they were, managed to fend them off with powerful kicks. This angered the dogs as they attacked again, meeting the same response and resistance. They backed off and continued their barking, which was likely to attract the attention of the security guards inside.

The intruders stayed calm and continued to keep the dogs at bay, before deciding that they did not have the luxury of time to deal with the dogs as well as complete their mission. Knowing that their remaining colleague was still undetected gave them a small measure of comfort as they quickly retreated towards the fence. They did so by walking backwards and facing the dangerous dogs, wary of the canine guards and that they'd be climbing over the fence and its razor wire with no protection, which had been left at their entry point.

As soon as they reached the fence they quickly turned and began to climb. The dogs, sensing their chance, moved quickly and each grabbed an ankle as the agents tried to make good their escape. It took several kicks to the snouts for the dogs to release them. They then had to navigate the razor wire which proved to be just as painful, both agents receiving multiple wounds.

The whole thing lasted just a couple of minutes. As the dogs continued to bark at the rapidly retreating invaders, their colleague had planted the explosives and left via the entry point, removing the plastic mat that protected him from the wire. The mission had not gone to plan but at least some damage would be done.

They were all back in their van within minutes and away from the area, bloodied by the dogs and the razor wire, but safe.

'Damn those hellhounds,' one of the agents said as he tried to stem the flow of blood from his ankle.

'I can't stop the bleeding,' said his equally savaged partner. 'Hand me the first-aid kit.'

'Did you complete the mission?' asked the driver as he handed the small kit to him.

'Partly, my explosives are in place, but it won't be enough

to destroy the whole factory,' said the successful—and pain-free—agent.

'I will let them know,' the driver said, dialling his handler. 'Phase three partially complete, total destruction not guaranteed.'

The C4 exploded as planned, two hours later. The destruction was not as complete as it had been at the Iris Aviation factory, but caused enough damage that it would need to be closed for several months for repairs, delaying production of the Steel Defender orders. It was still a damaging setback.

Due to the hacking of the Rayburn Technologies CCTV systems, nobody would ever learn of the heroic and valiant attempts by Tom and Jerry to see off the intruders. They would never find out that had it not been for the dogs, the entire factory would have been levelled.

The Chinese agents would be more thorough with their research next time.

The team arrived and parked up two streets away, waiting for the signal from Andy that it was safe to move in. The roads were quiet at this time of the night and there was no passing foot traffic anywhere near the warehouse.

'I've sent Mo and Amir out to check the area on foot just in case there's more of them in the vicinity. I'm about to launch Tim, so wait for my signal before moving in,' Andy told Kendra when she called for an update.

'Will do. I'm a bit nervous about this, Andy, this could backfire on us big time when Rick finds out.'

'Then just lie to him. Tell him you hired some people to do what the police couldn't. You know how long it takes for them to sort their shit out, the longer we wait the less chance Rick has of getting out of this alive.'

'Agreed. Hopefully he'll see it that way, too.'

'Okay, Tim is on his way now, I'll give you live updates once he's over the warehouse, which will be in about thirty seconds.'

'Standby on that, I just got a message that Mo is calling Dad,' she said. 'I'll speak to you later.'

'All received and understood,' Andy said, hanging up.

'How's it going, Mo? Trevor asked the twin when he called.

'All good here,' Mo said. 'We've walked around the perimeter and can't see anyone parked up or looking out of the ordinary. We'll stick around and keep an eye out but I'd say you're good to go.'

'Thanks, Mo,' Trevor replied, hanging up and sending Kendra the thumbs-up emoji.

'It's a green light from the twins,' he added when she messaged back. 'And it's a green light from Andy. Tim is in place and there's no change. We still have one guard at each entry point, five members of staff in the main warehouse, and four men guarding Rick.'

'I guess we're ready, then?' Darren asked.

'Yep. Charmaine, you're up,' Trevor said.

'Rock and roll,' she said as she left the car and made for the rear of the warehouse.

Charmaine's point of entry had been identified as a short fence in one corner where the warehouse dumped their cardboard. There were several neat stacks of flattened boxes, seven or eight feet in height, waiting for the recyclers to pick them up. It was no problem for Charmaine to scale the fence and enter the yard unnoticed. She could see the small shed that had been placed near the rear shutters where the security guard was currently sitting, watching a game show on his tablet. Side-on, through the window, Charmaine could see the flickering light from the device on his face.

Before making her way towards the guard, she double-checked to make sure there were no CCTV cameras. Fortunately, the two cameras in the yard were both facing the shutters and the monitors were clearly wired to the shed that she was heading towards. It was unlikely that the guard would see her approach, as she would do so out of the field of view of the cameras and then reach the shed door unnoticed, which was at the end farthest away from the shutters.

Charmaine was diligent as she approached at a good pace, looking for any likely hazards along the way. It was important to remove this guard or the team would not be able to gain entry with any element of surprise.

'So far, so good,' she muttered to herself as she approached the final ten feet towards the shed door.

Before opening the door, she put on her tactical helmet and M50 gas mask, necessary for the next step. She then took a small canister from her pocket and removed the plastic safety cover. Holding it at arm's length, her thumb ready on the actuator, she opened the shed door and went in. The guard was stunned at the strange apparition that had entered his shed and remained immobile for a second or two, long enough to give Charmaine time to squeeze and aim the CS spray directly into his face. The mask protected her from the effects very well, the only downside being the slight vision impairment.

Her aim, though, was true, and the guard started to splutter and wave his arms defensively in front of him. The small confines of the shed made it difficult, but she was able to get close enough to kick him hard in the groin. He fell like a sack of potatoes, giving Charmaine the opportunity to zip-tie his wrists together, and then his ankles. The guard was clearly distressed and so Charmaine looked around and grabbed the bottle of water he had started drinking from. She poured it on his face, washing away some of the effects of the spray and easing his distress. She then taped his mouth shut with gaffer tape, leaving him completely helpless on the floor but relatively unharmed.

'Over to you,' she told Trevor when he answered her call. She then looked around the shed and saw the two monitors that were pointing to the shutters. She turned everything off and cut the wires to the system with her pen-knife. There was no chance of any recordings now that could prove problematic later.

Darren and his five friends quickly scaled the fence at the same place Charmaine had, and followed her route to the shed silently. The old metal shutters were down and the only way into the warehouse was through the small door that was an integral part of the shutters, which the team hoped would be unlocked. As the security guard was less than ten feet away from the door it was deemed secure enough for them not to lock it, in case he wanted to use the toilet inside.

The team checked their equipment and put their gas

masks on, some armed with CS spray and others with their trusted Axion tasers, each with thirty thousand volts, more than likely to put the toughest man down in seconds.

Rory tried the handle to the small door and nodded as he opened it inwards slowly, watching intently for any trouble inside. He pushed the door fully open and stepped in, giving his team the thumbs-up. They all entered and spread out in the loading bay, heading towards the part of the warehouse where Rick was being held. They stopped just short of the door they believed would lead them to the four guards.

Darren called Andy before they entered.

'How's it looking, Andy? We're about to breach, so tell me it's safe to go in.'

'That I can't do, mate. What I can tell you is that the four men are still at the table and that Rick hasn't moved at all. When you go through the door, you'll be less than ten feet from them, so be safe, okay?'

'Will do, cheers,' Darren said.

He pointed to the door and Rory went forward again to repeat the procedure that had led them inside. He grabbed the door handle and turned to his team. Holding up his free hand, he counted down from three and then pulled the door open swiftly. Darren was first in, followed by Izzy, Clive, Martin, Jimmy, and Charmaine. Rory followed behind them.

The four triads were in the middle of an intense Texas Holdem poker game, with two of them heads up and waiting for the final river card to determine their next move. There was a stack of chips in the middle and none in front of the two players, indicating that someone was about to lose everything. Their training kicked in when the door was pulled open, allowing what looked like seven police officers to run in towards them.

The two non-playing gangsters were first to react, picking up the vicious meat cleavers that were leaning against their chairs. It was an instinctive move for them; they preferred the cleaver to their handguns tucked into their belts. They were the first to be sprayed by Charmaine and simultaneously tasered by Jimmy and Martin, the voltage causing them to shake uncontrollably as they fought against it. They failed and the cleavers fell from their hands as they too fell to the ground, the charges continuing their work. As this was happening, the two players chose a different path, going for the handguns first.

'Look out!' Charmaine screamed, as the rest of the team went for the armed men. The gangsters both raised their arms and aimed the guns as they were both sprayed and tasered. It was too late to stop them from firing and both were able to do so. The first shot was high, thanks to the effects of the taser, but the second shot was true and struck Izzy in the chest, knocking him backwards and down.

'Izzy!' Darren screamed, as the team started to secure the guards. He knelt beside his friend, who seemed unconscious and was not moving.

'No, no, no!' Darren said, unzipping Izzy's jacket to examine the wound. He saw that the bullet had struck Izzy's vest and was embedded deeply into the fabric, but there was no sign of any blood.

'Why is it always me?' Izzy suddenly said, his brow furrowed as he reacted to the pain from the impact.

Darren laughed and punched him playfully in the arm.

'You're a bloody magnet for this shit, aren't you?' he replied. 'Last time it was a knife, this time a bullet, what next? A bloody tank?'

'I hate to break this up, guys, but we need to move quickly,' Charmaine said.

Darren helped Izzy up and looked around. The four guards were now trussed up with gaffer tape over their mouths.

'The staff would've heard the shots, so Izzy and Martin, you two watch that door.' Darren pointed to the only way into the main warehouse. 'Jimmy, Rory and Clive, go get our man. Me and Charmaine will cover you if anyone bothers us. Let's go!'

Jimmy unlocked the door leading to the small room where Rick was being held. The captive was no longer slumped but wide awake, thanks to the two shots, his eyes now closing to acclimatise to the light pouring into the dark room. The windowless room stank, a bucket in the corner the only sign that they'd let him up to relieve himself.

'Are you lot TSG?' he croaked, watching the masked team enter, referring to the *Territorial Support Group* who were usually tasked with raids not involving firearms.

'Whatever you say, boss,' replied one of the men. They freed him from the chair and raised him slowly to his feet.

'Can you walk?' asked one of the rescuers.

'I... I think so,' Rick said, trying to move his feet forward. He failed and almost collapsed to the ground, only to be caught by his rescuers.

'Okay, we have you, just relax,' said one of the men. Rick was supported out of the room and towards the back of the warehouse as the team began their exit.

Izzy and Martin gave the thumbs-up as they joined them, suggesting that the warehouse staff would not be causing a problem.

'I put a wedge in the door, they won't be able to get in

easily,' Martin told Darren as they carefully navigated Rick through the small door in the shutters.

'Okay, keep your eyes peeled,' said Darren, 'they may not have been able to get in but they sure as hell would have called for backup.' They continued towards the back of the yard where they had all climbed the fence.

As they rounded the tall stack of cardboard they saw that Trevor, Greg, Danny and Zoe had prepared for an easy exit by cutting a hole in the fence big enough for their needs. They all navigated the hole and turned right towards the river, where Andy had told them to go. Trevor had sent his three young boxers to retrieve their cars and bring them closer. They were waiting for them around the corner, along with Marge, which Mo had driven as Andy prepared Tim's retrieval.

They bundled Rick in the back of one of the cars and within seconds they were away from the area, using the side roads to avoid going past the warehouse or any cameras.

The team had taken off their helmets and gas masks when they got to the cars, the gear now stashed in the boots. Rick was alert to the fact that the people that had rescued him were young, but clearly capable.

'Which unit are you lot from?' he asked, his voice still raspy and a little slurry.

'Don't worry about that now, mate,' said one of the men, who handed him a bottle of water. 'Have a drink and we'll get you back nice and safe in no time.'

'Rick drank the entire bottle; his guards had not been kind to him and had rationed food and water to break his spirit. He then remembered Duckmore and Critchley and placed the blame entirely on their shoulders.

'I need to speak to my bosses, they need to know it was a

couple of ex-police officers who are responsible for my kidnapping and that they're in bed with a bloody triad gang,' he said to the front passenger, who seemed slightly older and in charge.

'Take it easy, mate, we'll sort all that out when we get you to safety, okay?'

'If you can give me a phone I can call them now,' Rick said, insisting.

'We can't do that, just wait until we're safe and everything will be fine, okay?'

Rick was seasoned and experienced in most types of policing. The hairs on the back of his neck were telling him something was not quite right. Had he gone out of the frying pan into the fire?

'Seriously, what unit are you from? Don't tell me to wait otherwise I'll kick off and you won't like it. Are you even police?'

The front passenger turned to face Rick. The smile on his face suggested he wasn't a threat but after what Rick had been through, he didn't want to take any chances.

'Rick, all you need to know for now is that we're the good guys and we came to rescue you. We're not police, but we are on your side.'

Rick looked at the man and the other two with him in the car. He was confused.

'Look, I don't know you people, okay? I'm grateful that you rescued me, but I don't know you from Adam and that's enough of a red flag for me.'

'That's fair enough. Let's just say that your colleagues would've taken way too long, and your friends didn't fancy your chances as a result. Your friends figured that you needed help and asked us to get you out, which we did. You can ask all the questions you want later, when we get you to safety. Does that work for you?'

Rick nodded; he couldn't ask for more, really. He held his hand out to the front passenger.

'I'm Rick. Thank you, all of you, for getting me out of there,' he said, shaking the man's hand.

'I'm Darren, Rick, and you're very welcome.'

7

Kendra had stayed behind at the factory, constantly in touch with Andy, Mo, and Trevor throughout the rescue, so she was aware they had succeeded. One thing continually bothered her–how would Rick deal with seeing her involved in a clandestine operation? She mulled the question over and over in her mind and came to the same conclusion each time: badly.

Knowing that time was short, she called Andy to ask his thoughts.

'Honestly, I think this could work very much against us,' she told him.

'You're probably right, K, but his life is more important than that, isn't it?' Andy replied.

'Of course it is, but look at what we've achieved this past year, how much effort has gone into it, how much of a difference we've made, and how many people we've achieved it with. I don't want to risk all that, Andy, we still have so much to do.'

'Well, I can only think of one way around this. One way

where we get him to safety and keep our operation a secret from him,' he replied.

'What's that?'

'We continue the deception. Instead of bringing him here we take him somewhere safe and leave him for the police to pick him up. That way he doesn't see you, or me, or the factory. We limit who he sees to those in the car with him now. But we only have minutes to decide. Are you up for it?'

'Absolutely, where did you have in mind?'

'I know just the place.'

DARREN TOOK the call from Andy when they were just a few minutes from the factory. He'd noticed that Rick was becoming aware of his surroundings so the call had come at a good time.

'Before you answer, don't speak anyone else's name,' Andy said, before Darren could respond.

'Okay, what do you need?' Darren asked.

'I need you to change direction and go back to Dagenham, to the Qupi warehouse where you-know-who was taken from, remember?'

'Yes, I do,' Darren said, 'and then what?'

'Take our friend to the office upstairs and tell him that his colleagues will be there to pick him up in ten minutes. Leave him there, call 999 to inform them and then come to the factory,' Andy continued.

'I understand,' Darren said, 'we'll go there now.'

'Change of plan, driver,' he told Rory. 'We need to go to the warehouse where our young boxer friend was a guest, remember?'

'Yes, I do, not a problem.'

'Is something wrong?' Rick asked, noticing a change of demeanour in his rescuers.

'Yeah, we need to take you somewhere else so that your colleagues can pick you up and take you some place safe,' Darren replied.

'I thought that was where we were going anyway,' Rick said, confused.

'We were, it's just that they wanted you out of sight, in case anyone was looking out for you. I'm sure they know what they're doing.'

'Fair enough, I understand. Those bastards Duckmore and Critchley still have mates in the force, so it's probably just as well. I'm sure they'll be pissed off that I escaped and that I know they're at the bottom of all this,' Rick replied.

'Duckmore and Critchley, you mean those two bent cops who quit and disappeared?' Darren asked, surprised by the news.

'I bloody wish they'd disappeared, but it seems they're back with some vicious plan to take over London. They're a nasty pair of shits, those two.'

'From what I've heard, you're not wrong,' Darren said. He covertly unlocked his phone and sent a message to Kendra.

'*Your mate says Duckmore and Critchley are behind his kidnapping. Seems they're up to something big.*'

Kendra was stunned to see the message and it took several moments for her to think of a response.

'*Ask him what they're planning,*' she typed.

'What do you think those two arseholes are planning?' Darren asked Rick.

'I honestly don't know, other than they're now in bed with the Chinese triads. There's been a lot of activity going on there so it wouldn't surprise me if it was gang related. Those two must have found a way to get cosy with them, because they don't usually like to work with outsiders,' Rick replied. 'They must have something very important and very useful to them, who knows?'

'*He doesn't know,*' Darren messaged.

'*We'll chat when you return,*' Kendra replied.

'Well, you know what they say. The bigger the organisation the bigger the fallout,' said Darren.

'Let's hope so, Darren, let's hope so. How are you lot involved in all this?' Rick asked.

Darren thought for a few seconds before responding.

'Let's just say our little team doesn't like waiting for red tape when it comes to helping people, and leave it at that,' he said.

'Mate, don't mind me, it's just my inquisitive nature, I always like to know what I'm getting involved in. I can't complain, those bastards had something very nasty lined up for me, and you guys saved my arse. They were quite happy to show themselves to me which suggests they were gonna get rid of me, so I can never thank you enough.'

'The pleasure is ours, Rick, I can assure you.'

'Can't bloody wait to have a shit and a shower... in that order,' said Rick.

The journey took fifteen minutes and Rory parked a little farther down from their destination, in the unlikely event anyone was watching. All the businesses in the industrial estate were closed and in darkness and the area was free of activity. Their destination, the Albanian gangsters' warehouse, which had been abandoned after they had been 'removed', was in the Sterling Industrial Estate in Dagenham. Knowing about its history and the fact that it was still under lease to the Albanians made it an obvious choice–albeit an ironic one–for somewhere to safely leave Rick until his colleagues could pick him up.

'We're here,' Darren said as they came to a stop.

'Where's here? Everything is in darkness, what's going on?' Rick asked.

'Rick, I need you to trust us, okay? We're going to drop you off and call for your colleagues to come and pick you up when we're safely away from here, which will only be a few minutes. We can't get involved in any investigation and we don't want anyone to know who we are. Can you understand that?'

'What do you think is going to happen, Darren? You saved my life, for God's sake, you're not gonna get into any trouble for that,' said Rick.

'Maybe not, but like I said, we want to keep a low profile and we can't do that if we're being interviewed and what we've done goes on record. You yourself told us about the bent cops, we can't risk people finding out about us, mate.'

Rick nodded, understanding his rescuers' need for anonymity.

'I understand,' he said. 'Again, I can't thank you enough for saving me, guys. I'm not the biggest fan of all this clandestine stuff but you have your reasons and I respect that.'

'I appreciate it,' Darren said, 'now let's get you inside so we can make the call.'

They walked the short distance to the warehouse, where

they found it securely locked. Jimmy disappeared around the back and a minute later opened the door from within.

'The window?' asked Darren, guessing that was the point of entry.

'Yup,' said Jimmy.

Closing the door behind them, they used their phones' torches to make their way up the stairs to what had once been the gang leader's office. There wasn't much left; the team had cleared all the valuable furniture out, but Rory was able to find a couple of plastic chairs in the kitchenette next door.

'I'd say make yourself comfortable, but this is all we could find, sorry,' Darren said.

'That's alright, mate, better than the last chair I was in,' Rick said.

'We're gonna leave you now, please sit tight until your colleagues arrive, okay?'

'Yeah, I will, don't worry.'

Darren reached out and shook Rick's hand.

'It was a pleasure making your acquaintance, Rick. Look after yourself, maybe we'll meet under different circumstances next time, eh?'

'The pleasure was all mine, Darren, and all you guys. Please thank the rest of them for saving my hairy arse.'

The team went back downstairs and out towards the car. When inside, Darren turned to Jimmy.

'Jimmy, we'll make the call now, but I need you to stay and keep an eye out, to make sure he doesn't leave, or anyone else other than the cops decide to go in. You okay with that?'

'No problem, there's lots of places I can hide and watch from.'

'We'll be parked close by until he's picked up, then we'll come and get you.'

'Great, I'll catch up with you later,' Jimmy said, getting out of the car and disappearing into the shadows.

'Okay, Rory, take us somewhere else mate, not too far,' Darren said, taking a phone out of his jacket pocket. It was one Trevor had given him to use, which couldn't be traced back to anyone. He dialled 999.

'Which emergency service do you require?'

'Police.'

'Please hold for the police.'

'Thank you,' Darren replied.

'Metropolitan Police, can I take your name, please?'

'Please listen carefully. Your colleague, Detective Sergeant Rick Watts, has escaped his captors and needs medical attention. He is currently safe, but alone, and is waiting for you to pick him up from the warehouse at seventeen, Sterling Industrial Estate in Dagenham. The door to the warehouse has been left unlocked. Do you understand?'

'Yes, sir, I understand. We'll send someone round shortly. Can I take your name, please?'

Darren ended the call and then quickly removed the battery and SIM card from the phone. He snapped the SIM in two, intending to dispose of everything later.

'Let's get out of here,' he said, as they left the vicinity.

Two hundred feet from the warehouse, Jimmy crouched behind some bushes which were in the deepest shadows of another building. Nobody would see him, but he had a clear line of sight to the warehouse.

'Let's hope the boys in blue don't take long,' he muttered to himself, brushing some inquisitive ants from his trousers.

He didn't have long to wait. Two police cars arrived within

four minutes, their blue lights flashing but no sirens. All four police officers entered the warehouse, the lights coming on inside seconds later. Jimmy had to wait five more minutes before he saw Rick being escorted to one of the cars by two of the officers, the car leaving almost immediately. The remaining car stayed; the officers left behind secured the scene in case there was any forensic evidence.

It was a waste of their time; no evidence of Rick's rescuers would ever be found there.

Jimmy was able to slink away without being seen and was picked up two streets away by his friends.

'Went like a charm,' he told them.

'Let's get back to the factory; I for one could do with a nice cold beer,' Darren said.

'And a kebab?' Rory asked.

'Yeah, and a kebab. Why not? I think we've earned it today, don't you?

Kendra took the call from Darren, who quickly informed her that Rick was back in safe hands.

'Great news and great work, guys. Did he seem okay with you?' she asked.

'He was fine. He asked a few questions, as expected, but other than learning my first name he doesn't have a clue about us,' he replied. 'There's a lot of Darrens in London so I doubt he'll even look.'

'Great. We'll see you back at the factory in a bit, then,' she said.

'All good?' Trevor asked. The rest of the team were back safely, where they would debrief and relax after the day's work.

'Yeah, Rick was just picked up by the locals, so all is well. That was a good plan, Mister Pike,' she said, turning and bowing to Andy.

'The pleasure is all mine, Miss March. It was very much a team effort, wasn't it?'

'That turned out well,' said Trevor, 'but it's left me asking more questions than before.'

'Agreed. We may have won this battle, but it seems there's a big war rumbling in the background,' Kendra said. 'We really need to find out what the hell is going on.'

'Like how those two arseholes Duckmore and Critchley are involved, you mean?' Andy asked.

'Especially that,' said Kendra. 'Those triad gangs are brutal and rarely work with others, so how the hell did they get involved with them? What could they possibly offer the triads that would bring them into the fold like that?'

'Well, if anyone is going to find that out, it's you, love. As good as Andy is at hacking, he won't be able to get into the police network, so you're going to have to do something when you're back at work.'

'Honestly, I'm not sure who I can speak to about them, Dad, they were roundly hated by everyone.'

'Well, love, maybe the two new guys are worth having a chat with, what do you think?'

'I'll give it a go, one of them seems friendly enough. Maybe I'll speak with him tomorrow,' she said.

'In the meantime, I'll do some digging around the dark web to see if anything is brewing there,' Andy said, standing to leave. 'I'll catch up with you both tomorrow.'

'See you later, Andy,' Kendra said, waving him off.

'Come on, love, let's go and speak to the team. Darren will be with us soon, we can have a proper catch-up,' Trevor said.

'It's been a hell of a day, Dad. I bet they're all knackered. I'll get some drinks and snacks together and meet you there in a bit.'

'Bring some beers too, as many as you can find. The team have earned them.'

8

K endra was in the office the following day, eager to speak to Rick and to find out if the NCA detectives had any information about their predecessors. When she arrived early in the morning, she was surprised to see so many people already there, the room buzzing with excitement.

'What's going on?' she asked Jill when she sat at her desk.

'They found Rick safe and well!'

'That's fantastic!' Kendra replied, acting as enthusiastically as she thought was appropriate, 'where is he?'

'He's in protective custody while they interview him,' Jill said, 'I don't think we'll see him for a few days.'

'Can we talk to him?'

'I tried calling as soon as I found out, but his phone doesn't seem to work. The kidnappers must have smashed it when they took him,' Jill said.

'That's a shame, it would be great to find out what he knows, maybe we can help find the bastards who took him.'

'I have a feeling the NCA boys know more than they're

letting on, maybe we should cosy on up to them and find out. What do you think, K?' Jill asked.

'I doubt that would work, Jill, especially with DS Sisterson. He's very serious-looking, isn't he? Maybe I'll ask his mate, DS Adair, he seems friendly enough.'

'Okay, let us know if you have any luck. I for one am happy Rick is safe.'

'Me too. I'll be back in a few minutes,' Kendra said, walking towards the corner desks where the two NCA detectives were sitting.

Weirdly, DS Jim Adair was wearing a bright-yellow-and-green Norwich City football shirt and black jogging bottoms, which was not what the NCA considered acceptable clothing for work.

'Is your suit at the dry cleaners, or something?' she asked, smirking at the detective sergeant and pretending to have been blinded by the brightness of the shirt.

'No, it isn't, and this is the sixth time someone has asked me something similar. I was at home last night when I got the call that DS Watts had been found, so I came straight over without changing. I wasn't intending to be here all night, but I was, so here I am,' he said, standing and giving a twirl.

'That's very admirable of you Sarge, I'm guessing you have some good news? I mean apart from supporting a dodgy team.'

'What I can tell you is that he is safe. He's been checked out by the doctors as he was given a bit of a beating, but thankfully there's no broken bones or anything serious to worry about,' Adair said.

'Did he say much about his captors?'

'Never you mind, Detective,' Sisterson snapped.

'Remember you're not involved in the investigation so please allow us to do our job.'

'I was only asking about my boss and my friend, Sarge, I didn't mean anything else by it,' she said, backing off. 'I'll leave you to it.'

She nodded at Adair who looked rueful and apologetic, while Sisterson ignored her and continued typing away.

Well, at least I know who to talk to next time, she thought, walking back to her desk.

'You were right,' she told Jill when she returned to her desk. 'That Sergeant Sisterson is pretty abrupt. His colleague is much more amenable, though, so I'll try and speak with him alone later.'

'Good luck with that, we haven't had much of it with the NCA lately so don't be too disappointed if they rebuff your advances,' Jill said.

'There's no harm in asking, is there? Anyway, what else is going on? I was told in no uncertain terms that we don't get involved with Rick's kidnapping, so why is it so animated in here today?'

'Something about a couple of attacks on factories around London, companies that produce military hard-ware. We have several on our patch, so they've asked us to look into assessing the security on them, just in case,' said Jill.

'That's odd, are they connected in any way?'

'Not that anyone is aware of,' said Jill, 'I just do as I'm told.'

Do you fancy coming along to check a factory in Barking that produces engines for fighter jets? Should be interesting.'

'Yeah, why not? What time are you going?' Kendra asked.

'I was planning to go after lunch, if that works for you?'

'Great. I'll catch up with some admin for now and see if I can collar DS Adair on his own before we leave.'

'Good luck with that,' Jill said, 'have you seen what he's wearing today? He's a brave one, that's for sure.'

Brodie Dabbs paced around the small lounge of the flat he had been imprisoned in. The second-floor two-bed flat was one of the new ones in the same complex as those that were now accommodating the Chinese triad gangsters. He shared the flat with his two guards, one of whom was always awake to ensure that Dabbs did what he was told.

'Damned bastard, he should've got back to me by now,' he muttered as he paced the room, 'after everything I did for him.'

He ignored the piercing stares of Ailun, who Dabbs had been calling Alan, his guard at the time. The other guard, Huang, was taking the time to sleep while his colleague had the watch. Their job was to ensure Dabbs did what he was told and to report back to the Red Master with daily updates. Dabbs had reached out to several associates in the last couple of days, especially to those who relied on his logistics.

Today's task was to have contacted the Turkish gang responsible for most of the heroin imported into North London. Dabbs had sent a message to Halit Kaplan, his contact for years, for whom he had facilitated many successful imports via the docks. Duckmore wanted Dabbs to arrange a meet so that he could discuss future business now that he had taken over. Kaplan had not responded.

'Don't look at me like that, Alan, I showed you the message and you know I sent it. If that bastard doesn't want to talk to me it's not my fault,' he shouted at his guard, who stared at him.

'And I told you to call him, not text him,' Ailun replied, in flawless English.

'Why don't you ever listen to me? Kaplan will never answer a call from an unknown number, why don't you believe me when I tell you that?' Dabbs said.

'I'll believe it when I see it. Try now,' Ailun said, the smile that was forming on his lips looking strangely out of place against his unnerving stare.

'Fine, but don't blame me if nothing happens.'

He had written down many numbers from his phone before it was taken away from him, as per Duckmore's orders. He was only to reach out to his connections that relied on his business, nobody else, including his family. He looked at the list and then dialled the number, glancing along the list and confirming that he had written the name *Trevor G (gyms)*. It was a shot in the dark but if an opportunity arose, he would try and reach out to Trevor in the hope he could help him out of his predicament.

The number rang and Dabbs put it on speaker so Ailun could hear. There was no response.

'You happy now? I told you he wouldn't answer, he's a stubborn bastard, that one,' Dabbs said, ending the call.

'Then call the next one, the hash dealer from Hackney,' Ailun said unflinchingly.

'Fine,' Dabbs said, dialling the number. *Think, Brodie, think! How the hell can you get out of here?* was all he could think of as he waited for an answer.

If Dabbs' connections had found out he'd been usurped then there was every chance most of them would ignore him. If that happened, then Duckmore would have no more use for him. Which meant his life would come to a swift end.

He needed to escape... and soon.

IT WAS FAST APPROACHING lunchtime when Kendra saw an opportunity to speak to DS Jamie Adair. She overheard him tell Sisterson he was going out to get some lunch from the local sandwich shop and that he'd be back in half an hour. Knowing where the shop was, Kendra waited a few moments before making her move.

'I'll be back in a bit, just getting a bite to eat before we head out,' she told Jill.

She followed Adair on foot to the shop just a few minutes away and waited outside for him to make his purchase.

'Ooh, that looks nice,' she said as he came out, munching on his first bite.

'Mmm-hmm,' he said, surprised to see her, his mouth full of tuna mayonnaise.

'Don't worry, I won't steal it from you. I just wanted a word,' she said, laughing.

'What did you want to see me about?' he said, having downed the first scrumptious mouthful.

'I sense you're more open to working with us than your colleague is, so I thought I'd take a gamble. Was I wrong?'

He shook his head, wrapping the sandwich up for later.

'He can be hard, at times, but he's a good cop, is JP,' he replied.

'JP?'

'Jon Paul, but don't call him by his first name, he doesn't like it unless he knows you well.'

'He sounds much like a couple of colleagues of yours that we had unfortunate encounters with,' she said.

He smiled, nodding his head knowingly.

'Ah, you mean our *ex*-colleagues, Eddie Duckmore and Dave Critchley. Those two wankers have caused us a shit storm, I can tell you.'

'They did that to us too, trust me,' she said.

'Listen, I'm nothing like those two so please don't judge me like that, it's all I ask for, okay?'

'It's James, right?'

'Call me Jim.'

'Jim, I don't want to waste your time, and I'm taking a gamble that you're one of the good guys, okay? Rick Watts is my boss and my friend, and I want to help find the bastards who took him. That's why I was asking earlier, and I understand your mate doesn't want us involved but you must see that I was asking for a good reason, right?'

'Of course I do. It's just that JP is being really strict with the interpretation of our orders and using it to keep you all at arm's length. Honestly, I don't understand why, because it's clear we could do much more if we worked together.' Adair was clearly frustrated by his colleague and wanted her to know that.

'I don't blame you, but can't you tell us what's going on?' she asked, pleading to his good nature.

He looked around in case anyone he knew saw them talking.

'It's Kendra, right?'

She nodded.

'Kendra, all I can tell you is that Rick was rescued by persons unknown and taken to an abandoned warehouse where a phone call was made to 999 detailing his whereabouts. He was there when the locals picked him up and he's now in protective custody,' he replied.

'He was rescued? He doesn't know by whom? That is odd indeed,' she said, surprising herself with her acting skills.

'The strange thing is that JP wanted to know more about his rescuers than about his captors, which is what pissed me off. That's why I'm happy to talk to you, because I have my suspicions. The only thing I ask is that you don't tell anyone we've talked, and we do any investigating together secretly, just the two of us. Deal?'

'Deal!' she said, shaking his hand.

'Why does JP want to investigate the rescuers more than the kidnappers? That is strange, right?' Alarm bells were ringing.

'I'm pretty sure I know why but I don't have any evidence,' he said, looking around once more.

'Why?'

'Eddie Duckmore and Dave Critchley were good friends with JP, that's why,' he whispered.

'Shit, really?'

'Yeah, which really hacks me off. JP really is a good cop but his friendship with those two was a big red flag for me. What JP doesn't know, though, is that I was posted with him to try and find out whether he had any knowledge of their criminality before they resigned, because the DPS are investigating them both.'

'Really? What for?'

'Apparently, they stole a box full of surveillance logs that were critical to a number of investigations. It meant the cases never went to court, and it was the only solid evidence against the defendants.'

'Who were the defendants?' she asked, the hairs on the back of her neck tingling in anticipation.

'The Ghost Dragons, a Chinese triad gang here in east London.'

Kendra waited until she was back at the station before she made her call to Andy.

'Your dad's here so I'll put you on speaker, just remember to keep your language clean, Miss March,' Andy said.

'What's going on, love?' Trevor asked. She couldn't see the withering look and the shake of the head he was giving Andy.

'I just found out some very interesting news,' she said. 'It turns out that Duckmore and Critchley stole some important evidence before they resigned, which led to some high-profile cases against the triad gang in east London, the Ghost Dragons,' she said.

'Really? What sort of evidence?'

'The surveillance logs, which were critical to the cases. They had to drop them as a result. I'm guessing Duckmore and Critchley took them to the triads and made a deal, other-wise there was no way they'd accept outsiders into the fold. This is a big deal, gents,' she added.

'So, what does that mean for us?' Andy asked.

'I'd suggest you do a deep dive into the Ghost Dragons

and find out everything you can. Something is brewing with them so if we can get more intel on them, it may help later. I don't trust those two bastards, so see if there's anything about them or Hurricane Solutions, the company they're supposedly working for.'

'All received and understood, I'll get right on that.'

'Is there anything I can do, love?' Trevor asked.

'Not at the moment, Dad. It may be worth checking over the new systems at the factory, make sure we're well protected, in case. If they were brazen enough to go after Rick then I wouldn't put it past them to start looking at his rescuers. According to my source, one of their ex-colleagues is working in our office now and likely passing over all the intelligence coming in about Rick's capture and the investigation into it. I just have a horrible feeling something will lead to us. Best to be prepared, eh?'

'Of course, leave it to me. In the meantime, you be extra careful, he didn't like you either, remember?'

'Don't worry about me, Dad. I can't help but ask why they took Rick in the first place, though; it's a risky strategy and I can't see what benefit there is to it. I'm hoping to speak to Rick in the next day or so, maybe I'll get some answers then. In the meantime, you look after yourself too, and I'll speak to you later.'

'Take care, love,' he replied.

'That is a good question,' Andy said as he stood to leave. 'Why go after Rick?'

≈

9

It was early afternoon when Kendra and Jill arrived at the Carter Mills factory in the Barking Industrial Park, spending several minutes at the security checkpoint before being allowed access into the facility.

'Well, that answers the question about their security,' Jill said, making a note, 'it's pretty good so far.'

'What is it that they manufacture here, again?' Kendra asked.

'They make engines and parts for military jets,' Jill said, 'they're one of the leading companies in the world for that, so they export a lot all over. Hence the good security.'

'Ah, okay. So why are we here, just to give them a heads-up that they may be blown up like the others?'

'Something like that, but a little more professionally.' Jill laughed.

'Who are we seeing here?'

'Her name is Geraldine Spencer, she's the head of security here. Apparently, she's ex-police, so it should be relatively straightforward,' Jill replied.

They were met by Geraldine in reception. The tall, well-dressed head of security was warm and welcoming when she introduced herself.

'Just so you know, I was in the Met, too, I served for twenty-five years and retired as an Inspector.'

'Why only twenty-five years?' Kendra asked, surprised that she hadn't completed the full thirty.

'I carried over some military service,' Geraldine said, 'I was in the army for five years, served in Northern Ireland and Cyprus.'

'Gotcha, sorry for being nosy, things like that always intrigue me and I can't help myself,' Kendra said, nodding.

'That's okay, I'd expect nothing less from a detective.' Geraldine led them into her nearby office. 'Please, take a seat.'

'Thank you. We're visiting all local manufacturers of military hardware as there have been several attacks in the last week. We just wanted you to be aware of this so that you can better secure your facility, in case,' Jill said, getting to the point.

'I heard about those attacks, very worrying. I can assure you that we have stepped up our security and brought in extra staff, we don't want to take any chances,' the security chief replied.

'That's good to know, I'll make sure the bosses are aware.'

'Do you know who is responsible?' Geraldine asked.

'Not at the moment,' said Jill. 'We don't think it's a coincidence that they were both manufacturing military equipment and were not yet discounting the usual suspects such as Stop the War Coalition or Greenpeace. Hopefully our investigations will find out soon enough.'

'But in the meantime, please tell your staff to be vigilant, this would be a hell of a target for them,' Kendra added.

'Don't worry, Detective, we have things in hand. We even recruited extra dogs and handlers, they will give additional twenty-four-hour coverage of the grounds,' Geraldine said.

'Great, you seem to have everything under control here, so we'll leave you to it,' Kendra said, standing. She gave Geraldine a business card.

'Please, if anything comes up, however insignificant, please don't hesitate to get in touch.'

'Thank you, detectives, absolutely I will,' she said, taking the card and shaking both their hands.

They left the factory, confident that it was as secure as it could possibly be, especially with Geraldine in charge.

'I can't see anyone attacking that place, it's like a fortress. Did you notice how many CCTV cameras they have? I doubt there's an inch that isn't covered,' Jill said, making notes as Kendra drove away.

What they didn't notice was the make and model types of the CCTV cameras, identical to those used at Rayburn Technologies.

Brodie Dabbs was getting increasingly desperate and nervous at the lack of response from his connections. Knowing them as he did, he also knew that if the roles were reversed, he'd likely do the same. He had seen and heard Ailun call one of his bosses and speak animatedly, suggesting that he wasn't happy with the progress made so far. His chances of surviving were decreasing by the hour, and he knew that if he didn't somehow escape then he'd be in the worst kind of trouble.

Ailun was now resting, and Huang had taken his place. They had dinner together, a Chinese ready-meal that was surprisingly tasty and filling. They had not spoken at all; Huang had occasionally stared at him across the table, no doubt to try and intimidate him, but nothing more. Dabbs had figured out that Huang was the one he had a better chance of survival against if they fought, but he was realistic enough to know that his chances were slim at best. He had to find a way to beat Huang without waking Ailun, and then escaping a building that was completely inhabited by their gangster colleagues.

He went to the balcony for a cigarette and looked down at the fifty-foot drop below, just enough to ensure death if he jumped. He was surprised at how quiet it was below and for a second there was hope that he could get away from these killers. He simply had to find a way–quickly.

The Chinese agents had expected their missions to get more difficult as they entered the latest phase. It was expected that the police and government agencies would sit up and take notice of the recent targets being involved in the manufacture of military equipment. The agents didn't care, they had planned carefully and knew all the targets they were to visit and destroy–or attempt to destroy, barring setbacks such as the one at Rayburn Technologies.

All of the targets had something in common, they each

used advanced CCTV systems manufactured in China. Each had ignored the warnings from the intelligence agencies about using such equipment and the likelihood of data losses and potential interference from Chinese intelligence services. And now they would all pay the cost for ignoring that advice.

The method was the same as the previous missions, disrupt the CCTV feed and replace with static imagery to show nothing on the screens, deploy the agents over the fence and plant the C4 where it would do the most damage. The one difference tonight was the potential of meeting guard dogs again. They had come prepared with an extra agent positioned away from the insertion point to distract the dogs with mouth-watering treats thrown over the fence, such as a variety of raw meats laced with high doses of horse tranquiliser.

At precisely two o'clock in the morning the agent dubbed 'the chef' was in position by the fence, a position carefully selected so that he wasn't seen. Unlike the CCTV within the compound, where there were no blind spots, not so much care had been put in place for the perimeter. The agent was therefore unseen and able to deploy his treats on the hour, just as the CCTV system was disrupted. He then blew into a dog whistle, silent to human ears. The two dogs heard the whistle and ran towards it, picking up the scent of the treats almost immediately, leaving their surprised handlers behind. As they ran towards their rewards, the three intruders clambered over the fence and split up, heading towards their designated targets.

The handlers reached their dogs too late to see what had caused them to run there, so they had no idea they had wolfed down three pieces of meat each. The effects of the horse tranquiliser were swift, and the dogs simply lay down as if resting. After just a few minutes they were completely out, oblivious to their handlers' attempts to wake them.

'What the hell is the matter with them?' asked one of the handlers.

'Beats me, mate. What do you think made them run here to this part of the fence? I've never seen them run so fast. There's nothing out of place, nobody has tried to cut the fence or climb it, so why here?'

'Well, I for one am not getting into the shit because my dog is sleeping on the job, so let's just keep this between us, right? They probably ate a rat or something.'

'I'll get a bucket of water, that'll wake them up,' the colleague said, walking away.

By the time he returned with the water, the Chinese agents were back over the fence, into their waiting van, and away from the area.

'Phase four is complete,' the driver reported to base.

Brodie Dabbs hatched his plan and bided his time before making his move. He knew now how he'd leave the apartment, and he knew how to incapacitate Huang. He waited a couple of hours, knowing Ailun would be in a deep sleep, before making his move. Huang had seen his captor pace the room relentlessly for days now, so it was not unusual for him to do the same around the lounge, where Huang sat on a sofa watching Chinese TV. Dabbs cursed a few times and started to circle around the sofa.

The first time he did it, Huang stared at him as the mad

Englishman swore at those that had let him down so much. After the fourth time, Huang ignored him and paid attention to the TV. The fifth time, he picked up the heavy crystal glass ashtray from the sideboard, and as he walked behind Huang, continuing to curse, he hit him on the back of the head as hard as he could.

The guard slumped forward, immediately unconscious. Dabbs continued to curse and turned the volume up a notch, maintaining the appearance of normality in the event that Ailun was disturbed. He quickly frisked Huang and removed his phone and wallet. He unlocked the phone by placing it in front of Huang's face and then quickly changed the settings so he could use it later. He went to the balcony and took down the washing line from the wall. Acting swiftly, and expertly, he tied Huang up and stuffed a kitchen towel in his mouth so he wouldn't be able to speak when he woke. Dabbs then went into his bedroom and returned with four bedsheets, two from each of the beds in the room, which he tied together, giving a length of around twenty-five feet when tied to the railing.

Looking down at the drop below, Dabbs gulped but knew he had no choice. It was dark, and he was confident he wouldn't be seen as he unfurled his escape ladder over the side. He went to the sofa and grabbed the cushions, all of them, and carefully dropped them down below, one-by-one, giving him a tiny amount of protection for his landing. Taking a deep breath, he clambered over the side and grabbed the sheets with both hands. He was surprisingly fit for his age and didn't struggle too much on the way down. When he eventually neared the end, he looked down at the remaining twenty-five-foot drop. Slowly then, he continued one hand at a time until he had nothing left to hold on to, and looked down again and aimed for one of the cushions below.

'Here goes nothing,' he whispered, and let go.

He landed hard, surprisingly on one of the cushions, but it didn't stop the sharp jarring pain in his back or the badly twisted ankle as he landed in a heap.

'Shit!' he whispered again, putting his hand to his mouth to stop himself screaming out from the pain.

He got up gingerly and tried to put weight on his injured ankle. It was a bad idea. He slowly limped away from the apartment block and towards the road beyond the new estate. The pain was bad but his will to live was greater.

Brodie Dabbs would live to fight another day.

The detonations at the Carter Mills factory were timed and went off at four in the morning. They were hugely damaging and cost the lives of five workers. The three distinct explosions ripped through the main factory and destroyed hundreds of millions of pounds worth of equipment and stock, engines that were being readied for shipment to overseas clients. More damaging was the delay in fulfilling orders and the cost of rebuilding the facility. Although it wasn't their only manufacturing plant, it was their biggest and most prolific, as well as being their flagship plant. It was a devastating blow to the company and to the local economy.

Two guard dogs slept through the entire thing, waking up hours later away from the burning factory, safe and well and very thirsty.

～

10

'Listen to me very carefully, love,' Brodie Dabbs whispered into the phone. It had taken five attempts before his wife finally answered, swearing at the caller of an unknown number.

'Brodie? Is that you, darling? Where are you?' she replied, shocked to hear her husband.

'Stop talking, love, we don't have much time before they notice I've escaped. Pack only what you need and go to your Uncle Pete's place, do you understand me?'

Cheryl Dabbs recognised the code for going to her Aunt Pauline's place in Wales immediately. Although highly unlikely that anyone would be snooping on the call, Dabbs wasn't comfortable speaking freely on the gangster's phone.

'I understand, Brodie. Are you going to be alright?'

'Yes, don't worry about me. I'm gonna stick around for a while and see if I can sort this mess out. Listen, love, when you leave, make sure you smash your phone, okay? I'll call you at Pete's if I need to, do you understand?'

'Yes, I understand,' she replied.

'Park up at a station and leave the car, just in case. I don't want you taking any chances while these bastards are around,' he added.

'Okay love, I'll get ready now. Stay safe, do you hear me?'

'I do. Love you, pet,' he replied.

He dialled another number from the piece of paper he'd written all his contacts on. He wasn't expecting the man to pick up, but he wanted to leave a message that he'd be in touch very soon.

He was right: it went straight to voicemail.

'Trevor, it's Brodie. Listen, mate, the triads have taken over the gang and the shit has hit the fan. I need your help so listen out for my call tomorrow, I'll catch you up then.'

He ended the call and then dismantled the phone, throwing the battery in one direction and the SIM card in another. If they were tracking it, this was as far as they'd get. He continued to limp towards safety.

Brodie Dabbs was a lucky man, despite his current circumstances and the intense pain he was in. It seemed like an age before he was able to leave the estate but when he did, he found himself on a main road close to a taxi office where two drivers were enjoying a nap while they waited for the next call. He took out Huang's wallet and removed a hundred pounds in cash, waving it in the face of the first driver to wake.

'Take me to Loughton in Essex, my friend, and I'll give you another hundred if you can get me there quick. You good?' he said, smiling at the shocked driver's greedy smile.

'Get the other hundred ready, friend, I'll have you there in no time,' said the driver, rushing out of the office towards his car, with the escaped former gang leader close behind.

Although he had lost his empire, Brodie Dabbs was no

fool. He had back-up plans, like most leaders, and Loughton was the one safe house nobody else knew about. He would ask the driver to drop him off a good half mile away from his intended destination just in case the triads started asking questions at the cab office; he would take no chances. Once at the well-stocked and secure safe house, he would plan his counterattack–and there would be hell to pay.

Eddie Duckmore and Dave Critchley watched as the container was unloaded from the freighter straight onto the back of a lorry. It was the third such container from the ship that had arrived from China on a Panamanian registry. The intelligence agency had planned the journey carefully so that anyone checking would see a freighter carrying toys from Taiwan, a friendly nation and regular trading partner, and not a ship carrying a dangerous cargo sent to foment carnage and death in London.

Each container was packed with lethal Type 95 automatic rifles, QSZ-92 and QSZ-11 semi-automatic pistols, several months' worth of ammunition for all, Type 18 fragmentation grenades, combat vests, and much more. It was enough to start–and maintain–a small war. Now that Duckmore controlled the docks, it was easy for them to keep them supplied with everything they needed.

'One more to go,' said Duckmore. 'What a lovely evening we're having, eh, Dave? Perfect for starting a messy power grab and tying up our ex-colleagues for years to come. The perfect distraction for our friends from the east.'

'What do you reckon they're up to, Ed?' asked Critchley.

'Haven't got a clue, mate. To be honest, I don't give a shit. I'm happy to be their distraction, they've given us everything we need to take over as much of London as we want, so I'm all in. And while we're doing that, we'll be able to give some payback to those arseholes in Ilford,' he said, rubbing his hands.

'Shame Watts escaped. You not worried about him telling the Met it was us who grabbed him?' Critchley asked.

'Not at all. They won't find us, and by the time we're up and running we'll have new identities and new faces, remember? We were gonna do that anyway, when they find out about the missing surveillance logs. It just means we bring it forward a few weeks, that's all.'

'Fair enough. I just wish I'd hit that bastard harder,' Critchley mused.

'Don't worry, my old friend, you'll get your chance. I have no doubt we'll be seeing that bastard and his cronies again.'

Ailun woke to find Huang tied and bleeding heavily from a nasty cut on the back of his head. He was still unconscious. He called his team leader and explained. Within minutes, dozens of triads were out searching for Dabbs. Ailun had explained that Huang's phone and wallet were missing, so they tried to track the phone, but the trace ended close to the apartment block.

After a short search, the triads returned to their camp empty-handed. The team leader went to the apartment where he was met by Ailun and the now-freed Huang, whose head was being bandaged by a colleague. He seemed dazed and remained seated when the team leader approached him.

'How did this happen?' the team leader asked sternly.

'He... he hit me... from behind,' Huang slurred.

'How did you allow the stinking gweilo to get behind you?' the man shouted.

'I... I... didn't...' were the only words Huang was able to say before he lost consciousness again. They were the last words he would ever speak. Brodie Dabbs' blow had fractured his skull and caused a bleed that needed hospital treatment, not a bandage from a friend. His body was disposed of in the foundations of another house that was being built on the estate. He would not be missed.

~

Trevor woke to Brodie's message and immediately called Kendra.

'Morning, love. Sorry for the early morning call, but something's happened that you need to know about. I received a message from our old mate Brodie Dabbs who says that a Chinese triad gang has taken over his operations, which is very bad news. He's going to call later with more information, but I wanted you to know. Can you speak with Andy and see if he can work his magic on the computer?'

'I will do, Dad. This is getting very confusing, though. The Chinese have popped up a few times now in the past few days. What do you think is going on?'

'Well, if anyone can find out, it's Andy. Are you going in to work today?'

'Yeah, I was just leaving. I figured I'd see if there's anything more about Rick's kidnapping; maybe it's connected to the same triad gang, what do you think?'

'I don't believe in coincidences like that either, love. Find out what you can, and we'll catch up later,' he said.

'Alright, Dad, speak later,' she said. She dialled Andy immediately.

'Sorry to disturb your beauty sleep, Mister Pike, but something has come up,' she told her yawning friend.

'That's not a sentence I'd ever thought I'd hear from you,' he said, before changing the subject quickly. 'Sorry, what's up?'

'You should be sorry, it's way too early in the morning for that,' she replied. 'Anyway, Brodie Dabbs called Dad and left a message that the triads have taken over his operation. Can you have a look online? The Chinese are starting to appear all over the place, so we think something big is brewing.'

'Blimey, that's a big deal, Kendra. If they've taken over one of the largest gangs in London and they're involved in capturing serving police officers, they have hit the ground running. I'll have a delve into the dark web and see if anyone knows anything there,' he said.

'Call me if you find anything, I'm off to work now to see if I can find anything there,' said Kendra.

'Understood, I'll speak to you later.'

Kendra paused and considered the situation. She couldn't see any connections between the gang takeover and Rick's kidnap.

What am I missing? she thought.

∽

The office was buzzing again when she arrived less than an hour later. There were heated exchanges and urgent conversations going on throughout the large open-plan workspace, some with people she didn't recognise.

'What is it now? And who are those people?' she asked Jill, who had just ended a phone call.

'The shit's hit the fan, that's what's going on, K. They blew the bloody factory up during the night, the one we went and saw yesterday.'

'What? But they had extra security and seemed really switched on about the whole threat, how is that possible?'

'There's a couple of theories, one being an insider threat, but I doubt that because of all the other attacks. It's pretty clear what the targets are, London factories that manufacture for the military. That's who they are,' she said, pointing, 'the government has sent a bunch of military advisors here to rip us a new arsehole. They're attaching themselves to us as we go out and speak to as many other factories as we can, so they can see for themselves what the security is like.'

'Shit, with everything that happened with Rick this is the last thing we need,' Kendra said. She looked over at the two NCA detectives who seemed unperturbed by the activity in the room, carrying on with their work.

'Tell me about it,' said Jill.

'I have to go and ask them, I don't give a shit if mister serious tells me to sod off, I need to know,' she told Jill, walking over with purpose to the two men.

'How's it going, gents? I thought I'd check in and see how the investigation is going.'

'And I thought I told you it wasn't any of your concern,' DS Sisterson replied, looking up from his computer.

'Technically that's not what you said, but I get the message. Just tell me if you're making any progress, that's all,' she said, 'surely you can do that?'

'I can, but I choose not to, so please leave us alone and go and do some police work,' he said, looking back down to his keyboard and continuing to type.

Kendra looked over to Jim Adair who rolled his eyes in apology. She would speak to him later when he was alone.

'Fine, but ask yourself what you would do if the shoe was on the other foot, Detective Sergeant, and then maybe you'll understand why we ask.' At that, she turned and walked off.

'Maybe you shouldn't be so harsh on them, JP,' Adair said to his colleague.

'What the hell do you care?' Sisterson replied, 'sod this lot. The sooner we sort their mess out, the sooner we can go home.'

'Yeah, I get that, but have you ever thought that we might be able to sort this mess out quicker if we had their help? This team are switched on, JP, we could use their help, if you ask me.'

'Well, I'm not asking you, Jim, so just drop it, will you? I don't like this lot and I certainly don't trust them. They're the ones who grassed on Eddie and Dave, remember? If it weren't for this lot, they'd still be with us.'

'Mate, they're not with us because they quit after they did bad things, okay? You would have done the same as this lot if you were in their position and reported Eddie and Dave,' Jim said, seeing an opportunity.

'No, I bloody well wouldn't, Jim. You never grass on your mates, never!'

'Even if they're committing criminal offences?' Jim said, staring back at his angry colleague.

'I don't want to talk about it anymore, let's just get back to work, shall we?'

'Well, I do. If you think it's okay to ignore what those two wankers did then you're out of order, mister. I bet you're still in touch with them, aren't you, all sympathetic with them now that your mates are gone,' Jim pressed.

'Shut the hell up, Adair, what I do with my mates is none of your fucking business, and I suggest you be a bit more respectful. You hear me?' Sisterson stood, facing off against his colleague.

'What are you going to do, JP? You going to tell your mates on me? Maybe you can screw up some of our investigations too, just like they did before they resigned in shame.'

The words were damning and Sisterson took the bait. He lunged forward and grabbed a fistful of Adair's shirt, drawing him close.

'I told you, Jim, drop it. There's no evidence they did anything wrong, and they resigned, remember? There's nothing to stop me from speaking to either of them. What I do in my spare time is none of your fucking business,' Sisterson hissed, his eyes bulging.

'Hit a nerve, did I, JP? What are you going to do, hit me? Go ahead, there's a dozen people in this room who will queue up to kick your arse and arrest you if you do. Go ahead.'

Sisterson pushed him away roughly and sat back down at his desk.

'Eddie said you were soft, and he was right,' he muttered as he resumed his typing.

'Yeah, well, Eddie can sit and spin, for all I care. We're better off without him and the sooner you see that, the better,' said Jim. He had heard enough to confirm his suspicions, that Sisterson was in touch with Duckmore and Critchley and passing on intelligence to them.

He sat down and thought of a way to deal with the situation. It would be difficult to find evidence of anything untoward, so his job was far from finished.

Kendra had noticed the scuffle and nodded, knowing what she had to do.

Time to take this up a notch, she thought.

Kendra and Jill were tasked with returning to the Carter Mills factory to see if they had missed something or if there was any shred of evidence of the attack. With them was Marcus Allen, one of the government security advisors that had been sent to investigate.

'So, how do you become a security advisor for the government, Marcus?' Jill asked.

'I guess I was lucky, detective Petrou,' he said. 'When I was leaving the army, they suggested I look into government jobs that utilised my skillset, and the rest is history.'

'Oh, cool, where did you serve?'

'All over, I specialised in asset security and cyber-resilience. They used to send me to all our overseas stations to make sure they were fully protected. I guess I did a good job, and this was a natural progression.'

'Marcus, we had a good look around the factory yesterday and their head of security knows her stuff, so we're as perplexed about this attack as everyone,' Kendra said.

'I'm sure you did all you could. I do things a little differently, detectives. I will approach the site as an attacker and find ways to get in. If I can do it, then someone else can. And, I always find a way in,' he said.

'Well, if we can learn something then maybe we can protect the rest of them better,' Kendra added, hoping he was right. 'We're here,' she said, as they arrived at their destination.

They met again with Geraldine Spencer at the security checkpoint and introduced her to Marcus. She looked tired, having been on site within thirty minutes of the attack.

'I'd offer a drink in my office, but as you can see, there's not a lot of my office left,' she said, indicating to the smouldering mess.

'We're very sorry, Geraldine,' said Kendra, 'but we need to ask a few questions and check the site to see what we all clearly missed. Do you have any thoughts on that?'

'Honestly, none at all,' she said, as they walked around the wreckage. 'Our security has been the most robust we've ever had. I drafted in four extra security guards just for the night shift, along with an extra dog, I gave training to all staff and asked them to point out any weaknesses, I did at least three perimeter assessments, and the entire site is covered by the latest CCTV hardware and software. I can't think of anything we missed.' She shrugged her shoulders in frustration.

'I can,' Marcus suddenly announced.

'What, you can see something that was missed?' Jill asked.

'Yes, I can. I can see immediately, even though we haven't covered the perimeter, that your CCTV coverage is focused within the site itself, which has left a few blind spots externally and means someone could have approached the fence unseen. They may have been seen once within the perimeter, but that is certainly a weak point in your system,' Marcus explained.

'But does that matter? If our coverage within the perimeter is a hundred percent, surely any intruders would have set the alarms off?' Geraldine said.

'I agree, but you have wrongly assumed that your coverage *is* a hundred percent,' he added, looking down at his notepad. 'My understanding is that you were advised, approximately eighteen months ago, to install domestic or European security systems that would be more robust against outside interference. Is that correct?'

'That's right. We decided to choose the market-leading brand instead, which we researched thoroughly and found it to have more advanced features and more frequent updates than the competitors from Europe and the UK. We simply chose a better system.'

'You may have chosen a better system, Miss Spencer, but the system you chose was manufactured by an overseas company that is owned and managed by their government and was subject to intensive rigorous checks which showed it was susceptible to interference. In fact, we made it publicly known that we recommended against their use. You chose to ignore that advice,' he said.

'Wait, are you saying someone messed with the CCTV so the attackers could gain access without being seen?' Kendra asked.

'That's exactly what I'm saying, Detective March, with some confidence too,' Marcus replied.

'So, the security system that we believed to be the best is responsible for the destruction of the factory?' Geraldine asked. 'Is there evidence of this?'

'One of the advantages of their systems, Miss Spencer, is

that they are always in absolute control. There will be no evidence and we will not mention it publicly that an overseas government could have been responsible for attacks on British soil, which could be construed as an act of war. We have other ways of dealing with these situations, and deal with them we will, I assure you.'

'Unfortunately, it's a little late for Carter Mills,' Geraldine said. 'It will take years to recover from this.'

'But why would they want to attack our factories?' Kendra asked, confused by the overall picture forming in her mind, including Duckmore and Critchley's involvement.

'We have a theory I can't share, but what is a priority now is to ensure that no further attacks take place. We need to get back to the station so that I can make some calls. Miss Spencer, thank you for your time, I wish you luck with the rebuild,' he said, shaking her hand.

They were back in the car and on the way a few minutes later, the smoke still rising in the rear-view mirrors as they left the area.

'Bloody hell,' Jill said, 'how are we going to write this one up?'

'You won't be writing anything up, Detective. That's my job and I'd ask that you both keep the conversations and theories to yourself for now. I insist,' Marcus said.

'Don't worry about us, Marcus, our lips are sealed,' Kendra said, lying and hoping that this was the breakthrough they needed.

∾

11

That evening, Kendra met with Trevor and Andy to discuss what they had learned during the last day or so. Kendra explained her findings from the visit to the Carter Mills factory and Marcus Allen's intuitive assessment.

'Bloody hell,' said Andy, 'I knew those CCTV systems were rumoured to be under foreign government control but it's the first evidence of it ever happening here.'

'That's just it, though,' said Kendra, 'there is no evidence. There will be no trace of anyone ever messing with the system who can ever be traced back to China. That's why he wants to keep it all quiet, so our own government can respond appropriately.'

'This is some serious stuff we've gotten ourselves involved in,' Trevor added, 'maybe we should step back and let the secret squirrels do their thing.'

'You may be right, Dad, but I don't think we should step away fully. I think we should use this information to our advantage and probe a little more into their operations. I'm especially keen to find out what Duckmore and Critchley are hoping to gain out of it.'

'I have an idea, but we may need some help from the good cop from the NCA,' Andy said.

'I think he'd definitely help if there was a way of proving their involvement in crime,' Kendra replied. 'What do you need?'

'We need to get a message delivered to Detective Sergeant Sisterson. I'm guessing he'll only open it from a trusted source, though,' said Andy.

'Oh, so you want to deliver a virus so you can clone his phone?' Kendra said knowingly.

'You catch on fast, Detective March. I figure if he's in touch with Duckmore and Critchley he'll want to update them with what has been going on, especially now he's had a row with his NCA buddy.'

'Okay, get it ready and send it to me. I'll speak to him tomorrow and see if he's up for it.'

'I think you may need to use a little deception though, K, just in case. I'll mock up a photo that suggests evidence-tampering, a CCTV still image or something like that. Jim Adair can then continue his argument with Sisterson by implying he has evidence of Duckmore taking the surveillance logs. He won't be able to resist opening it, which will allow the virus to infect his phone.'

'That's pretty sneaky, even for you, Mister Pike.' Kendra nodded in appreciation.

'Remind me never to open anything you send me!' Trevor said.

'Well, it may be a little late, Trevor. Remember that laughing cat meme I sent you last week?'

'You'd better not have, you little...'

'Dad, he's messing with you,' Kendra interrupted, laughing. 'You're messing with him, right?'

'Yes, of course,' Andy said, smirking.

'You know what, two can play at that game,' Trevor announced. 'If you don't promise you're messing about then I won't tell you what I did to Marge this morning.'

'You're just making it up,' Andy said, the smile vanishing. 'I've been with her all day, so you couldn't have.'

'No? Even when you did the inventory check during your lunch break?'

Andy froze, unsure, wondering how Trevor would know he'd been checking inventory unless he'd seen him.

'Wait, I didn't tell anyone about that. What have you done to Marge?' he demanded.

'What have you done to my phone?'

'What are you two children doing? Can we please resume our very serious discussion?' Kendra said loudly.

'Fine. And for the record, I *was* only messing with you,' Andy replied, sitting back down.

'Good, I'm happy to hear that,' Trevor said.

'And? What did you do to Marge?'

Kendra shook her head and rolled her eyes.

'Nothing, I just left a little surprise for you, that's all,' Trevor said, laughing. 'I'll sort it out after the briefing, you'll never know anything has happened.'

'You used the bloody toilet, didn't you?' Andy said, aghast, standing again. Trevor continued to laugh.

'Dad, really?' Kendra stifled a laugh.

'Sorry, I've been wanting to do it for ages. I'll sort it out, I promise.'

'Enough of this, now, Dad. We need to stay focused on what is going on, okay?'

'Okay, from my end, I spoke with Brodie Dabbs, who, as you know, was also captured by the triads. They held him captive at a new development near the warehouse, a new housing estate that's being built. According to him, there's hundreds of them there and they are planning to take over everything in London. He was kept alive to contact all his old connections to set up meetings with them and Duckmore. This is a massive power-grab and Duckmore and Critchley are slap-bang in the middle of it.'

'He's smarter than we thought,' Kendra said. 'Removing evidence that helped the gang avoid lengthy jail terms that would have disrupted their operations was a smart move, because they really don't like working with outsiders.'

'We need to find out what the end game is, because I for one am confused as hell. I get the gang takeover thing, that's control and money. But the Chinese connection bothers me, especially with the factories being blown up. I know we don't have evidence it was them but why are they doing this?' Andy asked.

'That's what we need to find out,' Kendra said. 'With Duckmore in control of Brodie Dabbs' operations, especially the logistics side of it, they can pretty much do anything they want in London now.'

The following morning, Kendra arranged to meet with Jim Adair at the sandwich shop.

'Thanks for meeting me, Jim,' she said, handing him a coffee as he sat down.

'No problem, anything to get away from that grumpy bastard,' he said, taking a sip.

'I've got something to show you. Something which might help you find evidence against Duckmore and Critchley,' she said.

'Oh? What's that, then? We've looked everywhere and not found a bloody thing.'

'I have a friend of a friend who sent me a picture of Duckmore at the cabinet where they store the surveillance logs,' she said, showing him her phone.

The picture was of poor quality, but it showed Duckmore standing next to the metal cabinet that required a combination for access, which only a few people would be privy to. He was looking around surreptitiously to see if anyone was watching.

'It's not a great picture but it certainly shows him at the cabinet, which he vehemently denied. I mean, it isn't proof that he took the logs, but it's better than what we had,' Adair said.

'I thought you could use it to get Sisterson onside. If what you say about him is true, that he's a good cop but won't believe Duckmore is a rotten egg, then it may help change his mind about helping him. What do you think?' Kendra was hoping to entice him into delivering the message.

'I think that's as good a plan as any. I mean, I am positive he's helping Duckmore and Critchley but can't see me ever finding any evidence. If JP knows anything and sees this, he may come forward.'

'Well, there's only one way to find out,' she said, pressing the button and sending the message to Adair. His phone pinged immediately, confirming delivery.

'Okay, let's see where this takes us. Great coffee, by the way, thanks.'

'Trevor, what else did Brodie Dabbs say about his captors?' Andy asked, something niggling in the back of his mind. They had met in the canteen for a coffee.

'Like I said, he was asked to reach out to his contacts and introduce them to Duckmore so he would continue the operation as the new boss.'

'Yeah, I got that, but did he say anything else, whether he saw anything out of place or if Duckmore let anything slip? Something doesn't feel right about all this.'

'Let me think,' Trevor said, 'the only other thing he mentioned was that the bastards had turned his people against him by offering them double what he was paying, along with big bonuses later. They all accepted the offer, which is why he agreed to their terms. Not sure if that helps?'

'A little,' said Andy. 'That's a lot of money to fork out to such a big organisation. Where are those payments coming from, do you think?'

'Well, I doubt Duckmore or Critchley have that sort of money. It must be from the triads, right?'

'Yeah, but even for them it's a huge payout. Do you think the Chinese government is funding that as well? I ask because I'm going to try hacking into their systems to check their financials. I doubt I'll find any such payments going out from the warehouse business or related accounts. If my suspicions are correct, it'll be from untraceable offshore funds, which means the Chinese government are funding the takeover of London's gangs. Who knows what they want to do that for?' Andy mused.

'I thought you were checking the dark web for anything we're missing?' Trevor asked.

'I have, but it's not anything my connections will respond to quickly, it may take some time. I'm going back to check later.'

'Okay, in the meantime I'll let you know if Brodie reaches out again. He's using a burner phone and is lying low until it's safe for him to come out of hiding.'

'Right then, I'll catch up with you later,' Andy said, leaving the canteen.

What are those bastards up to? Trevor thought.

~

Brodie Dabbs had stocked his safe house well. It was the only one that nobody else was aware of, and one he visited weekly—alone— to ensure some semblance of normality for any potentially nosy neighbours. It was his back-up, his last resort if anything went wrong. The detached house was surrounded by tall, well-maintained hedges and always had a car parked in the drive to give the appearance of the home-owner being there. Brodie had even gone to the trouble of meeting the neighbours a few times and pretending to be an aloof, often drunk, frequently travelling businessman with an attitude problem, so they wouldn't try popping round for coffee.

The hidden safe in the cellar contained a dozen burner

phones, a hundred and fifty thousand pounds in cash, a hundred thousand pounds worth of gold bars, two handguns with ammunition, and a notebook with the secret bank accounts in Switzerland and the Cayman Islands, which nobody else had access to. Duckmore may have had control of the business bank accounts, but these ones were personal and very secret. There were several million pounds deposited in each account, more than enough for him to live a comfortable life away from the risks of his previous empire. He had been diligent in planning for the future over a number of years, it was always prudent to plan for all eventualities. Just like this one.

Brodie Dabbs had no thoughts about retiring in comfort just yet. He had an empire to win back and a lot of people to deal with, a lot of people who'd once been loyal and who had since stabbed him in the back. But especially the newcomers who had taken over, in a matter of days; decades worth of blood, sweat, and tears building a viable operation.

Brodie Dabbs had a plan. It wasn't just to win his empire back; it was also to pay back those responsible for its loss.

Jim Adair approached his angry partner, who was typing away at his desk. Sisterson looked up to see him standing there.

'Not in the mood, Jim, just piss off and go and do some work, will you?' he said, looking back down to his papers.

'Not before I show you something you need to see, JP.' Adair took his phone out of his pocket.

'I'm not interested,' came the blunt reply.

'Really? I thought you might be, it's a picture of your mate Duckmore with his hand in the cookie jar, but if you aren't interested, I'll just send it to the DPS instead. Maybe they can use it to finally arrest the bastard.'

'What are you talking about?' Sisterson looked back up at his colleague.

'You wanted evidence Duckmore was up to no good, well, I found it. It's a photo of him at the safe where the surveillance logbooks went missing, which he shouldn't have had access to, which he denied ever going near.'

'Bollocks.'

'It's fine that you don't believe it, JP, but you made a big song and dance about there being no evidence, so I guess you're just a hypocrite, right?'

Sisterson stood and stared at Adair.

'Just show me, will you?'

'I'll do better than that, JP, I'll send it to you and then you can decide what to do with it. How's that for not stabbing someone in the back? It puts you in an awkward position though, doesn't it?' Adair forwarded the text to his colleague.

Sisterson's phone pinged on his desk. He looked down at it and picked it up, hesitating for a second before opening the message. He frowned as he looked at the image. He zoomed in for a clearer view of Duckmore's face and the cabinet. Andy had done a great job in photoshopping Duckmore's face onto another officer's body; someone who had a similar build. The office image was taken from a CCTV still that he had easily gained access to.

'Where did you get this?' Sisterson whispered, clearly torn between his loyalty to Duckmore and his sworn duty as a police officer.

'I got it from a trusted source, JP, and that's all you need to know. Now, what are you going to do about it?'

Sisterson grabbed the jacket from the back of his chair and walked away without replying.

Jim Adair looked over to Kendra's desk and saw her watching. She gave a thumbs-up and nodded. He nodded back, before sitting down at his desk, suddenly full of remorse.

He's a good guy, he just made a bad choice, he thought.

Detective Sergeant Sisterson was furious as he walked out of the station and away from prying eyes. He felt betrayed by a friend he had stood by and defended vehemently against very serious allegations. The photo made him angry because it felt like a betrayal from a long-standing friend who had sworn his innocence. He took out his phone and called Duckmore, hoping to hear that what he had seen in the photo was wrong.

'JP, me ol' mucka, how are you doing, mate?' Duckmore said upon answering.

'Eddie, you swore you didn't take those surveillance logs, mate; you swore blind, and I believed you,' Sisterson yelled.

'Whoa, whoa, what the hell's the matter, JP? Why so angry?'

'I have a photo of you at the safe where the logs went missing from, that's what the matter is. You lied to me, you bastard.'

'What the hell are you talking about? There was no

CCTV footage of me or anyone taking those logs,' Duckmore said, knowing that to be the case as he had deleted that footage himself.

'It's not CCTV, it's a bloody photo taken by someone there on their phone, and it's definitely you,' Sisterson said.

'Mate, listen to me carefully. Whatever you've been shown is bollocks, there is no photo of me doing anything of the kind, okay? You have my word,' Duckmore knew for a fact that he'd been alone when he had taken the logs.

'How the hell do you explain the photo then, Eddie? How?'

'Where is this photo?' Duckmore asked.

'On my phone.'

'Send it to me now,' Duckmore ordered.

Sisterson did as he was asked and sent the photo.

'JP, that isn't me, mate. I don't know who's responsible, but someone is messing with you. I don't have a suit like that, and also if you look at the outstretched arm, whoever that is has a watch on their wrist. Since when have you ever seen me wear a bloody watch? I hate the things.'

'What, are you saying it's a fake photo?' Sisterson asked, confusion replacing the anger towards his ex-colleague.

'That's exactly what I'm saying, mate. What the hell is going on, is someone still investigating the missing logs?'

'I assume they are, yes. I also assumed they wouldn't find anything because you swore it wasn't you, and now this? Why would anyone implicate you like this, Eddie? Who has it in for you?'

'I don't know, but I will find out and put an end to it, okay? I promise. Tell me who gave you that photo, JP, and I'll sort it out.'

'Forget it, Eddie. I don't want to get involved in any of this shit. I've helped you where I could but if it means people getting hurt then I draw the line.'

There was silence for what seemed like an age, before Duckmore replied.

'I'm afraid it's too late for that, me ol' mucka. You've already helped me enough to get you in deep trouble with your firm. I suggest you continue to help me out, otherwise I'll have no choice but to send the recordings of our conversations to your boss. That won't look good on you at all, now, will it?' Duckmore said, his voice no longer friendly.

'You bastard, you did take the logs, didn't you?' Sisterson replied, realisation dawning without any evidence required.

'I want to know who sent you that bloody photo and I want to know everything about the investigation into me, Dave, and anything else that will help my cause. I want to know everything that's going on. Do we have an understanding, Detective Sergeant?'

It was Sisterson's turn to be silent as he considered the impossible position he now found himself in.

'We have an understanding,' he whispered. 'It was Jim Adair who gave me the photo. I have no idea about the investigation or anything else to do with you. If I hear anything I'll let you know,' he added.

JP Sisterson was a dejected figure as he returned to his desk, staring at the wall as he considered his next move.

≈

12

'Kendra, we have a situation.'

'What is it, Andy?' she said, having walked out of the office to answer his call.

'The cloned phone worked like a charm, and I was able to listen into the call between Sisterson and Duckmore. It appears the grumpy DS thought Duckmore was innocent of the allegations, but also that he's been passing information to him. Kendra, Sisterson was threatened with blackmail and told Duckmore it was Jim Adair who gave him the photo. Your mate is in danger, K; you need to figure out how to help him.'

'Shit, we didn't think of that. It's not going to be easy to tell him without giving the game away. How the hell are we going to do this?'

'There is some good news with the bad, which is a huge bonus for us. Sisterson sent Duckmore the photo, which means the virus is currently working its magic on his phone too.'

'Wow, is that even possible? Never mind, don't tell me.

Just monitor what that prick does and let me know. I'll figure out how to deal with the mess this end.'

'Good luck,' he said.

Damn, she thought, *this one is tricky*.

The solution was a simple and effective one but required a level of trust from Jim Adair that Kendra was unsure would be given. She arranged to meet him again at the café and took a deep breath in anticipation when he approached her table.

'You've heard something, haven't you?' Jim said as he sat down, instantly reading Kendra's expression as somewhat more serious than usual.

'I have, Jim, but I need you to trust me and not ask any awkward questions, okay? Just hear me out and then we can make a plan.'

'Well, that sounds ominous, but you have my attention,' he said.

'JP called Duckmore, as we expected him to. You were right, Jim, he believed Duckmore was innocent all along, but he did pass information on to him, which is not good. Duckmore is now blackmailing him, to keep the information flowing his way, and one of the things he had to do was give up the person who gave him the photo.'

'How the hell do you know all this?' Jim asked. 'Were you standing next to him when he called? How do you expect me to believe you?'

'The only reason I'm telling you is because Duckmore will come after you, I can guarantee that, and it won't end well. I'm telling you to keep you safe, you need to go into hiding. Right now, Jim.'

'Damn it, Kendra, you expect me to run away from this? I'm not scared of Duckmore, or his mate Critchley. They can go screw themselves.'

'It isn't just them anymore, Jim. They're working with the triads, the Ghost Dragons from Dagenham.'

'I don't believe that, Kendra. They don't ever work with outsiders,' he said.

'It's true. The surveillance logs were their way into the triads and now they're working together on something big. You're just another pawn in their way and they will kill you if they find you–without hesitation. Please listen to me,' she pleaded.

Adair slumped back in his chair and held his head in his hands.

'The damned fool. I told you he wasn't a bad cop, Kendra, just misguided. And now they have him by the balls, and now me, it seems.'

'That may well be the case, but he chose to put you in harm's way to save himself, Jim, so you have some thinking to do about how to deal with him.'

'There's only one way to do that, Kendra. I'll speak to him when we get back and see where that goes. Remember, we still don't have any admissible evidence against him or Duckmore. That photo certainly isn't enough; only a confession will save his arse.'

'Good luck with that, but in the meantime, you need to disappear, and you need to stay off the grid, okay? Tell your boss you need to take leave and then get rid of your phone, your car, and anything else that can be tracked. Do you have anywhere remote you can stay?'

'Yeah, I have family up in Yorkshire, I'll go and stay with them for a few weeks. I'll call you from there on their phone, if that's okay?' he said.

'Great. Now, go and deal with your mate and then leave as soon as possible. When we next speak, hopefully this will be all over and safe for you to come back.'

'Thanks, Kendra. I'll be in touch.'

Adair was true to his word and went straight back to see Sisterson.

'You've spoken to him, haven't you?' he demanded.

Sisterson avoided eye contact with his angry colleague who stood over his desk.

'Yes,' he whispered.

'He denied it, didn't he?' Adair said.

'He said it was a fake photo,' Sisterson said, finally looking up. 'Did you send me a fake photo, Jim?'

'I never took the photo, JP, I simply passed it on to you after it was given to me. Now, what are you going to do about it?'

'What the hell can I do?' came the reply.

'You can stop helping the bastard and help us put him inside, that's what you can do.'

Sisterson clenched his fist in anger, helpless and frustrated. He looked up again at his colleague.

'Jim, I'm sorry. I don't want to get involved in anything, okay? Now please, leave me the hell alone,' he said, looking away.

'Shame on you, JP, Shame on you,' Adair said. He picked his coat up and left, having quickly decided to take Kendra's advice and disappear for a while. He looked over to her desk and gave an almost imperceptible nod, which Kendra saw and reciprocated.

I guess I'd better get my hiking boots out of the loft, he thought as he left the building.

~

It had been a couple of days since she'd last tried, so Kendra thought it was time to try and get back in touch with Rick Watts. She called Rick's wife, Aileen, and was delighted when she answered.

'Hi Aileen, it's Kendra. How's it going? I thought I'd check in on Rick, hoping he isn't causing you too many problems?'

'Hi, Kendra, it's good to hear a friendly voice. All I've been hearing these past few days are serious, negative, demanding questions from your colleagues, it's doing my head in.'

'I'm sorry about that, unfortunately the investigators are just trying to do their jobs and will try and leech every drop of information out of your husband. I'm sure it will all be over soon,' she said.

'I hope so, love. Here, I'll pass him over to you.'

'Hi, Kendra, has the place fallen apart without me yet?' asked Rick.

'Actually, everything is running smoother than I've ever known,' she lied, laughing, 'you should stay off longer.'

'Trust me, as much as I'm champing at the bit to get back, I won't be rushing to do so. Those bastards did a number on me, and I have a fractured cheek and some very nasty bruised ribs that need to get better. It'll be a few weeks before I'm back.'

'I thought I'd give you a quick catch-up, if you're up for it?' she asked.

'Please, go for it.'

'There's no trace of Duckmore or Critchley, they've gone to ground knowing they're in deep shit for kidnapping you. They're in cahoots with the Ghost Dragons but we have no idea why. Also, they've taken over one of the largest gangs in London, with the triads' help, so there's that. Any idea why they grabbed you?' she asked.

'Honestly, I thought at first it was just them being petty wankers because of our run-in, but I think there's more to it than that, K, a lot more. I feel that I was almost like a diversion, know what I mean? Like a kill-two-birds-with-one-stone kind of thing.'

'Actually, I do. It's been bothering me from day one what their end game is, and nobody has a clue. There's been a lot of strange things going on around here, factories being blown up, gangs taken over, cops kidnapped. It's like a Hollywood movie,' she said.

'I don't know what to tell you, K. I'm stuck here at home with protection officers inside and outside my house, I just want whatever it is to end soon.'

'You need them there, Rick, who knows what Duckmore is capable of. It wouldn't surprise me if he came after you again, hence the officers there.'

'On top of that, I've had investigators from all over the place asking about the kidnapping. I've had our lot do their usual investigation, the DPS asking about Duckmore and Critchley's involvement, the NCA asking about my rescuers, it's been relentless. Even a couple of Ministry of Defence detectives came asking; God knows why.'

'Really? Ministry of Defence? How the hell are they involved, Rick?'

'Who knows?'

'Alright, well, the more people there, the safer you are, so just stay there for now, okay?'

'Yeah, I will, but I don't have to like it. I may try and sneak out for a laugh, see what they do when they find out. Just keep me in the loop, will you?' asked Rick.

'Of course. It's good to hear your voice again, boss, speak soon,' Kendra said.

She immediately called Andy.

'I think I have an idea what is going on,' she told him. 'The wider picture.'

'I think I know, too,' Andy said, excited. 'I was just about to call you and tell you about my latest foray into the dark web.'

'Okay, you first,' she said.

'A couple of contacts came through with the same intel,' Andy started to explain. 'It seems there's a few people on the dark web who work at Heathrow and were grumbling about the number of young Chinese men who had come through recently from Hong Kong, all with signed paperwork from judges and police officers. Something to do with a security show at the ExCel Centre?'

'Oh yes, the one we encountered on our boat trip,' she said.

'That's the one. Do you know who else was there?'

'Please, refresh my memory.'

'There was a huge security presence because the Taiwanese delegation were over to sign a huge trade deal with the UK, including some very lucrative military contracts,' he continued.

'And our friends the Chinese are not at all happy about it and started blowing up our factories. I bet if you check the factories destroyed recently, they all have something to do with that trade deal,' Kendra said.

'Already done it and confirmed it. A drone company, a jet engine factory, a missile defence manufacturer, all signed deals with Taiwan. Also, after doing more checking, the Minister for International Trade was almost killed in a hit-and-run incident a few days ago. The driver was Asian. This is big, Kendra; if evidence is found it could mean a potential military dispute with China, which will not end well for anyone.'

'This is way out of our comfort zone, Andy, we can't take on China, for God's sake!'

'I know, which means we need to work out what we're going to do next. Let's meet later, okay?'

'Will do. I'll let Dad know and we'll meet at your house, if that's okay?'

'Of course. See you later.'

What the hell have we found ourselves in the middle of? she thought as she prepared to leave work.

'That's a hell of a theory, love,' Trevor said after Kendra had updated him.

The trio sat in Andy's lounge, having decided to meet up away from the bustle of the factory. There was no sense in involving anyone else until they had decided their actions moving forward.

'I'm pretty sure it isn't just a theory, Trevor,' Andy added, 'and it seems more wide-reaching than just the triads and a couple of bent cops. Now we know there is a chance the Chinese intelligence services are involved, we can delve into the triad finances and see how it is they are funding all this, and it will give us a much better idea of their end game.'

'Listen, you two should know this is hugely complicated, right? We can deal with criminals, but foreign intelligence agencies? I think that's way out of our comfort zone.'

'For now,' Andy said.

'I like your confidence, Andy, but these people don't mess around. They kill for fun and use national pride as their excuse while they smile at you. I've dealt with their sort in the past, and they're much worse now,' Trevor warned.

'What do you reckon then, Dad? What should we do?'

'I have no problem with looking into the triads more, anything we find that can link to the intelligence agency or the government will be a bonus. Find out if we can get info on the men that came over, is that possible? I think we should focus on that for now and maybe looking for those two arse-holes Duckmore and Critchley.'

'Is there anything I can do?' Kendra asked, seeing that Andy would be busy.

'Yes,' said Trevor, 'you can contact the government investigator and ask him a few questions, maybe imply you have a theory that the attacks are linked to Taiwan. See what he says. If he tells you to keep that quiet, then we'll know our government knows, so we'll need to watch what we do in case we get in their way.'

'You mean we just back off from the big picture?' Andy

asked, disappointed. 'As much as I like gathering intelligence on baddies, I'd much rather be out there sticking it to them properly, not sitting on my backside hoping someone else does it.'

'Don't you worry about that, Andy. We'll still be involved, just not in any way that will put us at risk of discovery. I need to speak to some old colleagues of mine, we may be able to do something more, but it will mean leaving it to the experts,' Trevor said, smiling confidently.

'Oh, you mean British Army Intelligence?' Kendra asked.

'Them... and more.'

～

Andy spent several hours contacting his Heathrow connections on the dark web and finding out if they would be willing to send him the information. One of them declined, not wanting to risk losing his job. The other, though, was happy to assist... at a cost. After much enjoyable haggling, they settled on a price of one bitcoin, with an approximate value of just over twenty thousand pounds. For that, Andy would receive a list of the suspected triads and their documentation.

'I'm compiling the list for a report, so I have the information to hand,' the contact told Andy.

'What report?' he had asked.

'A few of us thought it coincidental that over two hundred men came over for a trade show and their documents were all signed and sponsored by judges, MPs, and other high-ranking officials including senior police officers. Nobody listened to our warnings, so I decided to send an official report so that something is in the system if the shit hits the fan,' the man replied.

'Good man,' Andy told him, 'if only more were as diligent. Check your wallet, the bitcoin should be there now.'

Andy had used funds taken from their first major adventure against the Albanian Qupi gang, which had filled their coffers with more than enough money to fund all their exploits. Twenty thousand pounds was money well spent if it meant they had the intel on the triads. How they would use it was a different matter altogether.

'Got it, thanks,' the man replied. Seconds later, the document was in the chat and downloaded by Andy. He looked over it quickly and saw it was, indeed, as the man had said. Names, UK addresses, passport information, and the sponsorship letters, which he would check over later. If what he said was true about judges and high-ranking officials being involved, then this was a matter of national importance that needed resolving urgently.

I hope Trevor knows what he's doing, he thought.

The following morning, after spending most of the night sorting out the intelligence, he decided to call Kendra, who was off work and home at the flat.

'Let me put you on speaker, Andy, Dad is here.'

'Oh, good, saves me having to repeat myself. So, I spent most of the night sifting through the intel I received from my airport contact. More than two hundred suspected triads came over, all allegedly to work at the International Security show that we encountered on our boat trip. What is worrying is that their sponsorship forms were signed by some very senior officials, including two judges, three Members of Parliament, two chief superintendents, and three senior civil servants, including one that works at MI5.'

'Bloody hell,' Trevor said, 'that's not good.'

'It gets better,' Andy continued. 'They're all shareholders or directors in a company that we are familiar with.'

'Don't tell me, Hurricane Solutions?' Kendra said.

'Yes, ma'am, which, as you know, is who our old friends Duckmore and Critchley now work for. Or *used* to work for, I should say.'

'What do you mean?' Kendra asked.

'When it was known they were responsible for Rick's kidnapping, Hurricane Solutions was one of the first places the investigators went to for information about them. According to the HR Manager there, they had both left a week earlier and were only signed on as contractors, if you believe that,' Andy said.

'So, what do we do now?' Kendra asked. 'We have some good intelligence, but if we find a way to discreetly report this then it's likely they'll have someone in place to warn them, or worse.'

'That's right, K. We really need to think about how we're going to do this, otherwise we'll be putting ourselves in the firing line,' Andy replied.

'Maybe not,' Trevor added. 'I spoke to several old friends last night who are more than willing to help with this mess.'

'Officially?' Kendra asked.

'Now that we know who is involved then we may be able to persuade them to do this on the quiet. You know, officially, but only when the bastards have been taken care of.'

'How the hell are you going to do that?' Andy asked.

'I'm going to see another old friend who will help with a smile, he hates corrupt bureaucrats more than anyone I've ever met. He has a lot of influence too and will definitely be able to do something on the quiet... but official,' Trevor said, smiling.

'Who can do that? It's not the police commissioner, is it?' Andy joked.

'Better. Much better,' Trevor said, his smile broadening.

13

'Trevor! It's been a hell of a long time, how the devil are you doing? It's so good to see you again,' said the man, shaking Trevor's hand warmly.

'Hello, sir, I'm sorry to turn up unannounced like this but I think you'll understand when I explain why.'

'Come on in,' said Admiral Sir Robert Jenkins, First Lord of the Royal Navy and Chief of Naval Staff, the man responsible for the fighting effectiveness, efficiency and morale of the Naval Service, and for supporting the management and direction of the Armed Forces. He led Trevor into a spacious, well-lit lounge with classical furniture and a vintage piano.

'Please, sit down. What can I get you to drink?' the admiral asked.

'I'm okay for now, sir, thank you,' Trevor replied, sitting in a plush leather Chesterfield armchair.

'It seems like a lifetime since we served together in Northern Ireland, doesn't it, Trevor? Tell me, what has the man who saved my life been up to?'

Trevor smiled, thinking back to the ambush that had

nearly cost them their lives. Trevor had been escorting the young lieutenant from the Special Boat Service to conduct a reconnaissance on a potential target. It was a joint operation with army intelligence that Trevor was attached to, and they'd been planning it for several weeks, working closely together as they prepared. Somehow, and very unluckily, they were spotted and attacked by an IRA unit as they left the scene, having completed their reconnaissance. They were both shot as the car they were in was sprayed from both sides of the road. Trevor managed to get a radio message off, giving their location when asking for urgent assistance.

He was hit in the arm and thigh, both flesh wounds, but was able to exit the car and help the SBS man to safety when the car had hit another parked vehicle and ended up in a ditch. The car caught fire almost immediately, and the thick black smoke had helped Trevor and the lieutenant escape unseen. The attackers had pursued the injured duo through a farmer's field and to a derelict farmhouse, where Trevor had held off the three-man unit, injuring two of them in the process.

Luckily for Trevor and his colleague, a helicopter had been dispatched to assist and was soon heard approaching the farmhouse. This was the signal for the attackers to turn and vanish into the dense fields, but not before spraying the house with one last act of defiance. The lieutenant spent several weeks in the hospital as he recovered from his more serious wounds. Trevor visited regularly as he recovered from his, and they became firm friends. Although they hadn't seen much of each other over the years, the pair had kept in contact enough for Trevor to feel comfortable about visiting and explaining the current situation.

'Sir, a situation has come up and I didn't know where else

to go. I believe it to be a matter of national security and of high importance, but going to the authorities would warn those responsible. I can't trust anyone else with this and I need your guidance and help moving forward,' Trevor said.

'Why do you think that going to the authorities would warn anyone, Trevor? And please, call me Rob, like you used to,' the First Sea Lord replied.

'They have people everywhere, including the police, judges, civil servants, even at MI5. The minute after I go to them the bad guys will know, and they'll disappear into the night without anyone ever getting to them. Plus, there's a good chance they'll take me out too, and maybe those close to me,' Trevor said.

'Why is it a national security issue, then?'

'Sir... sorry... Rob, we strongly believe that Chinese intelligence units, along with a local triad gang, are responsible for the recent explosions at the factories, along with an attack on a government official. It's all connected to the Taiwan trade deal with the UK, which includes a very significant amount of military hardware. They've come over to blow the hell out of everything and prevent the trade deal from happening.'

'Do you have evidence of this?' asked Rob.

'Yes, we have a printout of the triads that came over a couple of weeks ago, all with sponsorship letters signed by the corrupt officials, all who are shareholders in a security company that is linked to everything. They even kidnapped a police officer,' Trevor added.

'That was them? Why kidnap a cop? It doesn't make sense.'

'We think they're using a two-pronged attack. One is to take over gangs in London, which includes controlling docks and logistics routes, and causing as much chaos as possible.

The other is the attack on the Taiwan-related businesses and officials. I think they're trying to teach us a lesson we'll never forget, thinking we're still just a small island and no longer important in the world,' Trevor replied.

'Do they now? Well, we'll see about that, shall we? I need to make some phone calls, Trevor. The kitchen is over there, go and make yourself a cup of tea and a sandwich. I'll have one too. This matter needs attending to, and now.' Rob picked up the phone.

Trevor nodded and went to the substantial well-equipped kitchen just along the hallway. He made two cups of tea and two cheese-and-pickle sandwiches, remembering his old friend's favourite snack. He returned to the lounge to see Rob still talking on the phone.

'When you've spoken to them both, make sure you call me back, okay? And remember, this goes no further than the three of you, make sure to reinforce that point to the Major General and the Officer in Command. Thanks, Bill, I'll speak with you soon.'

He turned to Trevor, who handed him the tea and the sandwich.

You remembered!' he laughed, noticing the sandwich.

'How could I forget? Every time I saw you at the hospital it was a cheese-and-pickle sandwich, nothing else was good enough!' Trevor laughed.

'Well, we all have our weaknesses, Trevor. Anyway, that was the Judge Advocate, who is by now speaking with either the Major General or the Officer in Command. I have asked him to put a team together and to be ready for a briefing about a secret operation. When I get the green light, I want you to go to Poole and deliver that briefing,' the First Sea Lord said.

'Me? Sir... Rob, with all respect, I need to stay in the shadows with this one, I can't have anyone know that I am involved or who I am. Is there no other way?' Trevor pleaded.

'Ah, I see. I remember you doing something similar when your kid was young, keeping out of the way to keep her safe. How is she, by the way?'

'She's doing great, thank you for asking, and yes, it's critical that my involvement is kept to a minimum. I'll give a briefing, but I need to do it anonymously. I hope you're okay with that,' said Trevor.

'I'm sure it won't be a problem. When I hear back, I'll make arrangements for someone to meet you outside the camp and escort you in and out, will that work for you?'

'Yes, thank you. Do you have a number I can reach you on?'

'Of course,' the First Sea Lord replied, giving Trevor the number. Trevor dialled it so that Rob would have his.

'Done, so you'll contact me when you are organised and I will do the same if I hear anything more,' Trevor said, drinking his tea and taking a bite out of his sandwich.

'Yes. Now tell me more about what you've been doing these past few years, I'm intrigued to know.'

Trevor smiled as he drove away from his friend's house. It had been a positive and encouraging visit. It was still early but the authority in Rob's voice was reassuring. His phone rang and he saw it was Andy.

'Andy, what's happening?'

'I have you on speaker phone, Kendra is here with me.'

'Hi, Dad, where are you?'

'I'm just on my way back to your flat after visiting an old friend who will be helping us,' he said, smiling confidently.

'That's good to know, because we have some news, too,' Andy said, sounding excited.

'Take a deep breath, Andy, and tell me slowly.' Trevor laughed.

'I did some digging around on the dark web for more information and there is definitely chatter about a group of Chinese gangsters coming over. I then had a thought about how they communicate here, knowing they'd need UK SIM cards to use mobile phones, so I went back to the warehouse and surrounding area and mapped the mobile phones pinging from there,' Andy continued.

'What did you find?'

'There's a hot spot in a block of flats nearby as well as the warehouse where we rescued Rick. I checked the numbers and found that the majority of them were part of a bulk order of two hundred and twenty phones and the same number of SIM cards recently purchased and delivered to the warehouse.'

'Okay, so they have mobile phones, what is exciting about that?' Trevor asked.

'Well, for one, our old friend Eddie Duckmore paid for them on a credit card in his name, which is great intel. But mainly, we now have the numbers of two hundred and twenty burner phones, which we'll be able to trace as we continue monitoring them,' Andy continued.

'That's a good advantage to have, Dad,' Kendra said.

'Yes, it is. I'm guessing that the order was for the new arrivals, so it will be good to know where they are at all times.

The friend I just visited is going to help sort our visitors out while we can focus on Duckmore and Critchley. Any update on those two?' Trevor asked.

'Not a lot. Duckmore is smarter than we give him credit for. Since his call with JP Sisterson, he switches his phone off when he's not using it, so it's almost impossible to track him. He clearly doesn't trust the bloke now and is minimising phone use. He's sent a couple of messages, one to JP demanding information and one to a drug dealer in North London telling him to wait for instructions about a meeting. As soon as I know more, I'll let you know,' Andy said.

'Great. I think it's time we gather the team and let them know what is going on. Can you advise them that we'll meet with them tomorrow? You free for that, love?'

'Yes, it's one of my days off, so I'll arrange it for the morning,' she replied.

'Great, I'll see you in about half an hour when I get to your flat, I'll need to pack a small overnight bag as I have to go to Dorset. Andy, if you can pop over, I'll explain what's going on.'

'Sure, see you there soon,' Kendra said.

Trevor felt the familiar feelings that had come before important operations in the past, both nerves and excitement rolling into one strange knot in the stomach but accompanied with a warm glow.

It never goes away, does it? he thought, smiling to himself.

BEFORE ARRIVING at Kendra's flat, Trevor received a call.

Trevor, this is Brodie. How's it going, fella?' Dabbs asked, sounding cheerful.

'I'm good, mate, you sound happy, what's going on?'

'I tell you what's going on, Trev, I have a plan to get my operation back, but I'll need your help.'

'Happy to help, Brodie; and actually, you might get more than you expected this time. I've enlisted the help of some very powerful people to take on the triads.'

'That's why I was calling, to see if you could recruit a bunch of people to help me out,' Brodie exclaimed.

'I'm planning to do a lot more than that, mate. What were you planning to do with these people?' Trevor asked, intrigued by what Brodie hoped to do against an army of more than two hundred.

'When I was in trouble with the Albanians last month, I made contact with the police and asked them to help me out,' Brodie said. 'So, I reached out and asked them to help me again.'

'Seriously? You've enlisted the help of the police? How the hell did you manage that? How can the boss of one of the largest gangs in London get any help from the police?'

'Technically, it's now *ex-boss*, but that's not an issue. I know you may not like this and I'm asking you... *trusting you* to keep this to yourself, but I've cut a deal with them. In exchange for helping me take out the triads, I will give them information about the other gangs in London and their operations. It's a win-win, I get my operation back and thin the competition.'

'That sounds too easy, Brodie; a lot of things can go wrong. You know that, right?'

'Of course, I'm not an idiot. I'll always have a back-up plan, just as I did in this instance, so don't worry about me. Will you help me, then?'

'Yes, but hold off for a while, I need to know how things

are going to pan out in the next day or two. I need you to send me a number I can reach you on, this one you're using showed as No Caller ID,' Trevor said.

'I'll text you. When you know more, call me back, okay?' Brodie said.

'Of course. Glad to hear you so cheerful again, Brodie, it'll be good to have you back in charge again soon.'

They ended the call just as Trevor arrived at Kendra's flat. He saw her car parked and knew they'd both beaten him there.

Things are gonna get very interesting in the next few days, he thought as he walked towards the flat.

Kendra gave her dad a big hug as he walked in and brought him a bottle of beer as soon as he sat down in the lounge. Andy clinked bottles and nodded.

'Good to see you, old man. It seems you've been busy so tell us what you know,' he said, ignoring the withering gaze that his comment on Trevor's age caused.

'I'll give you that one as it is a big development,' he told them both, 'but remember not to push your luck.'

'Tell us, Dad, what's happened?'

'These attacks in London and the takeover of Brodie's gang are essentially an attack on the country, making it a national security issue. The problem is, many of the departments that deal with this sort of thing have corrupt officials in place, so we couldn't just go to the police or MI5 and tell them what's been going on.'

'But they must already know, Dad; Marcus Allen told us as much when he explained the issues with the CCTV systems. Surely the government are already doing something.'

'Maybe, but the fact they may have someone in that department could cause big problems. I'm guessing Marcus knows this and is being cautious,' Trevor replied.

'So, what are we going to do, then?' Andy asked, impatiently.

'I went and saw someone I trust and who despises corruption more than anyone I know. He's a very high-ranking official in the Royal Navy and can make decisions on deployment and logistics. When I told him about the attacks and about the corruption being likely to scupper any regular operation, he came up with a plan.'

'Okay, that's good, right?' Andy said.

'Yes, but it means I have to go and give a briefing to some very effective military people who are going to take out the triads,' said Trevor.

'Doesn't that put us at risk of discovery?' Kendra asked, concerned their operation would be found out.

'I've insisted I do it anonymously, so I think we'll be okay.'

'What do you want us to do in the meantime, while you're gone?' asked Andy.

'Do what you can to find Duckmore and Critchley. Also, brief the team tomorrow and tell them to be ready to help an old friend. Brodie Dabbs called me, and he has a plan to get his empire back. He's made a deal with the police but asked for our help too,' Trevor continued.

'Again, isn't that asking for trouble if the police are involved?' Kendra asked.

'Whatever we do, we'll do it covertly, so I'm not worried. If he asks us to accompany the police on raids then it'll be a flat rejection, but I doubt very much it'll be something like that.

Get the team ready and I'll call and let you know when he gets back to me, okay?'

'Okay. Sounds like things are finally starting to happen,' Kendra replied.

'This is some serious stuff we're getting involved with, so if we manage to pull it off without being discovered then it's a big deal for us all,' Trevor said.

'We'll be fine,' Andy said, 'just give us the nod and we'll prepare everyone like you asked. It'll be interesting to see what Brodie has up his sleeve.'

'Yep. That guy is full of surprises, that's for sure,' said Trevor.

14

E ddie Duckmore and Dave Critchley watched as the third and last pallet was unloaded from the freighter.

'That's the lot, Dave. Thirty tons of the best-grade marijuana that triad money can buy. That's around fifty million quid's worth, my old mate. And we're gonna sell it at a quarter of the street price,' Duckmore boasted.

'Why a quarter? Isn't that screwing us out of a lot of good money?' Critchley asked, bemused by the apparent charity.

'That's a good question, Dave, one I asked several times. The bosses want to flood the market to drive prices down so that other gangs lose business to rivals and come to us to buy. They want to cause as much chaos on the streets as possible, so the smaller gangs will be fighting it out and the bigger gangs will have to come to us. Our price will include taking out the competition. It's a fun plan and the police in London won't be able to cope with the repercussions. Anarchy will be the name of the game, me ol' mucka,' Duckmore replied, beaming at the thought of chaos in London. 'The future looks very bright indeed.'

'I still don't understand why,' Critchley said, 'the bosses would make much more money if they did business like the others. Why go to such lengths just to lose money?'

'It isn't about the money, Dave. It's about the power, and the ability to bring London to its knees. I'm pretty sure they're trying to send a very strong message. I couldn't care less, because we'll make a fortune out of it, me and you, and we'll be in charge of a hugely profitable venture for many years to come. They may lose money achieving their objectives in the short run, but we won't, we're getting our cut regardless.'

'Well, far be it for me to argue against that,' Critchley said, nodding in appreciation.

Duckmore rubbed his hands together as the last pallet was loaded onto the truck.

'Let the fun begin!' he exclaimed.

Trevor left for Dorset early the next day, aiming to get to the Poole barracks by midday at the latest. The three-and-a-half-hour journey gave him time to think about the briefing he was going to give to some of the most respected specialist soldiers in the world, the SBS. He had experience in dealing with the Special Boat Service, the navy equivalent of the SAS, but it had been a while since he had left the services himself, so he was slightly nervous about it.

Having received the call from Rob giving instructions on what to do and who to meet, he made sure to use an unregistered vehicle that Stav the garage man had provided, one that couldn't be traced back to him or which would identify anyone in the team. He carried a letter in case he was stopped by the police, confirming the sale of the vehicle and that he was booked in for a service. He also made sure not to have anything on him, credit cards or any other ID–just in case.

He arrived at a pub close to the Royal Marine Poole base for the pre-arranged meeting with Rob's contact. As he pulled into the car park, he saw the silver Range Rover he had been told would meet him, the driver still in the car, and he parked close to it. He locked his car and got into the passenger seat of the Range Rover.

'Morning, sir,' the driver said, nodding. 'I'm Bill, I've been instructed to escort you to the base for a briefing later this afternoon.'

'Hello, Bill. Please call me Tony. I appreciate you helping today,' Trevor replied, hoping he'd remember to use the same alias throughout his visit.

'You're very welcome, Tony. We're just a couple of miles away so we'll be there in no time. Here, put this around your neck and show it at the gate,' Bill said, giving Trevor a pass on a lanyard. He did as he was told and put it around his neck, the word *Visitor* showing in bright yellow lettering between the crest of the Royal Navy at the top and a serial number and that day's date at the bottom, printed in royal blue.

As promised, they arrived at the secretive base just a few minutes later. The base was home to four Sabre squadrons of the SBS, and as expected, the security surrounding it was optimal. The perimeter security fencing was protected by an advanced CCTV system and several different types of cutting-edge proximity detection sensors. The chances of anyone attempting to climb without being caught were virtually zero.

At the security gate, Bill showed his pass, which included a photo of him but no name, as was standard protocol with specialist servicemen.

'Our visitor is giving a briefing to Sirius and Poseidon units this afternoon, Corporal. He will be accompanied at all times,' Bill told one of the guards as Trevor showed the pass.

'Yes, sir, all received and understood. Please hold for a minute while we check the vehicle. If you can pop the boot, it will expedite the search.'

Two other guards worked swiftly to check the underside of the Range Rover, the boot, and the interior. They were methodical and efficient, so the check was completed within two minutes.

'Thank you, sir, please proceed.' The first guard nodded, indicating for the barriers to be raised.

Bill drove through and continued towards a number of low-level buildings in the distance. Trevor saw ongoing building works as the barracks were being redeveloped and improved, along with a large swimming pool and several playing fields, tennis courts and other open areas used for training. He saw several types of small naval boats moored at a pier and more anchored slightly offshore, no doubt used for the rigorous daily training exercises the SBS personnel undertook. There was much more that he didn't see as the car pulled up outside one of the newer buildings in the middle of the complex.

'If you follow me, Tony, I'll see you to the guest lounge where you can have a bite to eat and something to drink while you wait. Someone will come and collect you when you're needed, it shouldn't be much more than an hour,' Bill said as they walked towards the building.

The building in question was clearly one designed and

built specially for visitors where their interaction was kept to a minimum on the base. As they walked inside, they were met by a concierge who led them to a canteen with a dozen tables at one end and four sofas and a television at the other. The service area was a self-service buffet-type setup, with a modern coffee machine at the end. There was also a fridge filled with soft drinks and water.

'Help yourself to anything you need, sir,' the smiling concierge said, 'and if you need anything at all I'll be just outside at my desk,' she added.

'Thank you,' Trevor replied.

'If you're still here tonight I'll show you the bar,' Bill said, smiling at his guest, 'it's much nicer than this.'

'This is great, much better than anything I remember from my army days,' Trevor replied, 'I'll be fine here, thanks.'

'Well, help yourself to anything, and like I said, someone will be here in an hour or so to pick you up,' Bill said. 'I'll be around to escort you out of the barracks and back to your car when you're done here.'

'Thanks, Bill, I appreciate it,' Trevor said, shaking the man's hand.

He walked to the buffet as soon as Bill left, hungry after the long drive. Helping himself to a plate of lasagne with some salad and a bottle of water, Trevor sat at one of the tables by a window. The view wasn't great and designed to give very little away for any guests. The building was one of several surrounding a large, neat courtyard with some benches and small shrubs, so all he could see were the other building and the yard.

The lasagne was delicious, and he went back for a second helping. Once he was full, he helped himself to a cappuccino and sat on one of the sofas in front of the television. The news was on, giving an update about the recent wave of attacks on factories in London. The newscaster went to great lengths to say that it wasn't suspected to be terrorism related but rather a spate of unfortunate accidents.

If only they knew, he thought.

The significance of the situation was not lost on him. When he had started on the adventure with Kendra and Andy, he thought they would be dealing with criminals, not overseas governments and intelligence agencies. And now, here he was, briefing an elite group of soldiers about Chinese interference and attacks on domestic soil. He smiled at the thought, thinking back to when his daughter had approached him. His thoughts were soon interrupted.

'Sir, we're ready for you,' said a Royal Marine in uniform, no rank showing, who had just walked into the canteen.

'Thank you.'

'Follow me please, sir,' he said, turning smartly and leading Trevor out of the room.

They walked for perhaps three minutes towards an isolated group of buildings. The Royal Marine walked between two of them towards what looked like a raised berm in the middle of a courtyard. It was well hidden amongst the buildings and was clearly a place of importance. The soldier led him to the far side to the only entrance, which opened onto some steps leading down.

'We're going to our operations briefing room, sir. We use it for live operations as it is completely isolated from all buildings and is protected against electronic interference.'

He was led down a long corridor which sloped slightly downhill, taking them deeper underground. Trevor imagined it was very well protected against any form of attack. At the end of the corridor there were two doors, one on each side.

The Royal Marine led them through the door on the left into a vast auditorium, with seating in a semi-circle leading down towards a small stage, with a table, six chairs, and a single lectern. Behind them was a large screen currently showing the date, and the operation name: 'Trident Red.'

Less than half the auditorium was occupied and there was a slight murmur of voices.

Trevor was led down to the stage where he was met by another uniformed Royal Marine, again with no rank showing. The man extended his hand and shook Trevor's.

'Hello, Tony. I'm Ian, the Officer in Command of this operation. I've spoken with the First Sea Lord and the Judge Advocate, and they have both instructed me to give you the floor, sir. I'll start with the introduction and then pass the baton over to you, if that's okay?'

'That's fine with me, thank you,' Trevor replied. His nerves were gone, and he had automatically reverted to professional soldier mode, which gave him a feeling of pride and stirred up some very happy memories.

'Please, follow me,' Ian said, leading him to the chair closest to the lectern.

Once Trevor had sat, the Officer in Command walked to the lectern and tapped on the microphone. The room fell into an immediate hush, the men quickly showing their discipline.

'Good afternoon to you all, ladies and gents. Today's operation is a somewhat unusual one and of the highest importance due to its nature. Our sources have informed us that a number of facilities in London have been destroyed and government personnel have been attacked on our streets. There is a criminal organisation working with Chinese intelligence agents here on our shores who are trying to disrupt the trade agreement with Taiwan and also cause as much carnage on our streets as possible. These people mean business, and to add to the difficulty of the situation, it seems they have been assisted by trusted officials in government, police, even MI5. It is to that end that we have been tasked with this mission, which you will consider as Top Secret and which you are not to divulge to anyone outside of this room. Am I clear?'

'*Yes, sir!*' came the instant response from the audience.

'Good. Now the plan is to engage with this enemy and take them out of circulation as quickly and as quietly as possible. Our information is that there are in excess of two hundred trained soldiers, with some intelligence agents amongst them, who need to be taken care of. Additionally, there are the treasonous individuals that will need to be taken into custody, alive, and who will be interrogated to our advantage upon the conclusion of the operation. At this time, we will be deploying *Sirius* and *Poseidon* units to deal with the enemy personnel. We'll be assisted by a selected unit from Three Commando Brigade who will back up with logistics and armed support if and when required. Any questions so far?'

'Sir, is it safe to say that the operation will be conducted in London? If so, will there be a likelihood of innocent bystander casualties?' asked one person from the audience.

'At this time, we believe that the enemy have isolated themselves from the public and have taken over a new housing estate in east London. To that end, I'll pass you over to one of our sources, Tony, who will be able to answer many of your questions.'

He called Trevor over and spoke again into the microphone.

'Tony will give you more detail about the enemy and the locations involved. Feel free to ask anything that you think will help the operation,' he added.

Trevor took his place at the lectern.

'Ex-army intelligence can handle anything you sailor boys and girls can throw at us, so fire away,' he said, to much laughter and appreciation from the audience.

'The boss mentioned two hundred trained soldiers,' one man asked, 'can you expand on that please, Trevor?'

'Our understanding is that the Ghost Dragons, the triad gang that's also been operating in the UK for a while now, have sent two hundred of their finest warriors to back them up in their quest to take over the gangs of London. The triads train their men well and have armed them to the teeth,' Trevor said, 'but they are not soldiers in the same sense that you are, or I was.'

'Sir, you say they're looking to take over the gangs in London, I thought they wanted to screw up the trade deal with Taiwan?' asked another audience member.

'They do. Theirs is very much a two-pronged assault on our shores. They want to take over the gangs, and have already started doing so, in order to control logistics and bring more people and arms into the country. We're pretty sure they want to cause as much chaos as possible to divert attention from_their main objective, which is to stop us arming the Taiwanese with high-end military equipment. Everything else is a bonus.'

'I can't imagine that's an easy thing to do, sir, they just came over and took over the gangs?' asked the same person.

'They've had some assistance from corrupt ex-police officers, judges, and other senior officials who have a vested interest in the company that is running the gangs: Hurricane

Solutions. They stand to make billions of pounds, from selling drugs, to dealing arms, and much more. London could easily become a no-go area if they're not stopped,' Trevor said, reinforcing the seriousness of the situation.

'What are our orders when we engage with the enemy?' asked another audience member.

'I'll pass you back over to the OIC for that one,' Trevor said, making room for Ian to return to the lectern.

'As I mentioned, the British subjects will be taken alive unless they are armed and pose a threat to anyone. The rest, your orders are simple, if engaged then your orders are: shoot to kill,' he said.

'Tony, can you tell us more about the location of this estate?' asked one of the three men seated at the table on the stage.

'Yes, of course,' Trevor said, taking back the lectern. 'The estate is close to the river Thames in Dagenham and is being built on what was once part of the Ford complex there. The majority of the targets will be in the ten-storey tower block; we have seen the plans and know that each floor has four three-bed flats. There is also a row of eight houses that are holding more men and also—we believe—their leaders. There are no buildings overlooking the estate, and the closest is some minutes away. I informed the First Sea Lord of the location; do we have a map of the area?' Trevor asked.

'Yes, I believe we do,' Ian replied, waving to someone at the back.

The screen behind the stage lit up with a Google Earth image of the area. Although it was out of date and the buildings weren't all showing, it gave a good indication of the location, and ways in and out.

'This is where the tower block is,' Trevor said, pointing to a cleared area, 'and the houses are here. You can see there's only one road going in and out at the moment, that hasn't changed. They park their vehicles, mainly vans, here and here.'

'Will they all be in situ in the early hours? Or do they have a rota we should be aware of?' the same man asked.

'We believe most will be at the locations. There will also be some at the nearby warehouse they're using as their head-quarters, so that will need to be attacked simultaneously to avoid warning the others. They'll have some people there guarding their contraband and arms, I'm sure.'

'Anything else we need to know?'

'We have a list of all the burner phones the soldiers have been issued with, and will be able to let you know where they are in advance of the attack. Additionally, we can assist with camera feeds, drone footage, and anything else you think may be of use to you when the time comes,' Trevor added.

'We don't need that kind of help, Tony, we have our own people who'll be popping over for a visit later to install every-thing we need,' Ian said, smiling confidently.

'I can also get you information on the ancillary targets, the British contingent, names and addresses, et cetera. Two of them are ex-police officers on the run for kidnapping so they may be away from these locations,' Trevor said.

'Okay, well, we'll be a little stretched with the main targets so whatever you can assist with when it comes to loca-tions will be greatly appreciated. We'll take care of the rest,' the OIC replied.

'No problem,' said Trevor.

'We'll be looking to deploy early tomorrow, at zero-two-hundred hours, so make sure your kit is ready to go. We'll be going with small arms and ready to incapacitate and secure our targets, so plenty of zip-ties each, and evidence bags for each subject. I'll issue the order to dispense the *FenGas* as it'll be the best chance of taking most of them out without engaging direct- ly,' Ian continued. 'Anything else you think we need, just ask. I'll also speak to our colleagues at Three Commando Brigade to ensure we have back-up supplies. They'll be providing the transport and retrieval of all prisoners. Any questions?'

There was no response from the audience.

'Okay, we'll brief again before we move out. You're dismissed,' Ian said.

The audience rose and started to leave the auditorium.

'What's *FenGas*?' Trevor asked.

'It's the closest thing we have to knockout gas, which is a bit of a myth, as you know,' the OIC replied. 'It's an adapted derivative of the Fentanyl-based gas that was used by the Russians to take out the Chechen terrorists in Moscow a while back. Theirs was much cruder, and some people died. This should knock the triads out and keep them asleep for an hour or two while we gather them up.'

'Got it, thanks. Can I help in any other way?' Trevor asked.

'Not really,' said Ian, 'we'll be sending some people, as I mentioned, to install some cameras and give us an accurate mapping of the estate. From what you're saying we'll be stretched quite thin, so we'll use Three Commando Brigade backups more than usual.'

'Okay, how can we keep in touch? It'll help if we knew what was happening, so we keep out of the way.'

'Here's my number.' Ian handed Trevor a plain card with just a number on it. 'I meant to ask, and tell me to mind my own business, but how is it you're involved in this if you're long retired from the army?'

'Ian, that's an interesting story, and one that'll have to wait for a while. My team and I are trying to help out where we can and somehow, we've ended up in the middle of an international incident. We're great at dealing with criminals, but this is way out of our comfort zone,' Trevor replied.

'That doesn't really answer my question, but that's fine, I get it.' Ian laughed.

'We want to keep under the radar otherwise too many questions will be asked and too many awkward situations will follow, so thanks for understanding.'

'I'll call Bill to see you out. If anything comes up, be sure to let me know, okay? It was a pleasure working with you, *Tony*.' Ian smiled, shaking Trevor's hand warmly.

'Thanks, *Ian*,' he replied, returning the smile.

Bill arrived a few minutes later and escorted him out of the bunker and back to the Range Rover.

'It's a shame you never got to see the bar,' Bill said as they drove away from the barracks. 'Maybe next time, eh?'

'Bill, if there's a next time, then the shit would have hit the fan yet again,' Trevor said, laughing.

∽

15

'I wonder how your dad is getting on,' Andy asked as he continued his searches.

'From all accounts, I'm sure he'll be fine. He's full of surprises, is the old man, so nothing like that will faze him,' Kendra replied.

'Well, hopefully, by the time he's back, he'll find everything in order just as he asked. The team are ready to rock and roll and the phone tracking is working well,' he said, adjusting one of the three monitors he had running simultaneously for just that.

'Tell me again how you've done this,' Kendra said.

'It's relatively easy when you know how, and you have the right software. For example, having the phone numbers and identification numbers made it easy to trace the burner phones as they move around. You can see on this monitor that they're pretty well bunched up around the tower block, the houses they're using, and the warehouse, in the main. There's a few that seem to stay clear of the others, here on second monitor. They're driving around London, no doubt looking for more targets, and then returning to the same house on the estate, the one on the end. My guess is that they're the agents who have been blowing everything up. This third monitor shows our old friends Duckmore and Critchley. As you can see, they spend a lot of time at the warehouse; I guess they think they're safe there. With this information, it will make it easier to deal with them when Trevor gets his mates in to help,' Andy added.

'The ones that are driving around, can you pinpoint the locations they're paying attention to? Maybe we can give Marcus Allen an anonymous tip,' she said.

'Shouldn't be too difficult, although this lot frequently turn their phones off, so it may be sporadic but better than nothing.'

'It's amazing how much trouble you can get into by having a phone, isn't it?' Kendra said, shaking her head. 'Is there no way around it?'

'Not really, except the old, trusted way of turning it off and taking out the battery. No signal goes out to be tracked, and if you know it's a possibility you can just use a phone and bin it straight after, moving on to another,' he replied.

'That's an expensive way of communicating,' Kendra said.

'Yeah, but burner phones can be quite cheap and basic, so they don't feel the financial hit like we would. Also, many have started using encrypted platforms, so their calls aren't listened to. Luckily, our mate Duckmore feels nice and safe, thinking his burner phone isn't known to anyone yet.'

'So, I guess we just wait for Dad to return so he can brief us on what we need to do next.'

'Yes. The team are ready to go. Their kit is out and prepped for any excursions and we have four cars and a van at our disposal; Stav has worked his usual magic. Also, if Brodie calls, we'll be ready to help there too,' Andy added.

'Okay, then we wait.'

~

Brodie had made his own list of those he wanted removing from the organisation. Knowing Trevor as he did, and not wanting to upset the new police partnership too much, he was resigned to dealing with the traitors in his organisation without using excessive and sometimes lethal violence. He had other ways of dealing with backstabbers; painful ways, but he'd make sure they would feel lucky to be alive by the time he'd finished with them. Those he couldn't reach would be taken care of by the police, in the main, and maybe Trevor's team, who he knew were very capable.

He looked at the names on the list and imagined the organisation without them: who he'd replace them with, how long it would take to recover, and most of all, what measures he'd put in place to ensure it would never happen again. He'd be starting on his own, so he needed to be selective and cautious as he began his quest for revenge.

'A few cracked heads and plenty of time in prison should do the trick,' he said out loud, smiling again for the umpteenth time, knowing he was almost ready to go into action.

~

Trevor arrived at the factory early evening, having endured a relatively stress-free drive back from the SBS HQ in Dorset. He saw the car park had more vehicles than usual and nodded in approval that the team were likely here, awaiting further instructions. He went in through the main doors and was greeted by Greg, who was still recovering from his terrible injuries at the hands of the Albanians.

'Evening, boss, they're all in the loading bay waiting for you,' he said, smiling despite the scarring on both cheeks, where he'd been knifed.

'Grab yourself a drink and join us, Greg. Make sure you lock the front door first,' Trevor said, waving and returning the smile.

'Sure thing, shall I get you one too?' Greg asked.

'Yes, please, a plain black coffee for me, I need to wake up a little.'

He could hear the murmur of voices as he made his way to the loading bay. As he walked in, he saw that the shutters to the bay were open and the team were milling around, chatting and engaging with each other like any other team at work. Most waved in greeting.

'We thought you'd got lost, Trev,' Amir said, as he approached the younger twin and his brother, who were talking to Andy and Kendra. 'Or did you stop for a nap somewhere? Is it an age thing? You should let us know about stuff like that, maybe we can get you one of those monitors so we know you're safe.'

'He just never stops, does he?' Trevor said, shaking his head. 'Keep your brother in check, Mo, will you?'

'That's impossible, and you know it,' the elder twin replied.

'How was it, Dad?' asked Kendra as she gave him a hug.

'Yeah, how was it, Trev?' Andy asked, coming in for a hug and stopping at arm's length thanks to one of Trevor's famous glares.

'It was fine,' he said. 'They're some very impressive people down there. We're falling back and letting them do all the hard work now, so we'll focus on Duckmore, Critchley, and anything Brodie needs help with. Have you told them?'

'Not everything,' said Kendra, 'just that they need to be ready for anything, and some background about the triads and the corrupt officials. I figured you'd let them know the rest, whatever it is you feel they need to know.'

'Okay, gather everyone around,' he said, taking the steaming cup of coffee. 'Thanks, Greg.'

Kendra ushered the team together. The team present was fifteen-strong. Trevor was able to call on more if needed, younger recruits mainly, but on this occasion, it was best to stick to the trusted and experienced members.

'Evening, everyone. Sorry to ruin your night but this one is as important as anything we've yet had to deal with. So much so, we'll be playing more of a support and bit-part to what is about to happen,' he started.

'Bit-part? Come on, Trevor, we're supposed to be growing and dealing with more serious stuff than just backing someone up, aren't we?' asked Darren, one of the six from Walsall who were now permanently based in London with the team. 'I mean, look at these boys, their champing at the bit, bless 'em.'

Although his comment was partly in jest, Trevor could understand the frustration of being left out of the action that was about to start.

'Well, as mean and tough as you guys are, the teams from

the Special Boat Squadron and Three Commando Brigade will always take primacy when it comes to matters of national security, that goes without saying,' Trevor said, smiling at the sudden shocked expressions ahead of him.

'Wait, you mean the SBS are coming to our patch? They're like the SAS, aren't they?' Jimmy asked.

'That's right, Jimmy, they are. I won't say who the better unit is because they're both as good as anything out there.'

'How's it going to work then, Trevor? Where do we fit in?' asked Charmaine.

'Okay, so the team from Poole, as we'll call them, will be arriving in the early hours tomorrow. They'll be taking out the triads in the tower block, the row of houses, and the warehouse. Thanks to Andy's tracking of the phones, we'll know where the majority of them will be at any time, so we'll be able to pass that information on. So, we need to stay away from there from this moment and focus on anyone who for some reason isn't there, and on helping Brodie Dabbs with his concerns, which are basically taking back his gang by removing one traitor at a time. We'll help take out anyone he needs to pave the way for his return, I imagine it'll be a half-dozen or so.'

'Will we bring them here?' Amir asked.

'Maybe. If we do, we need to make sure they have no clue as to our location, so take all phones, watches—you know the score—and make sure you put everything in the Faraday bags so no signal can be tracked,' he added. 'Blindfold them, if necessary, I don't want anyone recognising our location here.'

'What about Duckmore and Critchley, Trev?' asked Andy, 'how do you want us to deal with them?'

'Luckily, you can keep track of them now, Andy. Well,

with Duckmore, that is. If we can isolate them from the triads, we'll keep one car free to deal with them. Darren, can you and a couple of others take a car and deal with those two? Make sure you're all fully kitted up as they're both armed and dangerous, you can be sure.'

'Yep, no problem. I'll liaise with Andy about locations, et cetera. Where do you want them taking?'

'That's a good question. I think we'll keep them away from here. Maybe we can use the warehouse that our friend Rick Watts was left in for the police to pick him up? We can secure them there and call it in again.'

'That'll work. We'll drive by and see if we can still have access, it'll be quiet on the estate so shouldn't be a problem,' Darren replied.

'Okay, that's about it, really. Just make sure you have the protective gear with you when you leave, and try to get some rest now until we get the calls,' Trevor said.

'I can't believe we're working with special forces, how cool is that?' Amir said as the team started to disperse.

'Don't get too excited, Amir, the whole point is that they'll come in and take care of the triads without anyone knowing they've even been. Chances are, we won't see hair nor hide of them,' Trevor replied.'Damn, that would've looked great on my CV,' Amir said, thumping his fist into his hand theatrically.

'Why, are you looking for a new job, Amir?' Kendra asked, crossing her arms and staring at the twin.

'Hell, no! This is the best gig... ever! I was just trying to be funny, that's all. Clearly it didn't work. Why would I want to leave such a sweet job as this? I'm not crazy.'

'Some would argue against that, Amir. Mo, keep an eye on your little brother,' Trevor said as they walked to the canteen.

Trevor indicated for Kendra and Andy to join him. They sat with their drinks, away from the hubbub of the team getting themselves ready or resting until called upon.

'I haven't told them everything, it's best that some things are kept from them,' Trevor whispered.

'Like what, Dad? Can we know?'

'Well, for one, it's likely that they've sent people ahead already to install cameras and do a proper recce for the unit. They turned down our offer of help with drones and cameras. No doubt their equipment is superior.'

'Yeah,' said Andy, 'I'm guessing they have kit that isn't available on the market.'

'That's pretty much what they told me, so I just left them to it. They don't want any outsiders getting involved, so we'll stay well out of their way and leave them to it, unless they ask for anything. They have my number.'

'What's gonna happen to the triads they take out?' Kendra asked.

'They're being supported by a team of Royal Marines who'll give them back-up and help with logistics and the prisoner transport. I never asked where they'll be taking them, so I have no clue. I'm sure they know what they're doing,' Trevor replied.

'Do they know there's over two hundred of them?' asked Andy.

'Yes, I briefed them on numbers and locations. They seem very confident that they can deal, with only forty-odd of them with their Royal Marine back-ups. I for one would not want to meet them in a dark alley, that's for sure.'

'It's a relief that we're able to hand them over, Dad, they were gonna be a nightmare for us and I doubt we could've done much against them.'

'I agree, love, it was an easy decision to make,' Trevor replied.

'Right,' said Andy, 'if you don't mind, I'm going to go and check on our friends from overseas and our corrupt friends from closer to home. I'll let you know if anything develops.'

'Now we wait,' Trevor said.

'When we have more time, I want to know more about your secret life, Dad. Much more.'

'Well, that's a boring tale that nobody should ever have to hear,' he said, laughing.

'Oh no, you're not getting away with it that easily. I know for sure it wouldn't have been boring, so you'd better make some time for your daughter and get your story ready!'

'Yes, ma'am,' he said, mock-saluting.

'And I want to know more about Mum, too. Nobody seems to speak about her, and I know so little,' Kendra said, sadly.

'She would have been so proud of you, love, knowing what you have become and what you're doing now. I'm bursting with pride, she would have been twice as proud as me,' he said, stroking her cheek.

'I want to know everything, so don't spare the details, Mister Giddings,' she said.

'Well, that's never a good sign, when your own daughter calls you by your surname!' He laughed.

'You'd better believe it,' she said. 'Now spill the details, we have plenty of time.'

≈

16

Andy returned to the canteen several hours later, just before midnight.

'Have you two been here all this time?' he asked, having searched elsewhere first.

'We've been catching up,' Kendra said, placing her hand on Trevor's. 'Dad's been telling me some old war stories from his youth.'

'Ooh, I'd like to hear those too one day,' Andy said, looking at Trevor expectantly.

'We'll see,' he said. 'What have you found?'

'I wanted to wait until it was late before updating you, as most of the triads are now tucked up in bed at the tower block, with very little movement in the last half hour or so. There are thirteen in total at the wholesaler's premises, five of them are moving around a lot and eight are pretty much stationary, so I assume they're the guards. They're in the rear of the complex in the warehouse section where we grabbed Rick from. It looks like they went from four to eight guards, maybe because of the attack or because something else is going on there,' Andy said.

'What about Duckmore and Critchley?' asked Kendra.

'That's very interesting. They're both at the docks, in a building close to one of the loading bays and moorings. I checked and saw they've spent most of their time there in the past few days, with a couple of trips to the wholesaler's. God knows what they're doing there but they have four of our triad friends there with them, so Darren is gonna need some help.'

'Anyone else not where we expect them?' asked Trevor.

'There's a couple that are stationary at a restaurant nearby; they usually reside in one of the houses, so I'm guessing they're part of the management setup. Hopefully they'll be back before our friends from Poole arrive. Then there's another five that keep moving around, the ones we spoke about checking potential targets out in London. The rest are at the houses, hopefully for the night,' Andy added.

'Okay, that's not as bad as I thought. So, we have nineteen in total that aren't at the locations, but we know where they are. The rest are in place and ready to go. I'll call my contact in Poole and let them know,' Trevor said, walking away to make the call.

'For some reason I'm feeling very nervous,' Andy said, rubbing his hands.

'It's like that when things are out of your control, I wouldn't worry about it,' Kendra replied.

'Let's hope they're as good as Trevor is saying,' Andy said.

'Trust me; if anyone knows, it'll be Dad, and he is very confident of their ability.'

'I guess so. I'd better get back and keep track, in case your dad needs to update again before they strike,' he added, leaving Kendra alone to wait for Trevor.

He returned a few moments later.

'They're grateful and just waiting for the green light to strike. Where did Andy go?'

'He's monitoring the phones in case you need to tell our friends,' Kendra said.

'Not long now. I haven't heard back from Brodie, so I guess he's okay and doesn't need anything from us yet.'

'It feels weird just sitting here waiting for something to happen that we can't be a part of,' Kendra said. 'I'm not sure I'm a fan.'

'I know what you mean, it's easier when you're in control of something and not reliant on others. Still, this is a big deal, love, and the best people are on the case.'

'Yeah, I know. Anyway, while we're waiting, you can tell me more war stories, can't you?'

'I'd hoped you'd forgotten!' he said.

Brodie Dabbs was meticulous in his planning and execution, whatever endeavours he was involved in. Yes, he was a criminal and a former boss of an organised crime gang, but he was the leader because of his attention to detail and because he paid attention. It was why he was able to view the house of his former second-in-command, Zane O' Connor. He crouched behind a bush by the side of the wooden fence that surrounded O' Connor's back garden. The garden was a hundred feet long by fifty feet wide, well maintained with borders along both side fences, which mainly hosted well-trimmed bushes and evergreens like the one he was hiding behind.

Brodie had been to this house many times, having attended many barbeques and dinners hosted by Zane and his wife Penny. The patio area abutting the house was sizeable and modern, with a stainless steel gas barbeque the focal point. Zane often boasted about his prowess as a barbeque cook with his secret barbeque sauces and mixes that had always been well-received.

'*It's a shame I won't get to eat those ribs again*,' Brodie sighed as he stared at the house.

He could see the open-plan lounge and dining area, with its heavy patio doors offering an unobstructed view into the house. He could see Zane and Penny cuddled together on the sofa watching the television. Knowing they were the only two in the house made it easy for Brodie to bide his time until there was an opportunity to deal with the man he had once trusted the most after the loss of his younger brother. He shook his head at the thought of betrayal.

Brodie had waited for almost two hours and was starting to think his plan was going to fail. Fortunately, he saw Penny get up, give her husband a kiss on the cheek, and leave the lounge, probably for the bedroom.

'Here we go,' Brodie whispered; knowing Zane's tradition of having a cigar before retiring for the night was the only way he was likely to get close to him.

He didn't have too long to wait; just fifteen minutes later, Zane slid open the patio doors and stepped out. He took a deep breath and put the Cuban cigar in his mouth, having snipped off the end with the stainless-steel cutter on his keyring. He then lit a match and drew a number of deep breaths to light the expensive cigar. He inhaled and then raised his head and exhaled, nodding appreciatively as he regarded the cigar in his hand.

'Does it taste as good, knowing what you did, Zane?' Brodie suddenly said, stepping out from behind the bush and walking towards his old friend, the revolver pointing directly at him. 'Do you even think about what you've done and the consequences?'

'Brodie! Bloody hell, you're alive!' Zane exclaimed.

'Less noise, please. Is Penny still taking sleeping pills at night?'

'Yes, she'll be out like a light now. No need to involve her.'

'Why'd you do it, Zane?' Brodie asked.

'We thought you were dead, for Christ's sake, what would you have done in our place?' Zane replied, staring at the gun.

'After all the years we've worked together you didn't think to even ask? I was there, you know, and it took all of a minute for you bastards to turn against me,' Brodie said through gritted teeth. 'I thought we were a family, but you all clearly thought otherwise, didn't you?'

'Brodie, please, hear me out. I thought they'd killed you and the alternative was for them to wipe us out. Have you seen how many people they've got working for them now? There are hundreds of the bastards and they're all armed to the teeth,' Zane said, 'you would have done the same.'

'I would never have turned my back on you, never! I may have gone with it at the time, but I would've tried to discover the truth and find a way to stop them from destroying everything we've built. Of that you can be sure. You lot just took the money and ran without a thought.'

'Come on, Brodie, think about it, my friend. What would you have really done if offered double the amount and a stake in all future profits?' Zane asked, pleading his case.

'It was never about the money, and you know it, Zane. You were nothing when I brought you onboard and now look what you've got,' he said, pointing to the house and its surroundings. 'You have a great life, more than comfortable, and there's nothing you can't have if you want it. You just got greedy and stabbed me in the back like the traitorous scum you are.'

'Think carefully about this, Brodie. You're literally on your own, how the hell do you think killing me is going to solve your problem?'

'Who said anything about killing you?' Brodie stepped closer. 'I just want to hurt you,' he added, pistol-whipping Zane to the side of the head.

Zane O'Connor fell like a bag of cement, momentarily unconscious for a few seconds before attempting to raise himself up on his elbow. He shook his head to clear it, a trickle of blood running down his cheek from the small cut in his temple. Before he could recover fully, Brodie took a set of handcuffs from his pocket and swiftly put them on Zane's wrists, locking them in place securely.

'Now, you have a choice, Zane. You can come with me, quietly, or I'll knock you out and set your bloody house on fire. What'll it be?' Brodie removed the keyring from Zane's pocket, along with his mobile phone. Brodie held the phone in front of his prisoner's face to unlock it. He quickly changed the settings to remove the security feature so he could have access later, before switching it off.

'No... don't... I'll go with you,' Zane croaked, still groggy.

Brodie pulled him to his feet and walked him around the

side of the house. He unlocked the side gate and went to a dark-grey van parked a few yards away from the house. Unlocking the back doors, he pushed Zane inside, where he fell on his side and lay there. Brodie took out a couple of zipties and bound his ankles together for good measure.

'How does it feel to be trussed up like a chicken, Zane?' he asked, closing the back doors and getting into the driver's seat.

'Where are you taking me?' Zane asked, his voice now shaky.

'That's a damned fine question. I'm taking you to your top-secret safety deposit box that nobody is supposed to know about. You'll tell me exactly where to go, and you'll go in and get it for me, otherwise you'll leave me no choice but to bury you alive. Do we have a deal?'

'D... d... deal,' said Zane. There was very little point in denying anything; his fortunes had changed significantly in the space of a few minutes.

Brodie drove the van with care through the virtually deserted roads of suburban London. His destination was Islington in North London, and it took thirty minutes to arrive. Brodie squeezed through the gap between the seats and went into the rear of the van where Zane lay.

'Right, there's no point lying to me about this so let's be clear about something now, okay? We're going to go inside and you're going to do the whole biometric thing to retrieve your safety deposit box. Only after I've emptied it and we're safely away from here will you have my assurance that I will let you live. Do we understand each other?'

'Y-yes... Brodie, please, I won't give you any trouble, I promise,' Zane replied.

'That's good, because I'm about to send a message to my associate now and if they don't hear from me again in ten minutes then they will be setting your house on fire. Am I clear?' Brodie lied. He took out his phone and sent a message to himself so that Zane would believe he was contacting his associate. 'There, it's done, so I suggest we get a move on.'

'A-absolutely. Like I said, you'll get no trouble from me.'

'That's what I like to hear. Now, I'm going to untie you, so no sudden movements, okay?'

'I promise,' came the reply.

Brodie cut the zip-ties with his penknife and unlocked the handcuffs, returning them to his pocket.

'Okay, let's go, we don't have much time. Remember, I know about this place and their security, their cameras, so no funny stuff.'

He opened the back doors and helped Zane out of the back. Zane stretched his arms in relief, his shoulders slumped in defeat.

'I'm sorry, boss,' he whispered, 'I thought you were dead, please believe me.'

'I don't want to hear it, Zane, just help me get your box and we'll call it quits, how's that?'

Zane nodded and walked towards the building.

'I'll need my fob,' he told Brodie, knowing that he had his keyring. Brodie took it out of his pocket and gave it to him.

The building was manned only during regular office

hours but was available to its clients twenty-four hours a day, thanks to its high-specification security systems that had recently been installed. Zane pressed a plastic-coated circular fob on his keyring against the scanner at the door. The door buzzed and clicked open, allowing them entry to a foyer with an unmanned reception desk in the centre and two doors either side of it. Zane went towards the door on the left and used the fob again, which allowed them entry to a hallway leading to another door, which again required the fob for entry.

They entered a large, well-lit room with four cubicles, each measuring ten-feet-by-ten. The doors to the cubicles were glass. Zane used the fob once more to gain entry into the first one. Once inside, the glass door immediately turned from clear to frosted to allow for privacy. Zane placed his thumb on a biometric fingerprint scanner on the desk against the far wall. He then typed a four-digit PIN into the pad next to the thumb scanner. A green light and a long beep confirmed the identity of the account holder.

A whirring sound then filled the room as a large, internal robotic arm retrieved Zane's safety deposit box from the hermetically sealed vault. The robotic arm placed the box gently on the table on the other side of a steel curtain, which then parted once the arm had returned to its resting point. Zane then used a small key on his keyring to open the box and then stepped back to allow Brodie access.

'Take it all, Brodie, I deserve it,' he pleaded, hoping he'd survive the encounter.

'What do you think I'm after, Zane?' Brodie asked, smiling.

'I don't know, to be honest. Everything?'

'No, I couldn't give two shits about your valuables. I'm after one thing and one thing only,' Brodie said, looking into the box.

He saw six bundles of fifty-pound notes, worth five thousand pounds each. There were three green boxes with the gold embossed crown and the brand name Rolex. There were two gold bullion bars, at which Brodie nodded in appreciation.

'I see you took my advice about the gold, good for you,' he said, nodding.

'Just take it all, Brodie, please.'

There was a brown document folder under the money, which Brodie pulled out. He was hoping his hunch was right. He removed the documents inside and looked through them.

'Here we go,' he said, 'this is what I came for and this is what it's going to cost you to stay alive, Mister O' Connor.'

'Wait, you want the deeds to the farm in Essex? My dad's old place?'

'That's right, this is the price for your treachery and the price for your life. I'll leave you with the rest, your wife doesn't need to know about any of this stuff, or the two mistresses you have in South London.'

'But... but why? What's going on here, Brodie?'

'I'll tell you why, Zane. You were the one I trusted the most, but you still stabbed me in the back. The others did the same, but you were like a brother to me, so it pissed me off very much when you agreed to shaft me like you did. I know our lives are limited in this business but I'm planning for that, and this farm is going to play a big part,' Brodie replied, 'but you'll not know why, and you'll never ask. Do I make myself clear?'

'I'm too confused to ask why and just grateful to stay alive, Brodie. To be honest, I hate that bloody farm, I would have given it to you had you asked,' Zane said, smiling for the first time since their initial encounter.

'Well, you're an idiot, because I was gonna offer you good money for it before you became a turncoat, so now I get it for nothing,' said Brodie.

'Please, take it off my hands with my blessing, the tenant there is a gigantic dick who I can't stand. He's your problem now.' Zane laughed.

'Right, enough chit-chat, let's get out of here,' Brodie said, moving aside for Zane to complete the process.

Zane closed the box and locked it with the key. The robotic arm then whirred into life again and retrieved the box. Once it had picked it up, the steel curtain closed, and the box was returned to the vault.

'Let's go,' Brodie said, holding the folder tightly as they left the room. They were soon outside and back in the van, this time with Zane in the front passenger seat.

Brodie looked at him and shook his head sadly.

'You're a prick, you know that?' he suddenly exclaimed, starting the van and driving off.

'I know I let you down, Brodie. Please, let me try and make it up to you,' said Zane.

'What the hell can you do to help me?'

'I can help you with the rest of them,' Zane suddenly said. 'I know I can help with that, and I know you're doing this alone and don't have an associate threatening to burn my house down. I know you like Penny and wouldn't harm her. Please, Brodie,' he said.

Brodie stared at him, taking his eyes off the road momentarily to do so.

'You're such a prick,' he said, his voice much less harsh than the first time.

17

Kendra and the team stayed at the factory as they waited for news of any developments. Some of the team took the time to rest whilst others gathered in small groups and talked, much as friends do, into the early hours of the morning.

'Well, it's five to two, so any time now the shit will be hitting the fan in a big way for our triad friends,' Andy said as he slurped another coffee. He'd been going back and forth to the control room to check on the location of the subjects in case there were any changes that needed reporting. Fortunately, everything was as it should be, even the two from the restaurant were now back in their house.

'Let's hope they give 'em hell,' Trevor said, his legs crossed and resting on one of the canteen tables, his arms behind his head.

'They will, Dad. I know there's a lot more of them, but honestly, I don't fancy their chances. Those SBS guys will have a bunch of surprises in store, I'm sure.'

They'd been joined by Charmaine and the twins, with

most of their chats focused on the growing security business they were all involved with. Charmaine, in particular, made some very astute suggestions and recommendations for the future. In particular, she suggested that the company create an in-house research and development department to look at legitimate new security solutions they could sell to clients as well as use for themselves.

'Like what?' Trevor had asked, intrigued.

'I think we should aim big and target government departments including the military and blue-chip companies as clients, offering solutions they can't resist. For example, cyber-security is huge business at the moment, along with counter-terrorist solutions, and I'm talking hardware as well as software. When we started looking at bomb-proof and bullet-proof doors for the factory after the attack, I couldn't stop thinking of how many other companies would be interested in something like that,' she had explained.

'Okay, how about you put your theory to the test?' Trevor had replied, receiving a nod from Kendra, who knew where he was going.

'What do you mean?' Charmaine had asked.

'I mean, you're in charge of putting a research and development department together and looking at the best solutions you think our clients—and future clients—won't be able to resist,' he said.

'Really? Wow, that was unexpected, is that a promotion?' she asked.

'She has you there, Dad. You can't expect her to do all that work and not get more money, do you?' Kendra laughed.

'Of course, but let's trial it for six months and see how it goes. Is that fair? And there will be a limit on how much we budget for it initially, so be cautious with your spending.'

'Sounds like a plan to me, boss, thank you!' Charmaine replied, ecstatic that her ideas were being considered seriously.

'Trev, I have a business opportunity too,' Amir said, quickly jumping in to take advantage of Trevor's generosity.

'What's that, Amir?' asked Trevor, smiling knowingly, expecting either a joke or a silly suggestion.

'Well, the company is doing well, right?' Amir started, 'and it's right to look forward with a new department looking at new solutions. My idea is slightly different and more in line with personal development on a physical level as well as equipment.'

'Oh? What's that, then?' Trevor asked, intrigued and somewhat surprised.

'We have a lot of land on this plot, and even more surrounding it. Why don't we use that to build a training centre, where we can get our people fit and train them to become high-end personal protection officers? We can also have a larger showroom to showcase the security equipment alongside the training we offer to the clients. It's much more interesting to have a one-stop-shop for things like that, and there's a lot of money in this business with a requirement that is growing.'

There was silence as they all tried to compute what had just happened.

'Bloody hell, Amir, that's a great idea!' Andy exclaimed first.

'I won't argue with that, you're full of surprises, Amir,' Kendra said, fist-bumping him.

'He gets his ideas from his older brother, you know that, right?' Mo added, smiling proudly.

'Well, technically, they're my ideas that we discuss occasionally. I just thought it would be a good time to bring it up, that's all,' Amir said.

'It looks like we can kill two birds with one stone here, doesn't it?' Trevor said.

'How do you mean, Dad?'

'We can buy more land, that's not a problem, and we can build something modern and quick to set up. We'll build a training centre on one end and a showroom and research centre on the first floor. They can put those modern steel structures up in a couple of months, from what I've seen. It looks like you two can work together on this,' he said to Charmaine and Amir, 'and Mo can assist you both, if you're okay with that, Mo?'

'Count me in. I'll make sure he doesn't spend all your money.'

'This is my favourite part of what we're doing,' Kendra said, looking proudly at her dad and the people who now meant so much to her. 'Sitting together and planning for a better future for us all, how much better can it get?'

The conversation was interrupted by a message Trevor received.

'They're going in.'

Andy, Kendra and Trevor watched the monitors closely, hoping that the dots remained still, meaning that when the raid began, they'd be easy prey for the attacking forces.

'Where are we at with everyone, Andy?' Kendra asked.

'Not much change, to be honest. We still have eight, plus

five staff at the warehouse, four with Duckmore at the dock, and the rest in their beds either in the tower block or the houses on the estate. The five roaming agents are also back there now, in one of the houses, so the team are good to go.'

'Are they sending anyone for Duckmore and Critchley?'

'Not at the moment, love, they're stretched pretty thinly, so we're leaving them for last,' Trevor replied. 'they'll be sending a team of eight to deal with them once the main raid has ended.'

'So, Darren and his team can stay in the background until then?' Kendra asked.

'Yeah, there's no need for them to get involved, just keep eyes on the ground in case anything happens before the SBS team gets to them.'

'This feels weird,' Andy said, shaking his head. 'It feels wrong that we've done all the background work and can't get involved in actually taking out the bad guys.'

'We've been through this, Andy; we couldn't cope with that many baddies,' Trevor said, 'and they are highly trained assassins who would cause us a lot of hurt, I can tell you,' he added.

'I know, and it's the right thing to do, it just feels odd, that's all.'

'Don't worry. They should be in place soon, keep your fingers crossed and hope that within the next half hour the threat to our country and our communities from this lot will be over,' Trevor said. He crossed the fingers on both hands, knowing that any number of things could go wrong.

∾

Due to the layout of the new housing estate, the SBS operatives had correctly judged that the safest and easiest way to approach the tower block and houses would be via the river in rigid hull inflatable boats. The back end of the estate was the least developed and had no lighting in place yet, so they'd be able to approach stealthily. Once in place and the solitary guard in reception had been dealt with, the signal would be given for the lorries, driven by the Three Commando Royal Marines, to make their way and prepare for the second part of the operation, transporting the prisoners away covertly and to a holding site where they'd be interrogated before being dealt with in a legal capacity.

The boats approached the pre-appointed position where they'd be moored for the duration of the raid. They carried ten personnel in each, making them slightly overcrowded for the short time they were in use. They disembarked silently, wearing their night kit of navy-blue, with blackened faces. Their tactical helmets each had a small camera mounted on one side and night vision goggles on the other. Their gas masks were currently loose around their necks ready for use. Each of them carried an L34 silent Sten sub-machine gun, which was perfect for covert operations such as this, and a small backpack loaded with the equipment they'd need. What the silent Sten lacked in range it made up for in stealth, and as the SBS were expert at close-quarter combat, the weapon was perfect for them.

One of the men broke off from the rest and ran, crouching instinctively, towards the front entrance of the block. Free from his backpack and machine gun, he was armed with a resin baton, a high-powered stun gun, a couple of zip-ties, and a state-of-the-art lock-picking mechanism. He approached the entrance and looked inside towards the desk, guessing correctly that the guard would be asleep—which he was, his feet up on the counter and his head resting on the back of the chair. The soldier quickly inserted the lock-pick mechanism and pressed a button. A faint whirring sound came from within as it worked its way through the standard lock, before a click indicated success. Removing the mechanism carefully, he pulled the door open and went inside, aiming for the guard.

As the soldier approached the desk he looked instinctively around for other dangers or hazards that would complicate the operation. There were none. He walked behind the desk and positioned himself behind the sleeping guard, readying the two zip-ties. The man was a trained specialist and did not require the baton or the stun gun. He simply put the guard in a stranglehold and held it tightly until the man passed out, as he knew he would. Lowering him gently to the ground, the soldier quickly zip-tied him before taking out a radio from his pocket and signalling his team.

'Green light, boss,' was all he said.

Ten seconds later the remaining soldiers tasked with this block entered the building and quickly moved into position, a pair of SBS personnel covering each of the ten floors, two per floor. It would take several minutes as they waited for the unlucky duo selected for the tenth floor to get into position. Once there, the faint radio signal was received by each team.

'Tenth floor in position.'

Within seconds, each of the twenty backpacks were relieved of the two bottles of FenGas, the fentanyl-based knockout gas, one for each apartment, with a hose attached to the bottles inserted through the letterbox and into the residences. Once this was done with each flat, the soldiers took their tactical helmets off and donned their military-grade gas masks. A minute later, another signal was heard on the radios.

The last message was also the signal for the lorries to be brought to the location by Three Commando Brigade, who were quickly in position near the entrance. Forty Royal Marines were deployed to assist the SBS, four on each floor. Their job was to help secure equipment, evidence, and to assist with the removal of the prisoners. They were quickly in position.

'Countdown... thirty seconds and entry.'

Each team was also equipped with the lock-picking mechanisms which would allow quiet entry in case the FenGas was ineffective, but confidence was high that it would work. The countdown ended and the locks were picked. Only two of the apartments had used the security measure of a chain, such was their confidence. Those two doors were quickly shouldered open with minimal noise as twenty specialists started to gain entry to the flats. They did so one at a time, quickly securing the sleeping triads who would not wake for a while, such was the potency of the gas. Each one was secured with zip-ties before the flat was searched for computers, phones, identification documents and anything else that could be used as intelligence, or even evidence after the operation was concluded.

The SBS had planned for a maximum of two minutes in each apartment, to enter and secure the occupants, with Three Commando assisting with the rest. They had estimated that it would take at least thirty minutes to remove more than a hundred and fifty unconscious bodies from the tower block and into the waiting vans. It was not an easy task and there was some nervousness about the length of time required to conclude the operation.

As it turned out, only nine of the triads were not fully affected by the gas and gave the attackers some mild resistance. The resin batons quickly placed them into the same unconscious stupor as their colleagues. The row of eight houses was also quickly subdued in similar fashion, where sixteen SBS operatives, two per house, quickly secured the occupants. The supporting staff completed their roles as equipment and evidence were secured.

Thirty-nine minutes later, the lorries left the estate, fully laden with a hundred and ninety-six captives, more than two hundred mobile phones, forty laptops, two hundred and seven Glock G17 handguns, twenty-three MP40 submachine guns, a great deal of ammunition, two hundred and ten watermelon knives, and some bonus cash in excess of a hundred thousand pounds. It was a fantastic haul.

The warehouse was raided at the same time, and the eight triad gangsters were quickly overpowered by the four SBS and two supporting Royal Marines who used the stun guns to great effect. The five workers were also rounded up and locked in one of the storerooms, their phones taken from them and a warning given to keep them quiet. As the soldiers checked the rest of the premises, they were stunned with what they found in the rear warehouse. A call was quickly made.

'Boss, there's tons of marijuana here, I mean tons of it. What do you want me to do?' asked the team leader.

'Is there a forklift there we can use, and any vehicles we can load?'

'Yes sir, two forklifts and four mid-sized lorries,' the team leader replied.

'I'll send a team to assist; you can start loading it up and we'll take it away,' came the response.

The support arrived within ten minutes, and three of the lorries were loaded with the pallets of marijuana. Thirteen minutes later they were gone, the warehouse left quiet, the staff left abandoned in the storeroom. They would not be able to describe the attackers in any way other than they wore dark clothing and carried guns.

The Ghost Dragons had been decimated, their army dismantled and in custody, their valuable haul taken from them, and their dream of disrupting London severely damaged. Someone would be paying a heavy price.

Eddie Duckmore was woken at two-thirty in the morning, unaware of the raids on his partners in Dagenham. Having decided to stay at the docks, Duckmore and Dave Critchley had made themselves comfortable in the union offices they had recently vacated. Conveniently located next to the moorings they now controlled, they were close to the goods coming in and far enough away from the partners that clearly despised them–except for the eight guards sent to assist them. They had spent the previous evening waiting for the next batch of drugs and weapons to dock, and the ship had arrived at eleven-thirty.

Duckmore had overseen the unloading of the pallets and their storage in the small warehouse beneath their offices, waiting for them to be picked up by the Ghost Dragon lorries in the morning. Once secure, they had all retired to the spacious offices, where Duckmore and Critchley each had a room and the triads shared two more between them.

The call was unexpected, and Duckmore, his old police instincts kicking in, knew something was wrong. He was correct in his assumption, but it was from an unexpected source.

'You rotten bastard!' JP Sisterson screamed down the phone, his voice slurred, his bravery due to the alcohol.

'What the hell is wrong with you?' Duckmore asked, now wide awake and angry.

'You heard me, you're a rotten bastard,' came the reply.

'Piss off back to bed, JP, or you won't like how this ends,' Duckmore grunted.

'I don't give a shit anymore. I'm a good cop. I helped you because you were my friend. You're just a nasty bent cop and I won't help you anymore,' Sisterson continued, his voice barely coherent.

'You haven't got a choice, mate, you either help or you go to prison, it's simple.'

'I do have a choice, you bastard. I'm turning myself in and I'm taking you down with me,' Sisterson replied, much to Duckmore's surprise.

'What the hell are you talking about?'

'You heard me. I'm going to the nick and turning myself in. I'm gonna tell them everything. I'll lose my job, but you'll be hunted down like the rat you are. It'll be worth it,' Sisterson said, his voice clearer and more confident.

'Don't be such an idiot,' Duckmore said, 'you'll be screwed just as much as I will.'

'I don't think so. All I did was help a mate who turned out to be a massive wanker, so like I said... I don't give a shit anymore.'

'JP, don't do this, mate. We can figure this out. I'll buy you that Aston Martin you always wanted, how about that?'

'I'll see you in hell, Eddie,' Sisterson replied, and calmly ended the call.

'Shit!' Duckmore shouted, throwing the phone at the wall.

It smashed instantly into pieces, something that set off alarm bells back at the factory.

18

'So far so good,' Trevor said, rubbing his hands as the calls started to come in. The raid was turning out to be a spectacular success, with no casualties at all.

'Don't get too excited, it looks like we may have a problem,' Andy replied, pointing to the monitor they'd been using to observe Duckmore.

'Where's the signal?' Kendra asked.

'That's what I mean by a problem: it's gone,' Andy said, 'and there's no trace of it anywhere.'

'I'll call Darren and let him know to look out for him,' Kendra said, picking up her phone. 'If he's on the move, they need to know right now.'

Darren answered immediately.

'Are you checking up on us, Kendra? We're too wound up to be asleep, you should know us by now!' He laughed.

'Well, you might have something coming your way right now, we've lost the signal to Duckmore's phone so he may be on the move.'

'No problem, we'll move to the junction and cover the

exit, it's the only way off the docks,' Darren said. 'I'll call if there's an update.'

'Thanks, Darren,' she replied, hanging up.

'Let's hope we've caught that in time,' she said to Trevor and Andy.

Darren was true to his word and moved their vehicle to cover the junction leading from the docks to the main road. Having hidden away in the back streets had not been a problem earlier, when the signal to the phone told them where Duckmore was, but now it would be down to some good old-fashioned eyes on the road.

'It's not ideal here, but it's the only place we can use to keep good vision on the junction,' he told Rory and Izzy, who both nodded. They were tired but wide awake, knowing that a lot was at stake, and that things could change very quickly.

'Looks like we're not alone here,' Izzy said, indicating to a vagrant sitting in a nearby shop doorway opposite the junction. The man appeared to be asleep, surrounded by several plastic bags filled with clothes and other belongings.

'He won't bother us, I'm sure. Poor bloke needs somewhere to sleep, right?' Darren said.

They all turned to look towards the junction. They could see bright lights in the distance, the docks themselves, where ships were unloaded twenty-four hours a day. The containers would be unloaded onto waiting lorries and there was a steady stream of them leaving, driving through the night to avoid the usual daytime traffic.

'What if they use one of the lorries to leave?' Rory asked, trying to see if he could recognise the driver of the lorry currently turning out of the junction.

'You can just about make out the driver so it shouldn't be too difficult. Plus, it's unlikely that they'd split up, so look for lorries with two or more occupants,' said Darren.

As they continued to focus on the junction, they were unaware that the vagrant who had appeared to be sleeping was now awake and walking stealthily towards them. Before they realised what was happening, the man opened the door and jumped into the back seat with Izzy.

'Whoa, steady on there, old man,' Izzy replied after reeling back in shock, waving his hand in front of his face in an attempt to disperse the pungent smell.

'Sorry pal, we're working and need you to go back to your doorway, it isn't that cold out there,' Darren said, his palms up to placate the intruder.

The vagrant started laughing, surprising them all.

'I thought you lot were better than this,' the man said. His voice was vaguely familiar to Darren.

'Do I know you, brother?' he asked.

'If you recognised me, I wouldn't be very good at what I do, so I'm happy to see that you haven't,' the man replied.

He started to peel off the long straggly beard and moustache, the woolly hat, and then an unkempt wig.

'Rick Watts, what the hell are you doing here?' Darren asked, alarmed and confused by the detective sergeant's appearance.

'Never you mind what I'm doing, young man. Remember I'm a bona fide cop, which I know you three aren't, so I should be the one asking that very question, shouldn't I?'

Rick replied, a determined grin making it clear he wasn't joking.

'Seriously, shouldn't you be resting at home? You were properly bashed up, those bruises are still there, and I doubt very much you're officially back at work,' Darren replied, equally determined.

'Maybe not, but I'm still a cop, Darren, and I want to know what the hell is going on with you lot. I know why I'm here, but what the hell does this all have to do with you? Spit it out, will you?'

Darren looked to his colleagues for some support but received nothing but raised eyebrows and a shrug.

'Some help you two are,' he said, shaking his head.

'Come on, out with it, I'm waiting,' Rick said, folding his arms.

'Look, it's complicated, okay? We're waiting to see if a couple of your ex-colleagues are gonna show themselves, that's all I'm going to tell you,' Darren replied.

'I guessed that much, it's why I'm here. Duckmore and Critchley, right?'

'How did you know about them being here?' Darren asked.

'Because those two fuckwits didn't think I was ever going to get away from them when they had me tied to a chair, and they stupidly mentioned something about the docks making them wealthy. I figured I'd come down and take a look for myself,' said Rick.

'Okay, I get that, but aren't you supposed to be at home with a couple of armed guards looking after you?'

Rick laughed out loud.

'The idiots who were keeping me company? I got bored of them after the first night, their conversation was dreadful. I couldn't just sit in my comfy chair and let these two bastards get away with it, so I sneaked out and got my old faithful ensemble out so I can keep watch. People typically ignore vagrants, so it's great cover.'

'Well, it certainly fooled us, so I guess you win the prize tonight, but it makes things very awkward for us. You know that, right?' Darren said.

'I do, but we're on the same side, Darren. There's no harm in working together and you'll get no grief from me if you let me stick around. I can do a lot of good and I'm great at keeping secrets.'

Darren looked again to his two allies and was met, this time, with appreciative nods.

'Fine. But as much as I like you... you stink. Can you get rid of some of that clothing?' he asked, grinning.

'Yeah, I get that sometimes. It's just the coat, I leave it stinking on purpose. I'll put my stuff in the boot, if that's okay?'

'Sure, go for it.'

Rick got back out and retrieved his bags and blanket from the shop doorway. He opened the boot of the car and deposited everything there, including the offending coat. He was back in the car soon after, smelling much better.

'That's better,' Izzy said, taking an exaggerated deep breath.

'You're a funny man, but it's true,' Rick said, smiling at his new companions. 'Got anything to drink?'

∼

Trevor received a call from Ian, the officer in charge at the Royal Marine base at Poole.

'Morning, sir,' said Trevor. 'How's it all going? I guess you're checking to see if we're still awake?'

'Not at all, old chap. We don't need to do that, we know everything, remember?' Ian laughed. 'Actually, I thought I'd give you a quick sitrep.'

'Thanks, I appreciate it. We're not quite sure what's happened as yet. Has it gone well?'

'In the main, yes, it has. We've had a few issues, nothing to concern yourself about. There were a few that weren't fully affected by the FenGas, who put up a fight. Three of our chaps suffered minor injuries, that was all.'

'I'd call that a success, then, wouldn't you?' Trevor asked, happy to hear the news.

'We'll see. The chaps you thought were intelligence agents have been split up from the rest and taken to a different location for questioning. There were a couple of bosses identified at the houses, they've also been taken separately,' Ian continued.

'What about the rest of them?'

'The majority of the hired guns have been taken to RAF Odiham in Hampshire where there is a large hangar we can use to process them. We're handing that fully over to Three Commando Brigade to deal with, they're top notch at that,' Ian replied.

'I'm guessing that will be interesting, interrogating them all,' Trevor said. 'Do you think they'll talk? They have a reputation of not co-operating, don't they?'

'Well, I don't think they'll have much of a choice in this instance. They will be treated as enemies of the state and a threat to national security, so I'm sure they'll collaborate when we tell them that we consider them terrorists as well as foreign invaders. We have ways, remember?'

'So, is that it? It's all done and dusted?' Trevor asked.

'We've done our job, it's up to the secret squirrels to do theirs and get the evidence they'll need to take it further,' said Ian.

'By that, you mean they'll keep it quiet and use the evidence as a carrot one day in the future,' Trevor said, nodding in understanding.

'Sadly, that is politics for you, old chap. If you don't like it then you should come back and do some real work, eh?' Ian laughed again.

Trevor laughed along with the specialist.

'I think I'm too long in the tooth to do that sort of work again, Ian, but I appreciate the suggestion. I'll leave it to you guys; you can do that stuff with your eyes shut. Anyway, there's still plenty for us to do yet, we still have the corrupt police officers and officials to sort out, don't we?'

'We're pulling out completely now. I know we said we'd assist with the rest of them, but we've been called in for something else. If you have any problems with that, you know where to find me, okay? I'll find a way of getting you the help you need. And thanks again for the heads-up, it was a tidy job well worth doing.'

'Thanks, Ian, and pass my regards and thanks to all those involved,' Trevor said.

'I will do; take care, soldier,' Ian replied.

Trevor grinned and shook his head at the reference, which brought back many more memories. He remembered that he wasn't alone and looked up to see Kendra and Andy staring, their hands out in anticipation of the update.

'Well? What's going on?' Kendra asked.

'Yeah, don't keep us in suspense any longer, old man,' Andy added, taking a step back.

'The job went well, and they've all been taken into custody by the services. Except for Duckmore, Critchley, and the five triads with them,' Trevor said.

'I thought they were helping with those, too?' Kendra asked.

'I know, but they've other commitments now so it's going to be up to us,' Trevor replied.

'I have signals for the five guards so hopefully the two cops will be close by, at the very least, right?' Andy weighed in.

'Let's hope so. I propose we send the twins in to have a good look, first of all, and then give Darren some back-up to take them out. Everyone involved will have to be fully kitted out for all eventualities, those bastards are lethal and armed to the back teeth,' Trevor added.

'I'll go and speak to the rest of the team,' Kendra said, stepping out of the room.

'I'll continue to monitor the signals,' Andy said, staring at the monitor. 'As you can see, the other signals have all disappeared, I'm guessing the phones have been turned off or sealed in Faraday bags.'

'That's good to know. The biggest part of the operation is done now, just these loose ends to tie up,' Trevor said. 'I just have a horrible feeling about those two, when they find out what's happened, their backs will be up against the wall, and they'll have nothing to lose. Who knows what they'll do.'

'Best we take them out as soon as possible, then,' said Andy.

Trevor nodded but couldn't shake the feeling that it was far from over.

Kendra quickly briefed the remaining team members, who quickly deployed to their allocated positions to support Darren. She asked Amir and Mo to stay behind for their briefing.

'I just wanted to be clear on what you are likely to face when you get close,' she told them.

'Kendra, we're not kids. We know how dangerous these people are, we'll be fine,' Mo assured her.

'I'm not suggesting you're kids or that anything will go wrong, Mo,' she said, 'but it's important for you to know that they are all as nasty as anything you've faced. The triads are trained killers who don't care about themselves, just getting the job done. And those two bent cops are not idiots, they are just as dangerous. They will have their backs against the wall. They're already wanted for kidnapping a police officer and dealing with some serious crimes, so they won't go down without a fight, I assure you.'

'We'll be ready for them, don't you worry,' Amir said, 'now I suggest we get going, unless there's anything else?'

'No, that's it. Take care, okay?'

The twins ran off to their car, eager to get stuck in.

'Finally, we get to do something, brother,' Amir grinned, as Mo took the driver's seat and started the engine.

Mo looked over to his slightly younger sibling.

'She's right, you know,' he said. 'Don't do anything stupid or reckless when we get there, okay?'

'Bro, it's cool, I'll be good, I promise,' Amir said. 'Have some faith, will you?'

'Yeah, well, it wasn't so long ago that you were hanging off a window ledge with one hand, so don't lecture me about having faith, little brother,' he said, grinning.

'It wouldn't be much fun if there wasn't some danger to it, would there? That's the whole point of parkour, the element of risk makes it exciting as anything,' Amir replied, grinning back.

Mo shook his head as he drove away, hoping that for once his brother would heed his warning. He had his doubts.

Kendra went back to Trevor and Andy, having seen the rest of the team off.

'They're all on the way. All kitted up, except for Amir and Mo who'll be going in and searching the docks. We should have enough people to deal with all seven, all being well,' she told them, stifling a yawn.

'That's great, thanks, love,' Trevor replied. 'Why don't you get your head down for a couple of hours, we'll wake you if anything happens.'

'I'm going to pop to the flat and pick up some fresh clothes and toiletries first, if that's okay. I didn't think we'd be here so long and am definitely not prepared. I won't be long, maybe an hour or so,' she said.

'Okay, we'll see you when you get back. Drive carefully, love.'

Kendra was soon on her way. The streets were deserted,

and it was still a couple of hours till dawn. A lot had happened in the last hour or two and it had seemed much longer. Despite the fatigue, she was happy with the way the operation had worked out. Just a couple of loose ends and they could all enjoy a well-earned rest.

'Almost there,' she muttered to herself.

19

'Anything at all?' Trevor asked Darren when he called.

'Nothing came past that looked like them, no,' Darren said. He stepped out of the car to continue the call in private.

'Trevor, there's something you all need to know,' he said, trying to find the words. 'We were keeping an eye on the junction when we had a visitor jump in our car.'

'What do you mean, a visitor?' Trevor said, clearly alarmed.

'It's Rick Watts, Trev. He was dressed up as a tramp and keeping a watch-out for Duckmore and Critchley. He recognised me from his rescue and decided to join us, we couldn't stop him.'

'Shit,' Trevor said. 'Does he know anything else, like who you're working with or anything like that?'

'Not at the moment, no. But every minute he's with us gives him another minute to gather more intel on us. If we slip up with a name or anything he can trace, it might come back to us all.'

'Okay. I'm guessing he's been stubborn and won't leave.'

'Yep. He's basically told us that he's the cop and we aren't, to stop messing around and let him help us. He's given his word that he won't do anything stupid but I'm still wary,' Darren said.

'That's all we bloody need, a police officer with a personal vendetta, who can identify us all and destroy everything we've worked for. As if we didn't have anything else to deal with.' Trevor sighed.

'What do you want me to do? We're keeping an eye out together, but what if we see them and he starts getting all *Dirty Harry* on us?'

'Mate, I don't know what to say to you other than be careful not to give anything away. You're all big enough and ugly enough to take care of yourselves, you'll figure it out as you go along. I trust you to do the right thing, okay?'

'I appreciate that. It doesn't help but I appreciate it.' Darren laughed. 'I'll keep you in the loop if we see anything.'

'Thanks, Darren. Take care, mate,' Trevor said, ending the call.

'Kendra is gonna love this,' he said out loud, shaking his head as he reached for the phone.

'What?' How did that happen? He's supposed to be under armed guard!'

'Clearly, they didn't do a good job, love. Anyway, there's

nothing we can do just yet, so sort your stuff out and get back. We can work on a plan then,' he said.

'Okay. Thanks for the heads-up. I'm almost at the flat so I won't be long back,' she replied, hanging up.

She was a couple of turnings away from her flat when her fears were confirmed—she was being followed. Kendra had received training in surveillance and counter-surveillance, and one of the cardinal rules was to keep a lookout at all times when driving to ensure that you weren't being followed. By now it had become automatic for her to do so, and tonight, that training and muscle memory had paid dividends.

She called her father back.

'What is it, love? Forget your key?' Trevor laughed.

'I wish it was something silly like that, Dad. I'm being followed and I may need some help,' she said calmly. 'Can you get Andy on the call too, please?'

Seconds later she heard his voice, somewhat nervous.

'You alright, K? Trevor says you're being followed. Any ideas?'

'Not yet. They're good, though, staying just far enough back so that it wouldn't spook anyone not trained. If I were a betting girl, I'd say they were police trained, which can mean only one thing.'

'Shit, you think it's Duckmore?'

'I'm hoping not, but I'm expecting the worst.'

'I'm calling Charmaine to divert to you, I think she's with Zoe, and I'll set off now myself. Andy will stay here and guide you somewhere safe, okay?' Trevor said, immediately rushing out. As he ran, he was dialling Charmaine.

Andy started typing furiously, bringing up a tracking programme on one of the monitors. He typed in some codes which showed up on a moving map. The codes were for the GPS trackers that the three were carrying.

'Kendra, I have you on the map. Charmaine and your dad are on the way. He's probably ten minutes away but Charmaine can be with you in two,' he said, looking at the three signals.

'Thanks, Andy. Where do you think I should I drive to from here?' she asked.

'Take the next left and head towards the High Street. You can maybe stop at the petrol station to see if they wait on the road for you. That'll buy Charmaine and Trevor some time,' he replied.

'Is it open this time of the morning?' she asked.

'Yes, it's one of those twenty-four-hour ones, so you'll be fine. It'll be well-lit so if they have any brains they'll stay back and wait for you,' he said, crossing his fingers.

'Okay, thanks. Keep the line open just in case.'

Kendra kept an eye on the car behind, being careful not to make any sudden moves. Taking the road towards the High Street was slightly out of the way but when she reached the petrol station it would seem a natural thing to do–or so she hoped. She reached the station less than a minute later and pulled onto the forecourt next to a pump. Without looking, she could see from her peripheral vision that the following car had pulled up behind a parked van on the opposite side of the road about a hundred metres back. The plan had worked. She unlocked the petrol cap on her car and started filling up.

'Oh goody, it's a slow one,' she muttered.

~

'Are you sure about this?' Critchley asked as he pulled up behind the parked van.

'Yes, I'm sure, Dave. I was a surveillance officer for a couple of years, and this is the perfect angle you want to have vision on the exit. Not too close and easy to pull out from when she leaves,' Duckmore replied.

'That's great, but not what I meant. Are you sure we should be going after her?' Critchley pressed.

'Why not? She's the one responsible for us quitting, remember? I hate the cow and I think she needs a lesson she won't forget,' Duckmore replied, smiling menacingly at his loyal colleague.

'I get that you hate her, Eddie, but shouldn't we be doing something a little more... productive? You saw what the cops did to the triads, if we hadn't driven up when we did, they might have nabbed us as well. I think we should take what we can and run for the hills, everyone will be looking for us now.'

'Well, we have our old mate JP to thank for our escape; although it was unintentional, it scared us enough to check on the gear, but you're right–if we hadn't turned up when we did, who knows where we'd have ended up?' Duckmore mused.

He was as angry as he'd ever been. His plans for taking over a hugely lucrative operation in the capital were now in tatters. He needed to vent his anger and the first person he could think of was Kendra. Having driven away from the warehouse that was being raided, they had driven straight for her flat, the location that Eddie had seared into his brain when still a police officer and eager to get some revenge on the upstart detective. As the streets were deserted, they had first checked her flat for the car she was known to own, before they relocated and then came across it by waiting at the one main junction that led towards her road. They didn't have long to wait.

As soon as they spotted her turning into the junction they had proceeded to follow, at a distance.

'Easy does it,' Duckmore had said, as he kept a healthy gap between the cars.

Despite Kendra taking an unusual route, they realised it was because she needed to fill up.

'Where are you thinking about grabbing her?' Critchley asked, as they waited.

'I think we should wait till she gets to her car park and grab her before she gets to her flat,' Duckmore replied.

'Where will we take her to?' Critchley asked, his concern mounting.

'Not sure where is safe, they may have raided all the organisation's premises, so we'll stay clear of those, I think. Maybe we can make her comfortable in her own place,' he replied, sneering. 'I fancy a good night's kip after all that's happened. I bet she has a comfy bed.'

'Come on, Eddie, what if a neighbour sees us? We shouldn't be taking chances like this, please think about it.'

'Stop whinging, will you? You sound like a broken record. I know what I'm doing, alright? We'll have some fun with her, give her a right good beating, and get the hell out of Dodge. Happy?'

'Far from it. Let's just do this quickly,' Critchley said, resigned to the delay. 'Is she still filling up?'

'Yeah. It's one of those automated pumps, so it's probably slower. Don't worry, she can't see us from there, we're golden,' Duckmore added.

Charmaine switched off the lights on her car and sat watching.

'That's them behind the van, isn't it?' Zoe asked, wanting to be sure.

'Yep. Andy's message said she'd be in the petrol station here, so once she leaves, I'm guessing they'll start following again,' Charmaine replied.

'So, what are we supposed to do?' Zoe asked.

'Trevor's a few minutes away so hopefully he'll have a plan. Other than ramming their car I honestly don't know what else we can do. They're probably carrying guns, from what I hear.'

'Great, I'm glad to be wearing the vest, then,' Zoe said, not entirely confident in its ability to stop a bullet.

'Don't knock it, girl. It might not be the most comfortable and it might not make you look as glamorous as you'd like, but that thing will save your life.'

'I'm glad to hear it. I couldn't care less about looking glamorous, how can you think that?' Zoe replied, playfully hitting Charmaine on the arm.

'You save that for the bad guys, girl, and make sure you hit a lot harder than that,' Charmaine said, smiling at her companion. 'Oh, here's Trevor.'

'How's it going, Charmaine? Is Kendra still at the petrol station?' he asked.

'Yes. She's been there a while, so any second now I guess she'll be on the move. Anything you want us to do?'

'No, just stay safely behind, she's on an open line to Andy so we're figuring out what to do. I'll be with you very soon,' he added.

'Okay, I'll call if anything happens,' she said. 'Oh, stand by, she's on the move now.'

'Thanks. I'm gonna hang up now so I can call Andy on the other line. I'll call back if I need anything,' he said.

'Okay, here we go,' Charmaine said, watching as Duckmore's car pulled out behind Kendra's.

'I think the safest thing would normally be to call for armed police, but it could take an age for them to arrive,' Andy told Kendra.

'Well, it might still be worth doing, but they're probably thinking I'm going home now, so that's where they're likely to have a go,' she said.

'Hang on, your dad is joining the call,' Andy said.

'K, can you hear me?' asked Trevor.

'Yes, loud and clear. What's the plan, Dad?'

'Not sure yet, I'm open to ideas,' he replied.

'I have one, but we need to move fast,' said Andy.

'I'm all ears,' Trevor said.

'Kendra, you need to call 999 and tell them you're being followed by armed fugitives and that you need urgent assistance from an armed unit. Drive towards your flat but then change course and speed up to try and get away from them. If you stay on the line and tell the operator you're being chased, she'll tell you the direction you need to travel to close the distance with the armed response unit making its way. Are you okay with that?' Andy asked.

'On it now. I'll be out of touch so if you can shadow me, Dad, Andy will tell you if I'm stationary or not. If I am, it means they've caught up to me, so I'll be trying to keep on the move whatever happens.'

'Alright, love, we're with you now, Charmaine and I will both shadow and can be with you in seconds. I'll let the rest of the team know what's going on, too. Please be careful and don't try anything silly, okay?'

'Don't worry, Dad, I'm a trained ninja, remember?' she said. Her laugh was the last thing they heard before she ended the call.

'She'll be fine, Trev, she's a tough cookie, is your daughter,' Andy said, not as convincingly as he'd planned.

'You can tell me that as much as you like, Andy, but it won't change how I feel. Now stop yapping and keep telling me where she is. I want to know every thirty seconds, and can you also get Charmaine to join the call,' Trevor said, his voice now all business.

Andy did as he was told, and Charmaine joined the call seconds later.

'Trevor, she's just turned into Broadmead Road and is heading west towards Woodford New Road,' Andy said. 'Charmaine, are you with us?'

'Yep, we're covering the offside and running parallel. Keep us in the loop with directions, please,' she replied.

'This brings back a few memories, I can tell you,' Andy said, 'so it's a left-left into Woodford New Road, be aware that she's heading towards the A406 North Circular Road which goes east and westbound,' he continued.

'Is she doing a rate of knots, Andy?' Trevor asked.

'It isn't too hellish; she's definitely breaking the speed limit, though, and I imagine she's being directed by the operator. Remember that the armed response unit will be looking to do a hard stop when they catch up.'

'Thanks.'

'Okay, she's now turned right-right onto the A406 heading westbound towards Walthamstow. She's picked up speed, so I imagine they're right behind her,' Andy said, his voice more nervous now.

'I'm just getting there, maybe twenty seconds behind,' Trevor said, 'and is that you right behind me, Charmaine?'

'It is,' she said, 'keep your eyes on the road, old man.'

Trevor shook his head and smiled.

'Hang on, it looks like she's slowing down, just after the roundabout at the junction with the A112 Chingford Mount Road. Can you see her yet?' Andy asked.

'I can see blue lights ahead, hopefully that's the armed response unit,' Trevor replied.

'Let's hope so,' Andy said.

Kendra had called the operator immediately and introduced herself.

'My name is DC Kendra March from the Serious Crime Unit and I require urgent assistance. I am being chased by a car that contains two wanted fugitives who I believe are armed and who were responsible for the recent capture and torture of a colleague. I'm in my private vehicle travelling away from my home address in Woodford Green. Can you please have an armed response unit attend to give assistance?' she said, as calmly as she could manage.

'Thank you, Detective, please continue with commentary as I call for armed assistance,' the operator replied.

'I'm currently in Chigwell Road, Woodford, and will be turning left-left into Broadmead Road shortly,' she continued.

'Thank you. I have two Trojan units en route, with an ETA of three to four minutes, via the M11. Please continue with the commentary and I will relay to them,' came the reply.

The Trojan units, armed response vehicles on call twenty-four hours a day, were specialist firearms officers trained in hard stops amongst other challenges.

'I'm now turning left-left into Broadmead Lane,' Kendra continued. She looked in her mirrors and could see the car following more closely now and in pursuit mode.

'That's right, suckers, keep coming,' she muttered.

'Sorry, Detective, what was your last?'

'Nothing, I'm about to reach Woodford Green, do you have instructions for me?'

'Yes. Turn left-left and head southbound towards the A406 please, Detective,' came the assured reply.

'Left-left it is,' Kendra said, doing as she was instructed.

'The Trojan units will be waiting at the junction with the B162 and will attempt a hard stop as soon as they join you. Do you understand?'

'Yes, I understand. Will you tell me what I need to do to assist them?' Kendra asked.

'Yes, as soon as they join you, I will pass on their instructions.'

Kendra sped up and came to a large roundabout.

'Operator, I'm just about to turn right-right onto the North Circular Road,' she said.

'You're doing a grand job, Detective, it's almost over.'

'That sounds ominous!' Kendra laughed.

'Okay, as you join the A406 you may see the two units waiting nearside, about half a mile from where you join it. As soon as you see them, I want you to slow down with the intention of stopping just after the next roundabout at the A112, not before it, okay?'

'All received,' Kendra replied.

She looked towards the nearside and saw the armed response units in wait, no blue lights, inconspicuously parked and facing the exit ramp to the main road she was on. She gently released the accelerator and started to slow down. She could see the roundabout ahead, and the exit, and was careful not to slow down too much to give Duckmore and Critchley an opportunity to escape if they saw that help had arrived. Hopefully they'd think she was breaking down.

'Come to Mummy,' she said as she watched her mirrors for a response.

It didn't take long, the pursuing car started to make ground quickly and was soon just a hundred feet behind her. It was here that she passed the point of no return for the exit and went underneath the roundabout that the operator had mentioned.

'Slowing down to a stop, passing under the A112 round-about,' she said.

'Well done, Detective, help will be with you very soon,' the operator said.

I bloody well hope so, Kendra thought as she continued to slow and as Duckmore got ever closer.

'This is madness, Eddie. She clearly knows she's being followed and now chased. Why are we doing this?' Critchley asked, wishing they were somewhere far from here.

'I told you, stop whinging. We're teaching this bitch a lesson she won't forget, remember? What will we look like if we give up after a little car chase? What's wrong with you?'

'She's probably calling for help as we speak,' Critchley added.

'Who gives a shit? By the time anyone responds, it'll all be over. See? She's slowing right down!'

'Damn it,' Critchley muttered as he watched the car ahead start to slow.

'She's probably broken down, this'll be easier than I thought.' Duckmore sneered contemptibly.

Their attention was so intent on Kendra that they never registered the two cars waiting near the junction, lights off, with three armed occupants in each car. As soon as Duckmore passed the junction they waited ten seconds before slipping out and joining the dual carriageway. The next thirty or so seconds would determine the fate of the two corrupt officers but potentially also that of Detective Constable Kendra March.

20

'Thanks for letting us know, Andy. What about the triad guards, are they still there?' Mo asked.

Andy had called to inform them that Duckmore and Critchley were no longer at the docks. Amir in particular was disappointed, until he remembered the triad guards.

'Yes, they haven't moved from the building they're in. I'm guessing they're fast asleep and completely unaware that those two have left,' Andy continued.

'Do we still go in or not?' Mo asked. 'Can we afford to leave five trained ninjas on the loose in London?'

'No, we need to take them out ourselves. You go and do your thing and I'll send some backup. I'll send Clive, Martin, Jimmy, Greg, and Danny to help. They'll have all the gear, so call them when you're ready for them to go in,' Andy said, pleased to be delegating.

'Will do. We're just parking up now, so all being well, I'll be calling shortly,' Mo replied.

'And don't let Amir do anything silly,' Andy added quickly, before hanging up.

'Chance would be a fine thing,' Mo muttered, looking over at his grinning brother.

Amir was over the fence in seconds and was joined by his brother when he gave the signal that it was clear to follow. Having reconnoitred the docks, they had decided to climb over the security fencing down a side street where it was unlikely that they would be seen by the sub-standard CCTV or by anyone passing. It was farther away from the building they were aiming for, but safer.

They navigated the dock yard quickly, walking between containers, buildings, and stationary vehicles, keeping to the shadows and sometimes climbing to avoid detection. It took longer than they'd liked, but they eventually got there.

'Bro, if it took us this long to get here on the quiet, how are the back-ups supposed to help us?' Amir asked. They hadn't considered their exit strategy well at all.

'Good question, Amir. I'm guessing there will be security watching the cameras twenty-four-seven, so we either need to stop them from doing so or find another way, which currently can't think of,' Mo replied.

'Yeah, but even if we take out the cameras, there's still a lot of people milling around; they're loading up all night, remember?'

Mo looked around and saw another lorry leaving. He

followed it to the gate where the barrier was raised without it being stopped.

'I guess we'll just have to steal a lorry, won't we?' he announced. 'You go and check on our sleeping beauties and I'll look for a lorry.'

'Sounds like a plan to me, bro.' Amir grinned before disappearing around the building. Mo saw a small office block next to their target building and tried the door. It was open, so he entered. There was enough light from outside for him to see that it was a locker room, with dozens of metal lockers along two walls and a table with eight chairs against another.

'Perfect,' he muttered, grabbing a yellow high-visibility vest and a hard hat from a hanger. He also picked up a clipboard from the stack he saw on a shelf. Stepping out of the building he looked like any other worker, so he walked confidently towards the nearby car park, where a dozen lorries waited for the morning shift and their allotted loads. The car park next to that had another dozen lorries fully laden and ready to go, waiting for the drivers to start the morning shift.

Mo made for the second car park, looking for a vehicle suitable to transport an additional five people. Most were standard containers, their doors securely locked, and, as such, unsuitable. He was just about to give up when he saw an opportunity that was just too good to pass up.

'Amir is going to love this,' he said, walking towards it.

∼

'Thanks for the update, Andy. We'll shadow them also,

just in case, but remember we have our guest still with us. Do you want me to tell him what's going on?' Darren said.

'Obviously, don't tell him it's Kendra, just that armed units are about to stop Duckmore and Critchley. Hopefully that will calm him, and he can go home with no damage done,' Andy replied.

'Okay, sounds good to me. He's a wily old dog but I like him, a good old fashioned no-nonsense type of guy, you know?'

'Yeah, but sometimes they can be the most troublesome, so be careful with him, Darren.'

'Will do. I'll catch up with you later.'

Darren walked back to the car and got in.

'Change of plan, gents. It seems that our friends have somehow left the docks without us spotting them and are now on the move about fifteen minutes away. The plan is for armed units to put a stop in somewhere on the North Circular Road. I told the boss that we'll shadow the stop, just in case anything goes wrong, but by all accounts, these armed units are pretty shit-hot, so I don't think they'll need any help. Still, we'd better get a move on as it'll likely happen quite soon,' he said.

'Slippery bastards,' Rick muttered, as Darren drove off. They were some miles away, so Darren did not hold back on speed. The deserted roads allowed for him to make swift progress.

'Izzy, call the boss and get an update, will you?' Darren asked after they'd been driving for a while.

'Sure thing,' Izzy said, and made the call.

'Anything to report, boss?' Izzy asked Andy, mindful of Rick's presence, careful not to mention names.

'They're about to pull onto the A406 so I imagine the stop will go in very shortly. How far away are you?' Andy asked.

'How far, Darren?' Izzy asked.

'About three minutes,' came the reply.

'You'll probably miss it but stay in the vicinity just in case,' Andy said.

'Will do, chat later,' Izzy said, relaying the estimate to Darren.

'Right then,' Darren said, 'let's see if we can do better.'

The car juddered as he changed down a gear and floored the accelerator.

'Two minutes it is,' Izzy said, laughing.

The operator continued to speak to Kendra as she slowed down further, approaching the bridge and the roundabout above.

'I want you to stop about a hundred metres or so past the bridge, so that it is too late for them to pull off if they spot the Trojan units, okay?'

'Not a problem,' Kendra said, her eyes fixed mainly on her rear-view mirror and the vehicle behind that was closing in.

'I'm under the bridge now, my speed is forty and slowing,' she said calmly, 'and they're now also under and past the point of no return.'

'That's great, Detective. Your help will be with you very soon. As soon as you see them put the stop in, you can pull away safely, but first I want you to come to a dead stop so that they do the same, okay?'

'All received and understood,' Kendra said, slowing to a crawl and getting closer to the kerb.

Still keeping an eye on the mirror, she came to a stop. The following car was only a few seconds behind and pulled up around twenty feet back.

'Here we go,' she muttered.

'See? It's like taking sweets from a baby,' Duckmore said, laughing as Kendra's car came to a stop.

'What now?' Critchley asked.

'Now, we put her in the boot and go and have some fun,' Duckmore said, taking his handgun out of his shoulder holster and stepping out of the car.

Critchley shook his head as he also stepped out.

'Be careful, Eddie, she'll not come without a fight, you know that, right?'

'That's what I'm hoping for,' Duckmore replied, walking carefully towards the driver's side, his handgun down by his side.

So intent were they on Kendra that they failed to notice the two cars approaching at speed from behind them. As Duckmore was half-distance towards his target, the Trojan armed units arrived on scene. They announced themselves with police sirens and an statement over the tannoy system.

'Armed police! Put the gun down and lie down on your fronts, arms spread out, both of you!'

Duckmore and Critchley turned around, shocked by the announcement, as one of the cars pulled ahead of them and the other stopped just behind. Two firearms officers exited from each vehicle, and in seconds two Glock 17 handguns were pointed at each of the corrupt officers.'You idiot, you've destroyed us,' Dave Critchley told his friend as he complied with the police request and lay down on his stomach, his hands spread out wide.

Duckmore took a split second to process it all, considering a gunfight against the prospect of a lengthy prison sentence. He was about to raise his handgun when he heard his colleague's words. They saved his life, as he laid the gun down carefully and lay down on his stomach as instructed. His head was turned towards Kendra's car, which he now saw driving away from the scene slowly. He was quickly handcuffed and then roughly searched by the armed officers, who gave instructions as they dealt with both men. Duckmore was oblivious and stared at the car.

'She played us,' Duckmore muttered. 'The little bitch played us.'

'Can you see what's going on?' Andy asked, nervous, having seen Kendra's signal come to a stop. He made the call to Trevor immediately.

'The armed units have taken them both down, Andy, and Kendra is away safely,' Trevor replied, the relief in his voice palpable. He had watched the incident unfold from above on the roundabout and watched as Duckmore paused before laying his weapon down. It could have ended up much worse than it did, and he was thankful.

'Thank, God,' Andy replied, breathing a sigh of relief.

'Andy I'll call in a bit, I want to speak to my daughter,' Trevor added.

'Sure thing. That was bloody nerve-wracking, Trevor, she did bloody well,' he replied, ending the call.

Trevor called Kendra immediately.

'How are you doing, princess?'

'You haven't called me that in a while, Dad, how sweet are you?' she mocked. 'Honestly, I'm fine, it went exactly as we'd hoped and those two will be banged up for years.'

'I couldn't give two shits about them, love. I'm just glad you're okay and this is almost over,' he replied.

'What do you mean, almost over? Isn't that everyone now in custody?' she asked, confused.

'There's five more at the docks that the rest of the team are taking care of. Also, there's the small matter of the corrupt officials involved in this from the start, remember? We have to figure out how to sort them out, too,' he said.

'I forgot about them. I guess we have a few more days before we can catch a breather, eh?'

'Yep. Get yourself back to the factory so we can catch up with everyone. See you there soon, love.'

'Okay, Dad, see you soon,' she said. She too breathed a sigh of relief; the last half-hour had been very tense, but she could now relax a little. Her phone rang again.

'It's me again, Detective,' the operator said. 'I just wanted you to know that both suspects are in custody and that the Trojan units send their thanks and regards for your efforts in their capture.'

'That's kind of you, thanks. Please also thank them, they

were pretty slick and that's two more nasty people off the streets, eh?'

'I will do. Take care, Detective,' the operator said.

Kendra turned the car around at the next junction and set off towards her flat. She noticed that it was starting to get lighter now as the new day dawned.

I'll be glad to see my bed later, she thought.

Darren made great progress and skirted the scene to avoid being seen. He too ended up on the roundabout and saw Trevor's car parked nearby, overlooking the police stop some two hundred metres away. Blue lights were flashing as he pulled up on the opposite side of the roundabout, slowing down with just enough time to see the two men being detained.

'Looks like they have it all under control,' he told his companions as he started to pull away. 'No need for us to stick around, I think it's time to get you home, Rick.'

Rick didn't reply, his eyes fixed on the scene below.

'Rick? We'll take you home now, okay?' Darren repeated.

'What? Oh, yes. Thanks,' Rick said, his gaze unmoved.

'You okay, mate? They've caught the bastards, it's over. You should be jumping up and down,' Izzy said, confused.

'Yeah. It's all good, thanks guys,' Rick replied, again staring at the scene, at the small car driving away from the scene.

A car he knew well.

Mo rejoined Amir, who'd kept watch on the building the triads were sleeping in.

'Find anything?' Amir asked.

'Yes, I've parked it around the back. I called the back-up team and three of them are joining us to help take them out. Should be here any minute,' Mo replied.

They waited until Danny, Clive, and Jimmy joined them. They each carried taser guns, zip-ties and duct tape, as requested by Mo, while he and his brother had the same. They also carried small cannisters of CS gas, just in case anything went wrong, but they preferred not to use them, especially as they would not be wearing their gas masks in this instance.

'How's it going, gents?' Mo said, greeting the trio. 'Any problems getting in?'

'No, it was just like you said, we climbed the fence in the side road and stuck to the shadows, easy peasy,' Jimmy replied.

'Great. Here's the plan. Our five friends are still fast asleep in this building. We believe they're on the first floor but it's a small building so it shouldn't be a problem getting to them quickly. Amir is going to get us in, so once inside, we go quietly and we use the tasers before they get a chance to respond, okay? Fast in, fast out, and we put them in the van I've commandeered and get the hell away. All clear?' Mo said. They each nodded in response.

'Okay, I'll go and sort our entrance out. Watch my signal,' Amir said, skipping off towards the side of the building.

He had seen a small side window to what he believed was a bathroom or toilet. His plan was to squeeze through that and open the door to the team. No stranger to getting in and out of awkward places, Amir's parkour skills allowed him to access places no ordinary person would even attempt to. Arriving at the window and checking that the coast was clear, he took out a small slim Jim and inserted it into the gap in the window frame where the simple standard latch was. It took but a second for him to slide it to one side, allowing him to prise open the window. He then lifted himself up and turned his body sideways to squeeze through the window and into what he could now see was the toilet.

Landing silently, he cracked open the door to see if it was safe to exit. He could see a room with several desks, chairs, and a sofa, and another room with a closed door. A staircase opposite led to the first floor. The place was silent. Opening the door slowly, Amir stepped into the room with the desks and looked around some more. He was unsure about the closed door to the other room and would leave that and the upstairs to his colleagues. He stepped towards the front door leading to the courtyard and slowly opened it. He raised his arm towards his colleagues, giving the signal for them to approach.

Leaving the door slightly ajar for them, he quietly moved towards the opposite end and the closed door, waiting to let his colleagues in when they were ready. They joined him within seconds. He silently gave hand signals to them, indicating the staircase and also the door he was standing by.

'We check this room first, be ready to move upstairs if they're not all in here,' he whispered. They nodded in understanding. Using his fingers to count down, Amir silently opened the door and pushed it wide open, revealing another large room which appeared to be a studio flat, with a bed, small kitchenette, table and chairs and a small sofa. It was unoccupied but there were signs of life: half-filled coffee cups, plates with food remains, and a holdall filled with clothes. There was another door, which Amir quickly approached and opened. It was a smaller room with a bed and chest of drawers, and a shower cubicle in the corner.

On their way back to the main room, Mo noticed a smashed mobile phone on the floor. He followed Amir, who went up to the first floor, and gave the signal for the team to follow. They did so, taser guns at the ready. There was a small landing with three doors. The middle door was ajar, which Amir opened slightly to reveal a bathroom. The other two doors were closed. Mo indicated for Amir and Clive to cover one, and for himself, Jimmy and Danny to cover the other. He held his arm up for them to wait for his signal, his other hand on the handle. His arm dropped and he quickly opened the door, not knowing what was in the room. Amir did the same.

There were three triads sleeping in the room that Amir and Clive entered and two in the room Mo went into. All five were asleep but quickly woke when the doors were opened, their training immediately kicking in. Fortunately for Amir and Clive, by getting out of the beds quickly, their targets made it easier for the taser barbs to take hold, and two of the targets were immediately given thirty-thousand-volt shocks. Unfortunately for them, the third triad was able to grab his watermelon chopper and rush towards the attackers. He aimed his first slash at Amir, who deftly sidestepped whilst still holding the taser gun and continuing to shock his man unconscious. The first slash missed but the triad was skilled, and backhanded Amir a second later as he recovered the swing.

The blow to the head was a hard one and pushed Amir back, still holding the taser gun but no longer squeezing the trigger. Fortunately, his man was still down and out. His vision was clear, and, in that split second he saw that Clive had also incapacitated his man and was turning towards him to help. Amir could see that there would not be enough time for him to do so; the triad had raised his arm above his head again and was about to slash down at him with a likely lethal blow. He raised the taser gun in an attempt to defend the strike, hoping that the plastic weapon would at least deflect the blow. It saved his life. The weapon did its job and was smashed for its efforts, leaving Amir holding just the handle, the dense batteries having been enough to prevent the chopper causing injury.

Despite avoiding the blade, Amir's arm was jarred from the impact, and he realised very quickly that he would not be able to prevent another blow.

As the triad raised his arm again, he suddenly screamed in pain as Clive's CS spray hit him square in the face, causing intense pain and blinding him. It was enough to prevent him from striking Amir again, as he slashed from side to side ineffectively, unable to see anything. Amir picked up a wooden chair and hit him flush in the jaw, hard enough to render him unconscious.

'Good shot, Amir,' Clive said, nodding in appreciation.

'Thanks, Clive, if you hadn't sprayed him, I'd be deep in the poo now. Let's zip-tie these bastards before they wake, I'm knackered.'

The pair quickly secured their captives and for good measure taped their mouths with the duct tape, deemed necessary until they were away from the docks.

In the other room, Mo, Jimmy, and Danny had fared a

little better against the two men they faced. Despite the failure of Mo's taser to make contact, Danny was there to make sure that both their targets were rendered unconscious and then swiftly secured. All phones and weapons were placed in the holdall retrieved from the room below and the five captives roughly manhandled down the stairs and into a heap on the floor.

'I'll be back in a minute,' Mo said, grinning as he left to retrieve their transport.

They waited for a few minutes until they heard the hissing of brakes being applied outside, and the gentle rumble of a large diesel engine idling. Amir went outside to take a look.

'You've got to be joking me,' he said, his mouth open in awe at the sight before him.

The Scania lorry was quite normal but the trailer that was hitched at the back was not. The heavy six-wheeler trailer had three electric vans loaded and secured. One was pointing forward and at a forty-five degree angle, another was facing away from the cabin, and the third van was the only one with all four wheels on the trailer.

'Well, nobody is gonna notice that, are they?' Clive asked when he poked his head out from inside, laughing.

'Really? That's our getaway car?' Amir asked, incredulous.

Mo got out of the cabin and walked towards them, gesturing theatrically towards the lorry and its contents.

'Well? Isn't it perfect?' he said, 'we'll stick our guests in the back and simply drive out of here.'

'Seriously? Couldn't we just take one of the vans?' Amir asked.

'They're electric and not charged, bro, I checked. Plus, they won't bother searching this, but they may stop smaller vehicles that look out of place. This will do the trick, don't worry.' Mo rubbed his hands together. 'Now, let's get them loaded and get out of here.'

They took the triad captives one at a time and laid them carefully in the back of the van at the rear end of the trailer. Clive, Danny, and Jimmy got in the back with them to ensure they stayed compliant during the journey.

'Let's go, then,' Mo said gleefully as he put the lorry in gear and drove off. As expected, the security barriers were raised automatically as he approached; nobody gave them a second glance and they were away from the docks safely, with their captives secure, a successful job.

Martin and Greg followed in the cars as the small convoy headed south out of London.

'Where are we taking them?' Amir asked.

'I spoke to Trevor, and he told me to leave them near an air force base in Hampshire. We'll drop the van off and call him so he can have someone pick it up. We'll come back home after that, shouldn't take too long,' Mo replied.

'If it's okay with you, I'm getting my head down for a bit, it's been a long night, my arm hurts, and I'm knackered. Wake me up when we get there, will you?'

'Will do, bro,' Mo said, glancing towards his younger brother who had already closed his eyes and rested his head against the window. Once again, his twin had had a lucky escape.

'You lead a charmed life, bro,' he whispered, grinning.

～

21

With most of the team back at the factory, they rested until the others made their way back from Hampshire. Mo had done as asked and parked the van half a mile away from the air force base, next to a service station. Having made sure that the captives in the back were still secure and unlikely to escape their bonds, they got into the two support cars driven by Greg and Martin and made their way back to London. Trevor did the rest, informing his contacts and making sure the keys to the lorry were left under the visor for the Three Brigade Commandos to return the vehicle to the police—after taking the five prisoners into their custody.

Kendra had taken a quick shower and changed clothes before making her way back to the factory, where Trevor and Andy updated her.

'Are you serious? Rick Watts just got in the car? What the hell is going on?'

'Yeah, that was our reaction, too,' Trevor said, 'but we think it's been contained well. No names were mentioned, and the guys have dropped him off home. He's seen Darren a couple of times, but he won't be able to connect him to you, I'm sure.'

'You don't know him, Dad. He's a bloody good detective and if anyone can figure it out it's him. We need to be very careful around him,' she said.

'Careful like encouraging a car chase?' Andy said, 'that was reckless, Kendra, it could've gone very badly wrong.'

Kendra saw the concern on his face, and maybe a little anger at the risk she had taken. She smiled.

'I couldn't think of any other way, Andy, and I had a ton of help and back-up, remember? I guess sometimes we have to be a little reckless to get things done. It turned out well, didn't it?'

'It did, but it doesn't mean I have to like it. I also recall you both being a little more forceful about me getting more involved, remember?'

'Yes, we did. And if you recall, we begrudgingly agreed to it,' she said, grinning. 'You were very persuasive.'

'We'll call it quits then, shall we?' Andy said, 'and great job, by the way, really great job.'

'Alright, alright,' said Trevor, 'enough of this mushy stuff, let's get back to business, shall we? How far away are Mo and the rest of them?'

'They're almost here. I'll go and get the rest of the team together for a debrief,' Kendra said, leaving them.

Trevor looked at Andy and nodded.

'I know you two have got this weird relationship thing going on, but I appreciate you having her back, Andy.'

'Don't even think about it, Trevor, I'd do anything for you and this team. We seem to forget just how much of an impact we're starting to have. We just prevented something hugely significant, you know? If it wasn't for Kendra... and you, for that matter, I'd be lying on my sofa in my dressing gown with a scraggly beard, unwashed, and drinking gin. I owe you both,' he said, 'especially Kendra.' He looked towards the door wistfully.

'Hey, don't underestimate the impact you're having, Andy. Give yourself a pat on the back occasionally, you deserve a lot of the credit.'

'Now who's being mushy?' Andy grinned.

'Let's go and speak to the team, they need to get home for some sleep,' Trevor said.

Trevor placed his hand on Andy's shoulder and guided him out of the canteen towards the rest of the team. Andy smiled; it was a meaningful gesture, as opposed to the typical affectionate slap.

He does like me, after all, Andy thought.

～

The team were finally assembled and reunited in the main room at the factory. Trevor, Kendra and Andy addressed them together.

'Guys and girls, it's been a hell of a long couple of days, but I think you'll agree that it was worth it, right?' Trevor said to them all.

'Why, what happened?' Amir joked, prompting a round of laughter.

'That's why we're here, Amir, so that we can update you on everything, not just your little breaking and entering adventure at the docks,' Kendra added, to more laughter.

'I'll crack on so you lot can go home and get some sleep, we're all exhausted,' Trevor said. 'So, this is pretty much where we're at. The entire triad gang have been rounded up, including some of the bosses and the Chinese saboteur agents. They're currently being processed by the military so that the corrupt officials don't get wind of anything too early.'

'We'll come to those later,' Kendra added.

'Our corrupt police officer friends are now both in police custody, thanks to some fine baiting and deflecting by Kendra here,' Trevor continued, 'although I think we all agree that it was a tad on the dangerous side.'

'But well worth it,' Kendra said, 'seeing those two on the ground being roughed up and handcuffed was just fab.'

She received a number of thumbs-up and many more grins in response.

'So where does it leave things, Trevor?' asked Charmaine.

'Well, there's a small matter of the corrupt officials. We know who they are because they were kind enough to sign off the immigration documents letting our gangster friends into the country. There's also the company they worked for, Hurricane Solutions, which we need to sort out, along with the Chinese wholesaler who was kind enough to help our invaders. I'm also keen to find out what Brodie Dabbs is up to; I imagine he's in hiding now trying to figure out how to get his empire back. We may be able to help with that, too, he's been a big help to us in the past.'

Those who had worked with some of Dabbs' volunteers in the past nodded in agreement.

'It's just some loose ends which we hope to tie up without getting our hands dirty. We should have enough evidence, but we need to pass it on to someone who can do something about it, and not another corrupt official,' Kendra said.

'That's not going to be as easy as you think,' Charmaine said. 'From what you've told us it sounds like they're all at it.'

'It isn't as bad as that, Charmaine,' Trevor replied. 'From what we understand it's a handful of prominent people but it's for their positions in the system that they were targeted. They're greedy for money but they'll lose everything as a result of their actions, we'll make sure of that.'

'In the meantime, unless anyone has anything to add, we suggest you get yourselves home. We'll be in touch in the next couple of days. Those of you who have work scheduled for the company take the day off, okay?' Kendra said.

The team stood and there were some high-fives and hugs as they said goodnight to each other, before leaving the room to make their way home.

'I think we ought to do the same, don't you?' Andy said, putting an arm around Trevor and Kendra's shoulders.

'Before you spoil the moment and do something stupid, I'm gonna point out that we're all exhausted and just want to get some rest,' Trevor said, looking Andy in the eye.

'Nope, I wasn't going to do anything of the sort, Trevor. As I said earlier, I'm just thankful you're both in my life,' Andy replied, giving them both a squeeze before letting go.

'Ugh, I'm gonna be sick,' Trevor said, putting two fingers in his mouth.

'Dad, be nice, he's just being a big softy, that's all. Isn't that right, Andy?' She looked him up and down seductively and smiled as he reddened.

'No. Not soft at all. Just trying to be good, that's all,' he said, his face turning ever more crimson.

Trevor was still laughing when they got to the car as Andy made his way to his camper van.

'That was a lot of fun,' Trevor said.

'It was, I'll make it up to him tomorrow with some custard doughnuts or something,' Kendra said.

Andy reached the camper van and looked back to see Trevor and Kendra get into their car, wishing that he was going with them.

'*You* love me, don't you, Marge?' he asked his beloved van as he opened the door.

∾

22

'Honestly, Brodie, if you'd have asked me, I would have given this to you ages ago. I don't give a rat's arse about it, you'd have been doing me a favour,' Zane told his boss as they toured the tired old farmhouse. 'You did good by me and I'm more than comfortable now as a result, it's the least I could do for you.'

'Yeah, well, don't get too sentimental just yet, Zane. It was only a few days ago that you stabbed me in the back, remember? It's gonna be a while before I completely forgive you... if ever.'

'Really, this again? You've rammed that down my throat every hour on the hour since you kidnapped me from my home. I told you many times, we had no choice, it was do or die,' Zane replied, exasperated that he was repeating himself again.

'Bollocks, not one of you put up a fight or any resistance,' Brodie said, 'I was there, and I heard you.'

'Again, we had no bloody choice. They made the offer while their guards were standing there with machetes and guns, the message was very clear, Brodie. Why don't you bloody believe me?'

'So, tell me, Zane. Of all my people that were there and who accepted the offer from the Chinese, who do you think feels the same as you? Who do you think was happy to take the extra money and listen to the new bosses without batting an eyelid. Who?'

Zane paused as he considered the question.

'That's not fair, Brodie. Their fate is in my hands now, is it? You trying to make me put them in the frame?' he asked.

Brodie stood inches away from Zane's face, glaring.

'No, Zane, I want you to tell me who I can trust and who I should get rid of. I want you to tell me who will save the organisation and who will happily destroy it. If you can't see what I'm trying to do here, then you can piss off back home... on foot. Maybe with a knife in your back, see how you like it.'

'I see what you're trying to do, and I believe you. If you're giving me the benefit of the doubt, then I guess you'll do the same for others,' Zane replied.

'So, don't make me ask again. Who's for us and who's against us?' Brodie asked.

'Honestly, I think most of them are the same as me, they only agreed to save themselves. I saw them look towards me, looking for guidance, and I could see it in their eyes.'

'Except for?' Brodie asked.

'I don't think Colin or Alby gave a shit, Brodie. They were smiling and rubbing their hands together when the offer was made.' Zane liked them both but knew instantly they were not loyal to Brodie, which is what Brodie was looking for — and which he needed.

'Anyone else?' Brodie asked.

Zane paused again, making sure he remembered

correctly. He didn't want to make a mistake and freeze someone out of the organisation, or worse.

'I got on with all these people, Brodie, so it sickened me to see their reactions. Frankie and Billy were happy with the new offer, too. Those four are the ones I think might not be loyal, maybe they never were.'

Brodie took a few steps back, continuing to stare into Zane's eyes. He could see the man was sincere.

'Right then, I'm glad that's sorted out,' Brodie said in a softer voice.

'So, what are you going to do now?' Zane asked.

'For one, I'm building a much tougher, taller wall of trust so that shit doesn't happen to me again. As of today, this is my base of operations, mine alone. I'm gonna fix it up and live here with the missus while you run the organisation in London on my behalf.'

'W...w...what?'

'You heard me. You're also lucky I don't stick that knife in your back. I may be getting on a bit, but I know how to judge a character, Zane. Yes, you fucked up, but you've been honest with me since and I appreciate that. I'm gonna help you get rid of those four fuckers, and we'll rebuild the organisation together. It'll be more streamlined, more efficient and a lot tougher to take over. I'm getting too long in the tooth for the day-to-day stuff so you can take over that, fresh eyes will be a good thing. That shit isn't happening again, do you hear me?'

'Bloody hell, Brodie. I didn't see that coming, mate. You sure about this?'

'I am. I have plans, some of them I'll even let you in on, but many I won't. I worked hard to get where I am and the fact that I lost it in one bloody night pisses the hell out of me no end. Now, are you in or out?' he asked.

'I'm in, with bells on,' Zane said, stepping forward to shake Brodie's hand.

'Don't let me down again, boy, or it'll be the last thing you do. Do you hear me?' Brodie whispered.

Zane wasn't intimidated and continued smiling.

'I won't let you down, boss, you have my word. On pain of death.' Zane's smile was becoming more focused and determined.

'Good, now let's put our heads together and sort out how we're gonna do this,' Brodie said, sitting at the table. He poured whisky into a couple of glasses and passed one to Zane.

'Cheers!' Zane said, as they clinked glasses.

Several hours later, Brodie and Zane left the farmhouse, having made plans for the future of the organisation. They drove to London mainly in silence, the significance of their conversations and plans not lost on either.

Before dropping Zane off, Brodie looked at his subordinate.

'There's no turning back. You sure you want to do this?' he asked.

'I've never been so sure in my life, Brodie. I know that if we... sorry, *when* we pull it off, we'll be stronger than ever and one of the most powerful organisations in the country, let alone London,' Zane replied.

'That's good. Now get back to your wife and let her know

that your lives are about to change massively.' Brodie smiled as he pulled up to Zane's house.

'Thanks, boss. I'll speak with you soon,' Zane said, shaking Brodie's hand and getting out of the car.

Brodie drove away, thinking about his plans with Zane but also those he hadn't discussed. He dialled a number that he had memorised as he drove towards his empty home. He'd call his wife tomorrow with the good news that their lives would be back on track. He missed her and looked forward to her returning.

'I'm guessing you're calling to discuss my offer?' a man said immediately upon answering. No greeting or small talk, straight to the point.

'I have. As long as you leave my organisation... *and me* alone, I'll agree to your offer. I just wanna be clear on one thing, though. If you ever double-cross me, I'll stop at nothing to bury you. Am I clear? This little adventure has made me realise a few things but has also taught me much more, so remember that before you make a stupid decision.'

The man laughed in response.

'I hear you, Brodie, don't you worry. I may be getting in bed with a wily old gangster like you but if it means we can bring down some of the other gangs in London then it'll be worth it,' came the reply.

'Then please go ahead and formalise the deal and we'll speak again soon, Detective Chief Superintendent Fisher,' Brodie said.

∽

The factory remained closed all day, with a notice placed in the window apologising for any inconvenience to visiting clients, of whom there were not likely to be many, due to most of the official security discussions being conducted remotely. The team enjoyed a well-earned rest, but Trevor and Kendra decided to meet with Andy at his house late in the afternoon to continue their discussions about what they'd be doing next.

Kendra was true to her word, so when Andy opened his door, she handed over a fresh bag of custard doughnuts.

'I bring a peace offering,' she said solemnly, as Trevor smirked and shook his head. 'Freshly baked and still warm.'

'What for?' Andy asked, 'what did you do?'

'You know what for, silly. I shouldn't have tried to embarrass you yesterday, it was mean, so I told Dad here that I'd bring these to make up for it.'

Andy blushed, having forgotten the incident, chalking it up to the usual high jinks between the three of them.

'I don't know what you're talking about, but I'll take these, thank you very much,' he said.

'There's enough for all of us, so don't get all greedy on us, Pike,' Trevor added quickly.

'Don't worry, Giddings, I'll cut it into small pieces for you so that you won't have to chew too much with your fancy new teeth,' Andy joked, grinning as he let them into the house.

'Before you threaten him, I'd like to point out that he was being nice yesterday and we weren't, so leave it please, Dad,' Kendra said.

'Fine, but if he cuts my doughnut into small pieces, I'll not be *leaving* it,' came the gruff response.

They sat in the lounge and Andy joined them from the

kitchen with plates for each of them and a teapot with the usual accoutrements.

'I thought we'd try tea for a change,' he said, grinning. 'You can't beat a fresh custard doughnut with a cup of tea.'

They tucked in, with no words exchanged as they devoured the sugar-coated treats.

'You were right, they do taste better with tea,' Kendra said when she had finished hers.

'Like I said, occasionally I come in useful,' Andy replied. 'So, what's the plan for today?'

'Well, we have the list of corrupt officials, I suggest we put together files for each of them, with all the evidence the police will need to charge them, and then research someone trustworthy to hand it over to,' Kendra said.

'Got any thoughts on that?' Trevor asked.

'To be honest, I trust all my team and the majority of the officers at the station, but I think we should stay away from them for now. After everything with Rick I'm a little wary,' she said.

'Can I make a suggestion?' Andy said.

'Sure, go for it,' she replied.

'Why don't we get someone else to hand it over? Someone that won't be ignored by anyone.'

'Perfect, who did you have in mind?' Trevor asked.

'The press, of course.' Andy grinned. 'And I suggest we make duplicate folders and give them to the most prominent crime journalists and let them fight it out between them as to who does the most damage to these corrupt bastards. They can also deal with any subsequent police investigation where they can hand over the evidence.'

'I think that's a great idea,' Kendra said. 'We can hand the folders over anonymously, it keeps us completely out of the frame, nobody will have a clue.'

'You were right, Andy, occasionally you do make yourself useful,' Trevor said, smiling.

'And now we can have a beer,' Andy said, leaving the room for a colder, more refreshing drink.

'I guess that is something to celebrate,' Trevor said, nodding in approval.

They decided what to put in the evidence folders while they drank their beers, having decided to keep things simple and uncomplicated.

Each person that signed off on the sponsorship letters would have their own folder, with a copy of said letter, and copies of bank accounts showing almost identical payments on similar dates with all the other suspects, paid from the same account that they clearly proved was controlled by an overseas company closely linked to China's intelligence services. They would include the information about the person they were sponsoring, with their criminal record and ties to the triads. Everything would be nicely lined up for the police to arrest, interview, charge and prosecute.

'So, all we need to do now is make copies of all the folders and decide who we'll be taking them to,' Kendra said, leaning back in her chair.

'Leave that to me. I've compiled a list of the best crime journalists who work for the most prominent news-papers and broadcasters. We'll stick to the top three and let them know that the same files have been passed on to two others. That'll get their competitive juices flowing, for sure,' Andy said, raising his nearly empty bottle as a toast.

'Okay, this is good and sorts out the dirty bastards. What about the Hurricane Solutions company and the Chinese wholesalers? Are we just gonna let them carry on as if nothing has happened?' Trevor asked.

'No way, they're not getting away with it! We have to take them down too,' Kendra said angrily.

'How about we get that investigator involved in Hurricane Solutions?' Trevor said. 'What was his name, again?'

'Marcus Allen,' Kendra replied. As the government security advisor, he would take great interest in the company that was complicit in the sabotage that affected the trade deal with Taiwan.

'That's the man,' said Trevor. 'He seemed switched on, if we can find a way to get the information to him, wouldn't he be able to sort them out?'

'I think he would,' Kendra said, 'so that's what we should do. Which just leaves the Chinese wholesaler. Any thoughts on how to sort them out?'

'I say we think of something that ensures they go out of business, with immediate effect,' Kendra said. 'Their ties to the triads and now the intelligence agency makes them a continuing threat.'

'Agreed, but what do we do?' Trevor asked.

'Andy, do you think you can hack their system?' Kendra asked, a plan forming quickly.

'I wouldn't be of much use to this team if I couldn't do that, now, would I?' Andy said, flexing his fingers, ready to start.

'I mean not just their computers, but also get login information to bank accounts and the like,' she added.

'Yes, I can. It may take a couple of days to get everything, but once I break into their system, I can grab the rest from keystrokes or insecurely placed login info, which most people love to leave lying around.'

'Great, then here's what I think those bastards deserve,' she continued, 'we hack into their system and grab every bit of intelligence we can, potentially to use later, and add it to our growing database. Once you've retrieved their login info to bank accounts, we start by taking everything they have and transferring it overseas, as usual.'

'So far so good, but will that put them out of business if they can get help from China?' Trevor asked.

'No, but if Andy can access their insurance account, we can cancel their insurances on the building, business, vehicles, everything.'

'And then what?' Trevor asked, sensing where she was going with this and smiling proudly.

'Then we burn the bloody place to the ground, and everything in it, including the vehicles,' she finished. 'As a bonus, if we time it so that we empty their accounts while it's happening, they won't have a clue for days that they've been robbed.'

'Yep, that would be a setback, for sure,' Andy said. 'Remind me never to piss you off,' he added, smiling almost as proudly as her father.

'Glad you approve, you can get cracking on that, then, while I help Dad make our lunch.'

'Is it my turn again?' Trevor said, 'really?'

'Yes, really. If you can't be bothered to keep track then it'll always be your turn, so finish your beer and let's go and see what Andy has in his fridge.'

Andy grinned as he watched them make their way to the kitchen. He opened his laptop and fired up the Cyclops programme to access the Golden Dragon Foods CCTV system, thereby allowing him access via a *back door* that was almost always overlooked. People and businesses generally trusted their security systems, so they never considered them a potential threat. It took a few minutes of gentle probing as he continued to search the system, recognising it immediately as a high-spec Chinese-made system that was likely accessible to the same intelligence service that had blown up the factories. Andy nodded and immediately started inserting extra coding so that nothing could be traced back to him or his computer. Grinning mischievously, he added a few red herrings that would lead the Chinese agents to a Russian hacker that Andy had faced off with on many occasions.

'Childish, I know, but I'd pay money to see the look on his face when they go after him,' he murmured.

Continuing, he accessed the network as expected via the CCTV programme that ran continually, twenty-four hours a day. That led to the servers and ultimately the nineteen computers that they serviced. Andy isolated the one computer that belonged to the manager of the facility and was soon searching through the files.

'Bingo,' he said out loud, as he found the folder where the manager had recklessly left all the information Andy would need.

'That was quick, what have you found?' Kendra said, hearing his cry and coming to investigate. 'I found his login info. He has a folder with a Word document in it with the company logins and, weirdly, an app that is linked to his phone that has all the financial logins. From what I can see, they have four different bank accounts: two for business and two for something else, probably to do with their extra-curricular spy stuff,' he replied.

'So, you can access them now?' she asked, excited by the swift development.

'No, these guys are switched on and have good security in place. I need to get into his phone and clone it so I can block any messages and intercept the two-factor authentication, otherwise money transfers won't be authorised. Once I'm into the accounts I can change all the security settings and divert everything to me. It may take some time, but I'll crack on while you're sorting lunch out.'

'It's ready, didn't you hear me calling?' she asked.

'No, I was in the zone, sorry,' he said, grinning. 'I'll get back to this after I eat,' he said, closing the laptop.

'Don't expect anything fancy, there wasn't much in your fridge or your cupboards, so you'll have to settle for a smoked mackerel salad and some olives,' she said, grinning back.

'Wow, okay, sounds very appealing. Lucky we still have some doughnuts left for dessert, eh?'

'Nope, Dad and I finished those off when we saw what you had in your fridge!'

'Then it's a good job I like smoked mackerel and olives,' he said, grimacing.

'You're lucky to have that. By the way, Dad has grabbed the last tin of beans and is having them on toast, he doesn't like smoked mackerel... or olives... or salad.'

~

23

Kendra went into work the following day. As she was part-time, nobody asked questions if she was away for an extra day or two; she always made it up, and as her work was excellent, nobody minded.

Having exchanged pleasantries with her co-workers, especially with Jillian Petrou, she sat and started working through her emails from the past few days. The station atmosphere was back to normal now that Rick had been found and was safely back home. Everyone had resumed their previous duties with the odd exception where officers had been retained on the investigation to top and tail the paperwork.

'Where's our NCA mate Sisterson?' she asked Jill. She could see—and she expected—that Jim Adair would still be absent but expected his partner to be here, working away with his head down and being typically unsociable.

'Wow, you haven't heard? Where have you been, girl?' Jill asked, her arms outstretched in mock surprise.

'I had some personal stuff to deal with, miss nosy pants. Now, spill the beans, will you?' Kendra replied.

'He came in yesterday, packed his things up and just sat there in his chair, staring at the wall. After an hour or so a couple of detectives came and arrested him, took him away in handcuffs and everything,' Jill replied excitedly.

'What? Do you know why?' Kendra asked.

'Apparently, and this is only speculation, he confessed to helping the douchebag. They were old mates, apparently, and he tried to help him out when he was being investigated. Other than that, I haven't a clue and he hasn't been seen since.'

Kendra wasn't surprised that the Directorate of Professional Standards, who only investigated the conduct of police officers, had finally caught up with Sisterson; she just hadn't expected it so soon.

'Wait,' she said, 'he confessed? How do you know that?'

Jill looked around surreptitiously, to check she wasn't within earshot of anyone else.

'I heard the DI talking about it with Rick,' she whispered.

Kendra laughed.

'You mean you were snooping, don't you?' she asked, giggling.

'Call it what you will, I've overheard a lot of very useful snippets using that skill. Anyway, that's what the DI said,' Jill said.

'Hang on, you said he was speaking to Rick? Has he been in?' Kendra asked.

'Yes. He's in now, still talking with the DI in his office.'

'I thought he'd be away for a while,' Kendra said, wondering why he'd come in so soon.

'Maybe he's bored at home, I know I would be,' Jill said, standing. 'Anyway, enough chit-chat, I have an interview to conduct. Nab you later for a proper catch-up?'

'Sure, see you later.'

As Jill walked away, Kendra saw Rick entering the office. He looked towards her and stood still for a second, before indicating for her to join him in his office.

Uh-oh, she thought, *this can't be good*.

'Shouldn't you be at home recovering?' Kendra said as she walked into Rick's office.

'Sit down, Kendra,' Rick said, stony-faced. There were still visible bruises, giving him a sinister appearance, not unlike that of a boxer who has just been through ten rounds.

'Everything okay?' she asked.

'Good question,' he said. 'I should ask the same of you.'

Kendra's confused expression made Rick waver and he smiled a little.

'Honestly, if you could see your face now, knowing what I know, you'd laugh out loud,' he said.

'Seriously, Rick, stop messing about and tell me what the hell is going on,' she replied, somewhat agitated.

Rick leaned forward, his elbows resting on the desk, as he whispered theatrically to his subordinate.

'I know what you're involved in.'

'What am I involved in, Rick?' she asked, alarm bells ringing in her head.

'Well, let's start with a few questions, shall we?'

'Okay, go for it,' she replied.

'What were you doing last night?' he started.

'I was at home reading,' she lied.

Rick smiled and continued.

'What about the early hours of the morning? Were you alone?' he asked, not wanting to be too obvious.

'Yes, Rick, I was alone in bed. Bit of a creepy question, that one, if I may say so.'

'Don't worry, I only have one or two more. How long have you had your car now?' he asked.

Kendra's alarms were wailing as she paused before answering.

'I don't know why you're asking this, but I'll play along. I've had it for about two years now,' she replied.

'Did you drive today or were you picked up? Last one,' he continued.

'Yes, I drove in. It's parked downstairs. Is this an integrity thing, you think I've been drinking and driving or something?'

'No, Kendra. I don't think you're drinking and driving or anything remotely like that. What I do know is that you're definitely lying to me. Now that worries me a lot, so my actions moving forward will now depend on how our conversation here goes from this moment onwards. Do you understand?' he asked, his expression grim again.

Kendra knew something was very wrong and tried to maintain a neutral expression.

'I understand,' she replied.

Rick picked up a brown folder from his desk and took out some documents. He spread them out in front of Kendra, watching her expression change from neutral to concerned.

'This is a transcript from the early hours of this morning, of a hard stop conducted by two armed response units. They were acting on information and an ongoing commentary by Detective Constable Kendra March who had called 999 to inform them that she was being followed by two potentially armed and dangerous fugitives, who happened to be ex-police officers responsible for my kidnapping and assault,' he said.

He paused to allow Kendra to respond. She had nothing to say.

'I know about this because I witnessed the stop seconds after it happened, where I saw your car driving from the scene. I wanted to be sure so I contacted the Information Room and asked for this transcript, which confirmed my suspicions,' he continued.

Kendra's stomach lurched.

'I... I... don't know what to say, Rick. I didn't think anyone needed to know,' she stammered.

'I haven't finished,' he continued. 'Do you have anything you want to tell me?'

She shook her head.

'Do you know how I was able to witness the stop and your car driving off?'

Again, she shook her head. Not so convincingly, this time.

'I witnessed it from the back of a car that had three very nice gentlemen in it, the same gentlemen who had rescued me from Duckmore and Critchley. I even know one of their names, Darren. Top bloke, he is, top bloke. All three of them were. And guess what?' he said.

This time she shrugged her shoulders in resignation.

'Nothing? Okay, I'll continue. They tried their best, you know, making phone calls away from the car, keeping names out of their conversations, that sort of thing. They're skilled, I'll give them that. But you know what they couldn't do?'

Again, another imperceptible shrug.

'They couldn't stop me from recognising that they were there to have your back in case anything happened. Do you know what that told me?'

This time she didn't even bother to shrug, she knew she was in deep, deep trouble.

'Still nothing? I'll tell you, Kendra. It told me that you know them and are probably working closely with them. That's what it told me. You're working with a non-sanctioned, non-commissioned, non-licensed and highly illegal team of people to do things that you should not be doing. Am I close?'

This time she met his glare and straightened her back, defiant in the face of the onslaught.

'Yep, I see I'm close. Unfortunately, that is about all I know, but it's enough, isn't it? It's enough for me to instigate an investigation into your actions and into any involvement you have as a serving police officer. I'm guessing it'll be the end of your career and a very likely prison term. How'd you feel about that then, Kendra?' he asked, his questions finally coming to an end.

'Have you finished?' she asked, her tone cold and some-what rebellious.

'I have. I'm waiting on you to respond, Kendra,' he said, leaning back and folding his arms.

It took her a few seconds to formulate her response. In those few seconds she could see no alternative but to answer in the manner that she was about to.

'I have nothing further to add, Detective Sergeant. If you

feel the need to instigate an investigation then please go ahead, but I will say nothing more on this matter. Until then, unless I'm under arrest, I'll be taking a few days off sick, so please excuse me,' she said, standing.

'Sit down, Kendra, I do have something I want to add,' he said, waving her back into the chair.

'I know you had something to do with saving my life. For that alone I will be forever grateful. For that alone I will not pursue any action against you or your team. For that and because of the fact that I can see how frustrating a job this is turning into, I need to ask a couple more questions.'

'I'm listening,' she said.

'Is your team involved in any murders?'

'No,' she replied.

'Does your team commit crimes that affect innocent people?'

'Not adversely, no.'

'Does your team commit acts that help innocent people?'

'Yes.'

'Have you been using police resources to assist with your cause?'

'Yes,' she replied, knowing that this answer alone would potentially lose her the job that she loved.

'Final two questions. Firstly, would you be able to continue with your cause if you had no access to police assets?'

'We would, but nowhere near as effectively,' she replied.

'Final question. What do I need to do to join your team?'

24

'It's great to hear from you, mate,' Trevor told Brodie when he'd called. 'What's happening on your end? Are you back in charge yet?'

'I'm making a few changes, Trev, me ol' mate. That shit isn't happening to us again, it was way too easy to take over and that was a massive wake-up call,' Brodie replied.

'Anything we can help with?'

'Not really. I just wanted you to know that I'm weeding out the problem areas in the organisation and placing Zane in charge of it in London. I'm relocating to Essex and my new farmhouse where I can run things from a distance. It'll be safer and more secure this way. I'll keep you in the loop if we need anything, and likewise, if you need a leg-up anytime, just let me know,' Brodie added.

Although Brodie had helped with manpower against the Albanian gangs, the team had now grown and no longer needed support in that way. It was deemed much safer. Trevor, his affiliation with Brodie going back many years, trusted the gangster and had helped him just as much, along with a number of youngsters who had preferred Brodie's lifestyle to his own, more legal way of living.

'That's a big change, mate. I'm sure you know what you're doing. If you send me the address I'll try and pop up one day,' Trevor added.

'I'm in the process of renovating it. The place looks and smells like shit, and my missus won't come anywhere near it until it's been sorted out. Give it a few weeks and I'll send you an invite,' Brodie said, 'we have a lot to catch up on.'

'Look forward to it, mate. In the meantime, you know how to find me, take care,' Trevor replied, hanging up.

Trevor leaned back and took a sip of coffee, thinking of his long affiliation with Brodie and the ironic relationship they had.

I made some solid friends in my army days, but Brodie Dabbs was a weird one, that's for sure! he thought.

His phone rang again. Seeing that it was Kendra, he smiled and answered straight away.

'Hello, love, you at work yet?'

'Dad, we have a serious problem. I'll meet you and Andy at his house in about half an hour, okay?'

'Sure, I'll see you there.' He knew that asking questions would not work, so he grabbed his car keys and left immediately.

'There goes my relaxing morning,' he said out loud as he made his way to the car.

~

Kendra was already there when he arrived twenty-five minutes later.

'She didn't say a word, just came in, grabbed a drink and sat down,' Andy said. 'Do you know what this is all about?'

'Not a clue, let's find out, shall we?' Trevor replied, walking to the lounge.

Kendra sat in the lounge with a bottle of beer in her hand, waiting for them to join her.

'What's going on, K?' Trevor asked, sitting opposite.

She looked back and forth at them both before replying.

'Remember I warned you that Rick Watts was a wily old goat and to be cautious with him? Well, he knows,' she said.

'Knows what?' Andy asked, confused.

Trevor had known that whatever Kendra needed to talk about was serious but hadn't expected this.

'He knows about us, love?'

'Yes, Dad. He knows about us. He saw me drive away from the stop yesterday and figured it all out. Caught me out with a few devious questions, too. That's not all,' she said.

'Is he coming after us?' Andy asked, knowing how resourceful his former boss was.

'Nope.'

'He's sending investigators after us?' Trevor asked.

'Nope.'

'Then what's the problem?'

'He wants to join the team,' she said, her eyes flitting between Andy and her dad.

Andy was the first to respond, his face clearly showing shock and confusion as he stood, his arms outstretched.

'What? Why? Is he serious? Bloody hell!'

Trevor was more sedate in his response.

'Kendra, are you telling me that your boss wants to join

our vigilante-slash-dispenser of justice-slash-crime-committing team?' he asked calmly.

'Yes, Dad. That's exactly what I'm telling you. As long as we don't kill people and are doing what we do to help people, then he's all for joining us.'

'And if we say no, what happens?' Andy asked.

'Nothing. He made it clear that he isn't blackmailing us, he won't tell anyone our little secret and we can carry on as normal. I believe him,' she said.

'Darling, if you believe him and trust him then I don't have a problem with him joining us. I do have a problem with him thinking he's your boss here, though, so we need to lay down some ground rules if we're gonna let him in,' Trevor added.

'Yep, he's already thought of that too. He doesn't want to get involved in everything, doesn't need to come here or get involved in our live operations. He wants to help from work, using the police databases and intelligence to do some good that way. He's also well connected and can guide us in other ways. Honestly, I couldn't find a good enough reason to say no. He's grateful to us for saving his life and he sees that we're doing a lot of good.'

'Man, he's gonna have a coronary when he sees me,' Andy said, laughing out loudly.

'Yep, he is,' she said, grinning.

'I guess that's settled, then. Let's not overload him too quickly. He doesn't need to know everything just yet, so we can keep some things back until he needs to know, is that fair?' Trevor said.

'Sounds like a plan to me,' Kendra replied. 'I'll let him know and welcome him aboard,' she said, walking out to make the call.

'I did not see that coming,' Andy said, shaking his head and sitting back down.

'Are you worried?' Trevor asked.

'No, Rick is one of the good ones. I honestly don't know how he'll react when he sees me. I was a bitter and twisted ex-colleague, remember? I never returned their calls and purposely kept away from them. When he finds out, I may get a slap from him, too,' Andy said, grinning.

'I'm sure he'll understand, Andy. Also, that's my perk, he can find someone else to slap.'

Kendra came back into the room.

'That was quick,' Andy said.

'I just told him that he was in and that we'd be in touch when things have calmed down a little. He's good as gold,' Kendra said, sitting back down.

'You ok, love?' Trevor asked.

'I am now, yes. Glad he's on board and not against us. I definitely need this beer,' she said, taking a swig.

'Amen to that,' Andy said, doing the same.

The trio ordered and then quickly consumed two large pizzas and a box of barbeque wings as they mulled over some questions regarding Rick and the future of the team.

'While you're both here, you should know that I have everything ready to go. Just give me the word and I can empty some bank accounts. Also, the files are ready for you to deliver to the journalists. As you can imagine, I didn't get much sleep last night, but I'm dead chuffed because I've been doing some of my best work.'

'That's great, Andy, well done,' Kendra said.

'I'll take the folders and get them to the journalists,' Trevor said. 'They're all based in London, so I'll use a bike courier to deliver them direct.'

'I'll speak to the twins about the wholesaler in Dagenham. Amir will love setting that place alight,' Kendra said. 'I'll call you when they're about to go in so you can do your hacking thing,' she added.

'Great, I'll go and grab the folders for you, Trevor,' Andy said, leaving the room.

'We may as well do this tonight; no sense in waiting, is there?' Trevor said as Andy returned with the evidence folders.

'Don't forget to put something together about Hurricane Solutions for Marcus Allen,' Kendra said, wanting all loose ends to be tied up. 'He'll be able to sort that lot out.'

'Don't worry, that's also ready to go. If you have an email address for him, I can send the file anonymously, he won't be able to trace it back to us.'

'Yeah, that works. I have his contact card, so I'll scan it and message it to you,' she replied.

'Is there anything else we need to do?' Trevor asked.

'I think that's more than enough, don't you, Dad?'

'Then let's put this saga to bed, once and for all,' Trevor said, grabbing the folders. 'I'll see you two later.'

'Bye, Dad,' Kendra replied as Andy waved him off.

'I'll go and get that data ready,' Andy said. 'Send that email over and I'll get it out now.'

'Will do. I'll call Mo while you're doing that,' Kendra said.

Mo answered after one ring.

'Wow, Mo, are you psychic or something?' She laughed.

'I wish. No, I'm waiting for that idiot brother of mine to call me back. What can I do for you?'

'We're going to cause some damage to our wholesaler friends tonight, and need you and Amir to go and set fire to their warehouse. You up for that?'

'Does a bear shit in the woods? You know better than to ask that, knowing full well that my brother loves burning things!' Mo laughed.

'Glad to hear it. I'll message you later when we're ready for you to go in. Can you prep Amir and be ready for tonight?'

'Will do, Kendra. Speak later.'

That should put the cat amongst the pigeons, she thought, thinking of the damage to the triad organisation that the fire and theft would accomplish. It wouldn't wipe them out, they had more soldiers in London and beyond, but it would take many years for them to recover fully, if ever.

Almost done, she thought, looking forward to a few days rest when it was all over.

BY THE EARLY EVENING, they met again when Trevor returned from his errand.

'All three folders have been delivered, let's see who does what and how quickly they do it,' he told Andy and Kendra.

'I imagine something will be in the news tomorrow, if they're as good as people say,' Kendra replied.

'Good, the sooner those corrupt bastards are taken out of circulation, the better,' Andy added.

'Mo and Amir have been to the wholesaler and checked

the area over again. They'll be going in the same way as our rescue party did and setting the fires strategically so that the place goes up quickly and too late for the fire brigade to save it,' Kendra said.

'I've also emailed our Government Security Advisor friend about Hurricane Solutions and linked to the folders we sent to the journalists. He will not be impressed that the company aided a foreign government to cause such problems and damage on our shores,' Andy said.

'So, now we wait,' Trevor said. 'I don't suppose it matters what time of the day or night the fire starts, does it?'

'Not really. Once the main staff have gone home, there are only half a dozen or so left overnight so we won't be putting lives at risk. I told Mo to make sure they factor into their plan for the staff get out safely,' Kendra said.

'Great. I suggest you call Mo and get them to do their thing in an hour. Andy, can you work your magic at that time also?' Trevor asked.

'Absolutely, I can,' Andy replied, rubbing his hands together.

'Already messaged Mo and got a thumbs-up,' Kendra said.

'Fab, should be an interesting night, love!'

The triad soldiers had woken from their stupor and were now sitting on crude benches in one of the unused hangars at the Royal Air Force base at Odiham in Hampshire, their hands cuffed at the front and their ankles chained to the rail that was securely screwed to the concrete floor. They'd been given a sandwich and a bottle of water and waited their turn to be interrogated by the anonymous investigators. They had not resisted after being threatened with handguns by the dozen armed Royal Marine Commandos who guarded them twenty-four hours a day.

The team leaders and bosses who had been captured had been taken to a separate building for more intensive questioning. The two dozen men were not so robust when away from their soldiers and threatened with solitary imprisonment for life for the crimes against the United Kingdom. Useful intelligence was gathered and fourteen of them claimed asylum, knowing that a return to China would mean instant death.

The five intelligence agents that were responsible for much destruction were taken to yet another building where they were prepared for their interrogation by the interpreter that had been assigned to them.

'My advice is that you all cooperate and tell them everything they ask for,' she had told them all, separately.

When the escort for the first agent went to retrieve him for questioning, they found him dead on the floor of his cell, his eyes wide open and a frothy white substance on his mouth. He was pronounced dead a short time later by the company doctor. Upon checking in on his four colleagues, the investigators found them all to be dead, with the same symptoms. It was later found that they had chomped on the cyanide pills embedded in their back teeth, instant death preferable over disgrace and dishonour due to the failure of their mission.

Despite this, much evidence was gathered by the investigators, more than enough to implicate China and its intelligence service in deliberate sabotage and potentially an act of war against the United Kingdom. This evidence was taken away and stored for use later, where it would become an invaluable tool when dealing with China on important matters.

In China, the organisers of the operation had realised that their mission had failed, and its objectives only partially met. Phone calls were made to the Ghost Dragons leadership in China, who in return made several calls to the UK. They had to act in some way to save face, and there was only one acceptable solution.

DUCKMORE AND CRITCHLEY HAD, as instructed by their solicitor, made no replies to any of the questions put to them by the interviewing detectives. They had both remained impassive as questions relating to Rick Watts' kidnap and assault were put to them, along with allegations of drug importation when a large quantity had been found at their storage facility at the docks. Even evidence including their fingerprints at the scene did not elicit a response.

'Just hope they screw the investigation up and we'll try and go for the sympathetic jury who will no doubt feel sorry for the way you were treated,' the solicitor told them.

They were now on the way back from the first hearing at the Magistrates Court, having waited for many hours, and made their brief appearance at the end of the day to confirm their details and that they'd be kept in custody without any chance of bail while they awaited trial. Their transport eventually arrived late in the day to take them back to their cells. They'd be taken the next day to a prison outside London where they'd remain until their case was heard, which was likely to be many months away.

As the armoured vehicle that was taking them away drove off from the court, the motorcyclist that was watching from a distance dialled a number and made his long-awaited call. 'It's on the move; our friend inside told us that it would be this one,' he said, getting onto the bike and starting the engine. Seconds later he was also on the move behind the van, following some fifty metres behind with several vehicles for cover. He was joined by his fellow surveillance colleagues who drove a variety of vehicles, all designed to follow subjects in London. Throughout the forty-minute journey to east London holding cells, the team gave regular commentary for each other's benefit, in real time, to ensure that their next course of action was successful.

The meticulous planning and the execution of the plan was a result of the phone call from China. As the vehicle carrying Duckmore and Critchley entered the last phase of its journey, the signal was given.

'Stand by, stand by,' the team leader said, 'Bison One, prepare to execute. Blocking units into position.'

'Received by Bison One,' came the response.

As the transport entered the industrial estate, quiet at this time of the evening, Bison One made its catastrophic entrance. The old dump truck, bought in cash to serve one last purpose, was fully loaded with seven tons of rubble and drove into the side of the prisoner transport at forty miles per hour. The armoured vehicle did not stand a chance and tumbled violently onto its side, sliding along for twenty feet before coming to a halt. There was a huge gouge in its side as its wheels continued to spin and the engine finally cut out.

'Leopard One, execute,' came the calm voice of the team leader. 'Blocking units execute.'

'Received by Leopard One,' came the reply, along with acknowledgements by several blocking units.

Seconds later, another cash-bought vehicle came into view, as simultaneously the road was cut off to vehicles by the blocking team and its imaginary roadworks. The JCB excavator was instantly recognisable by its yellow colour and the giant black lettering on its side as it trundled into view. Tired and faded from many years of use, it still had a mighty punch and was quickly at the side of the fallen prison transport. The excavator raised its bucket to the maximum elevation before releasing it into the side of the van where the door was. The impact from the dump truck had caused much of the damage already and had weakened the hidden hinges. It took four blows from the giant bucket before the door flew open, the hinges now sheared.

Three masked men ignored the unconscious driver and passenger and entered the van's rear where the prisoners were secured in their small cubicles. There were only two that were occupied and the occupants were both stunned but conscious.

Duckmore looked at the armed man standing before him, recognising the outfit and stance as those of the Ghost Dragons. He smiled, despite the pain from the blow he'd received to his head.

'Ah, our rescuers. Red Master is pleased,' he said, grinning at the man before him.

The man fired two shots from the Glock 17, one to the head and one to the chest. Instant kill shots. Duckmore's last act in the second of life he had left was to empty his bowels. He didn't even have time to register shock. Two more shots came from an adjoining cubicle as Dave Critchley met a similar fate.

The attack team were out of the van and away moments later. The dump truck and JCB were already abandoned, and the bollards and roadwork signs were also abandoned. The driver and passenger, now both awake, called for assistance, which would take many minutes to arrive.

Duckmore and Critchley were pronounced dead at the scene.

The attackers were never found, and nobody ever admitted responsibility.

25

Mo and Amir found no problems getting into the grounds of the Chinese wholesaler facility. Having already been victims of the incursion to rescue Rick, the owners hadn't considered that it could happen again so soon, so the security was much the same as it had been before the rescue. The twins both carried small backpacks with several plastic bottles that included paraffin, some lengths of cord and a couple of lighters each, just in case.

Having looked at the plans for the buildings and receiving the information from the rescue party who'd been here previously, they both knew where they wanted to plant the simple incendiary devices they'd brought. As they got close to the building line, out of sight of the CCTV cameras, the brothers looked at each other and gave the thumbs-up signal that meant they were parting ways. Mo went around the side towards the giant stack of wooden pallets that was waiting collection, along with a mountain of cardboard that had been tied in bundles and was destined for recycling. He wedged one of the bottles of flammable liquid into some cardboard, the top pointing slightly upwards to avoid spillage, and removed the lid. Placing the cord inside, which was filled with paraffin and other materials to allow for instant combustion, he lit the cord and walked away.

Their plan was a simple one. This fire would be the diversion that would bring the lone security guard away from his post and also some, if not all, of the warehouse staff to see what was happening. This would allow Amir easy entry inside, where he'd set a few more fires upstairs, while Mo would stay downstairs and do the same. All they had to do was avoid detection, and they'd achieve their objective: the total destruction of the premises and everything within it.

Amir was inside and upstairs almost the moment the security guard saw the glow from the fire and shouted for help. The offices were empty, so it was easy for him to open a couple of filing cabinets and throw the contents to the floor, making a nice heap of paper close to the wooden furniture. He placed one bottle and lit the cord before moving to another room, this time a storeroom that doubled as an archive, with floor-to-ceiling stacks of files along with a desk and computer. He grinned as he repeated the process and left the door open, moving on to one last room.

The boardroom was luxuriously appointed with deep navy-blue carpet and detailed wooden carvings depicting battle scenes from ancient China. The chairs around the ornate oak table were thickly padded, making them an instant target for Amir. Using his small pen knife, he slashed a number of chairs and pulled out the foam padding, scattering it over the chairs. He placed a bottle next to the table and lit the cord.

As he went back downstairs, he could already smell the

burning and he smiled at his successful mission. He made his way cautiously to the exit where he could hear the staff shouting in alarm at the roaring fire that they had attempted to put out. The security guard was with them. He slid along the wall and disappeared into the gloom, making his way towards their pre-appointed exit, where they had climbed in. He didn't need to wait for long, as Mo suddenly appeared out of the gloom, wearing a big grin.

'That was fun, bro,' he told his younger brother, 'I can see why you enjoy it so much.'

'You should listen to me more, you'd have a lot more fun if you did,' Amir said, as they climbed over and into the side road.

As they drove past a few minutes later, they could see that a number of fires had taken hold upstairs and also in the warehouse, below. The fire brigade would no doubt get there soon, but the fires were already so well established that they would struggle to put even one of them out. The fires would then merge into one huge one that would raze the building— and the business—to the ground.

'The fire in the alcohol section is gonna bring this whole place down on its own, bro. It was floor-to-ceiling with spirits in there, it's gonna burn really well.'

'I taught you well, Mo. Now, can we get a nice kebab on the way home?' Amir said, grinning as Mo took out his phone to make the call.

∾

'That was Mo,' Trevor said. 'The place is well and truly on fire. That's your signal, Andy.'

Andy's fingers flew over the keyboard as he instigated the programmes to access the four bank accounts. A few minutes later, the two-factor authentication codes were sent to his cloned phone where only he could see them. Once the codes were in his possession, it was just a matter of time before the transactions were made and the funds transferred to offshore bank accounts via two crypto accounts that would render them impossible to track back to the team.

Fifteen minutes was all it took to empty the four accounts and for the funds to be transferred to the two main accounts that Andy had set up in the Cayman Islands, in the names of *Sherwood Management Trust* and *Loxley Investments*. Funds that would go towards running the team and, most importantly, to help deserving causes and individuals.

'It's done,' Andy finally said, shaking his hands to relax his fingers again.

'How much, this time?' Trevor asked.

'Four point eight million pounds, minus some crypto fees. We can help a lot of people with that,' he said, smiling proudly.

'Great job, mate,' Trevor said, nodding in acknowledgement and respect.

'Yes, well done, Andy. Another great job,' Kendra said, giving him a peck on the cheek.

He blushed but knew better than to say anything, knowing it would come out as gibberish.

'How about something a little fancier to eat, tonight?' Kendra said, looking to each of them for support.

'I'd be up for that, we haven't cooked anything fancy for a while,' Andy replied, his blush gone. 'How about a nice lasagne with some fresh salad? It isn't the fanciest meal, but I could definitely enjoy some of that.'

'Sounds good to me,' Trevor said. 'I'll call the team and update them while you're doing that.'

'Let's go, mister blusher man,' Kendra said, grinning as she took Andy by the hand and pulled him towards the kitchen.

'When did I blush?' he said, feigning ignorance, 'stop making things up. I don't blush.'

'Really? Okay, let's see what happens now,' she said, taking out her phone.

'What are you gonna do with that?' he asked, confused.

'Looking back at him, she reached up and kissed him fully on the lips. She then stood back and held the camera phone up to his face as he gradually turned crimson.

'Not. Fair,' was all he could manage.

'No, but it was a lot of fun, and now I have proof,' she said, leaning forward and kissing him again, this time gentler.

'Evil woman,' he whispered, as he followed her into the kitchen, where she continued to laugh.

The news started filtering through the following after-noon. Fifteen government officials in senior positions, including three judges, two Members of Parliament, three senior police officers, and one executive officer at MI5 along with civil servants in prominent positions were arrested simultaneously, most at their places of work before they finished for the day. The press was there for each and every one of them, thanks primarily to the journalist who had taken the evidence to his police contact first. It was a huge coup for the journalist and significant news, despite the fact the police wouldn't disclose fully what evidence they had. The arrests were made under the Treason Act, leading to much speculation, none of it close to the truth, as the public intrigue grew.

One news story that wasn't made public was the arrest of several executives involved with Hurricane Solutions, as Marcus Allen used the evidence supplied to him to start the process that would lead to more convictions of treason and the complete closure of the company. Andy had contacted an associate on the dark web to confirm this, otherwise they'd have had no idea.

'My contact told me that the police had raided the offices just before lunch and taken all the executives away, along with all the computers and boxes of records. The staff were turfed out of the offices and the building locked up by police,' he told Kendra and Trevor as they watched the news about the other arrests.

'So that's that, then? The rest is down to the military, I suppose,' Kendra said.

'I have another snippet of news. Our chums Duckmore and Critchley were shot and killed yesterday when the van carrying them back to their holding cells was ambushed. They won't be bothering anyone else ever again,' Andy added, his voice sombre.

'Bloody hell. I hated the bastards but that's pretty harsh, isn't it? I'm guessing the triads took a dislike to their failure and wanted to tie up all loose ends?' Kendra asked.

'I guess we'll never know. I for one won't miss them,' Trevor said.

'Oh, I won't miss them, Dad. I'd have just preferred that they'd spent the next fifty years in prison, that's all.'

'Well, it's not for us to concern ourselves with them anymore, so let's just take a deep breath and enjoy some well-earned rest, eh?' Trevor said.

'How about a jaunt down the river in *Soggy Bottom*?' Andy asked, holding up his captain's cap.

~

EPILOGUE

Christine Marlowe stood on the steps of the Admiralty Building, standing proudly in front of the press, her arm in a sling.

'As you know, there were a number of attacks on companies that were involved in the production of military equipment to Taiwan under the recent trade agreement. This included Rayburn Technologies, Carter Mills, and Iris Aviation. The destruction of their factories was complete and devastating, but what the attackers failed to understand is the resilience of our nation and of the companies such as the ones that were affected,' she said.

She paused, standing upright, her expression defiant, before continuing.

'As a result of this onerous act of sabotage, the Government has pledged to fast-track support for all three companies so they can continue to meet their orders. Additionally, after consultation with Taiwan, we can now announce that we will in fact be increasing our support to them with a revised trade agreement for a longer period of time. This will include on-site support as we build new factories in Taiwan to help meet the demand and the allocation of funds to support the companies throughout the term of the agreement. So, to those responsible, I tell you this. Not only have you failed in your quest to sabotage our agreement, but you have in fact improved it and strengthened our relationship with Taiwan. We will come out of this much stronger, thanks to your evil intentions. I leave you with a parting gesture, one that the entire world is familiar with. Thank you very much.'

Christine Marlowe then raised her two-fingered salute, made famous by Winston Churchill.

The message was loud and clear.

THE END

BOOK 6 PREVIEW

'Justice'
Book 6 of the *'Summary Justice'* series
with DC Kendra March.

Prologue

Thirty years ago, London

'Goodnight, princess,' Amy March said to her baby, leaning down into the cot and kissing her on the cheek.

She stroked its warm face gently and pulled the woollen blanket over her, leaving just the chubby face exposed. The baby yawned and then smiled, struggling to keep her eyes open as her mother looked down at her.

'I can't believe you're already nine months old, you'll be running around in no time,' Amy said, imagining the tiny toddler running around at full speed and wreaking havoc.

Speaking to the baby always made her go to sleep quicker, and tonight it was no different.

Amy smiled as the baby finally stopped resisting and closed it eyes, continuing to smile ever so slightly as it slept. She stroked its little face once more and then left the small room, turning the light off on the way out but keeping the door slightly ajar.

'Thank God for giving me a baby that loves to sleep through the night,' she thought as she went downstairs.

In the kitchen she made herself a cup of chamomile tea, a nightly ritual that helped her rest well during the night, before sitting on the sofa in the lounge. The three bedroomed end-of-terrace house was less than ten years old and had been theirs now for just a year. The minute that she and Trevor had stepped foot inside to view it she knew that this was the house. Amy had smiled and turned to her beloved partner, nodding enthusiastically.

'This is the one, love,' she had whispered.

'Then this one it will be,' he had replied, kissing her gently on the lips and holding her hands against her slightly swollen tummy.

Their offer had been accepted and they moved in ten weeks later. Trevor, a soldier in the British Army, worked tirelessly during the few occasions he was on leave, making sure that it would be ready for the baby's arrival. The house was ready with a week to spare, so when they arrived back from the hospital with baby Kendra it was a fresh, new home for them, one to enjoy and cherish for many years to come.

Amy smiled at the memory, taking a sip of the chamomile tea as she thought fondly of her soon-to-be husband. The attraction had been instant when they'd met at an outdoor concert. He was with a group of squaddie friends and she with her cousin Tracey. They started dating and knew within weeks that they wanted to be together. It was a whirlwind, intensely romantic courtship, leading to disapproval from her father, and suggested restraint from Trevor's parents. They neither listened nor didn't care.

Only one thing bothered her, and that was the amount of time Trevor spent away from home, and the worrying effect it was having on him recently. He rarely spoke about his work, and she knew better than to ask too many questions. The last few times they had spoken had been a little strange... tense almost, as if something was playing on his mind but which he wouldn't share. Amy hoped that whatever it was that was distracting him so much would pass soon and they could go away for a much-needed holiday. She closed her eyes and dozed off, thinking of a sandy beach and the sound of waves.

Her dream then changed from the sandy beach to a darker moment from a week ago when she had heard someone trying to get into the house. She had quietly taken baby Kendra and hid in the loft, but only after calling the police and a nearby friend. She wanted someone, whoever it was, to come quickly. The police sirens had alerted the supposed intruders from gaining entry and they had fled in a car. Luckily, the friend, Charlie, had arrived in time to see a car speeding away from her road. He had taken the number down and given it to the police. Unluckily, the number had either been written down wrongly or the number was a fake one, so it wasn't traceable. The police did not investigate further and as there was no sign of attempted or forced entry the matter was quickly closed. The police told her and Charlie that they suspected it was a group of local teenagers whose MO was to out fireworks in people's letterboxes or other p ranks they found amusing.

It was the sound of the squeaky back door opening, the door that led from the kitchen to the garden, that woke her–that startled her, suspecting her subconscious had gone into overdrive. As she sat upright and turned towards the sound, her dreams of a perfect holiday were shattered by the appearance of two intruders, one male and one female, who rushed her before she could do anything. The former, a tall but stockily built black man dressed in jeans and an unusually bright orange t-shirt, grabbed one of her arms roughly. The latter, a tall, athletic white woman with dark brown shoulder length wavy hair and striking blue eyes, wearing a blue vest and brown shorts, grabbed the other arm, equally as rough.

'Let go!' Amy shouted, trying to wrestle free. Her immediate concern was for her sleeping baby, she prayed that Kendra would do her usual thing and sleep through everything and anything.

'She's a feisty one, this one,' the woman laughed, holding on tightly.

'Yes, she is. Her man is gonna be happy that we found her safe and well, eh?' the man replied, his gruff West Indian accent a contrast to the woman's American accent. For a split second, Amy thought it an odd couple to be here in northeast London.

'Please... take whatever you want, just leave me alone,' Amy pleaded.

'Now why would we do that, pretty lady? We want to take you to your man, make sure he knows you're safe and well with us, okay?' the man replied.

'My man? What are you talking about?' she asked, 'my partner is away working.'

'You mean, Tony? No, missy, he's been with us all this time. He's been a bad boy, you know, lots and lots of lies, so we found out who he really is and where he really lives and now, we are here,' he laughed.

'Tony? No, no, my partner's name isn't Tony, it's Trevor,' she pleaded again, praying they'd made a mistake.

'We know, dear, we know,' the woman answered, smiling malevolently at Amy.

'Time to go,' the man said, pulling her towards the door.

'No!' Amy suddenly cried, wrenching her arm free from the woman. She lashed out with her free hand and caught the man across the face with her fingernails, slashing the skin and drawing blood.

The man was strong and held onto her arm with a vice-like grip. He used his free hand to wipe the blood from his cheek. His eyes turned cold and angry, and as swift as a snake striking its victim, he backhanded her with his free hand across the side of her face.

Amy barely held onto consciousness as the vicious blow forced her back into the arms of the woman, who grabbed her free arm again, this time holding on tighter.

'Do that again, bitch, and he'll rip your head off,' the woman hissed angrily.

They dragged her from the lounge to the adjoining kitchen and dining area and out of the back door that led to her garden. The man placed his free hand across her mouth as they walked up the garden path running alongside the house and to the front, rivulets of blood running down his cheek from her scratches. Amy could see the gate had been opened and left ajar and her heart sank when she saw a white van parked on her drive, blocking any view her neighbours may have had of her abduction. As the approached the van the side door slid open and she was pushed roughly into the back of the van where another man grabbed her roughly and pinned her down while the woman taped her wrists behind her and stuffed a tea towel into her mouth, almost choking her.

'There you go, that wasn't too bad, was it?' the first man said, now let's go find Trevor, shall we?

'Boss, haven't you heard? The other, younger man suddenly asked.

'Heard what, man?'

'He had a fight earlier with Banjo and ran off. I thought you knew. They can't find him now and Banjo thinks he's the police,' the young man replied.

'Shit, that bastard. We need to phone the club and see if they found him yet, let's go,' the older man ordered angrily.

The younger man jumped into the driver's seat while Amy's captors stayed with her. The van moved off and was soon out of the estate and towards Hackney. They stopped by a telephone box soon after leaving the estate and the leader went to make a phone call. He was gone for a few minutes and returned angrier than ever.

'That bastard boyfriend of yours is a policeman, a damned fifth columnist, isn't he?' he shouted, referring to the term commonly used by the Yardies for infiltrators in their midst. 'They just raided my club and took three of my men away,' he shouted, kicking Amy viciously in the side.

Amy screamed in pain, confused and with no idea what was going on and what Trevor had gotten himself involved with. She made the decision to be defiant in the hope that it saved him from more grief later.

'Go screw yourself,' she shouted, 'he's not a policeman but he is a real man who doesn't beat women up.'

'Is he now? Well, let's see how much of a man he'll be when he finds out we have his woman, shall we?' the man laughed.

The van drove off and the driver was given whispered instructions by his boss. After just a couple of minutes they stopped, and the engine was switched off. It was dark outside and there was no passing traffic. When they opened the sliding door Amy could see they were in a remote area with no housing in her eye line, and very little street lighting. When they pulled her roughly from the back of the van, she realised that they were on a bridge that had recently been opened and part of a large construction project close to the M11 motorway.

'I'm gonna ask you one more time,' the man said, glaring into her eyes, 'is your man a policeman?'

Amy knew she was in deep trouble and looked around futilely for an escape. There was none. Her only hope was to tell the man what she knew and hope that she'd be spared.

'No,' she whispered, 'he's not a policeman. He's a soldier.'

The man looked at her and knew she was telling the truth.

'A soldier, eh? Then what is he doing working for me in my club?' he asked, his voice still menacing.

'Honestly, I don't know. He doesn't tell me about his work, I thought he was posted up North somewhere,' she replied truthfully. 'Please, sir, I think you've made a mistake. Please, just let me go. My man hasn't done anything to you, I'm sure.'

The man nodded and his expression softened. He took a penknife out and for a moment Amy thought that she was done for and stepped back instinctively. The man grabbed her hands and cut through the tape tying them together, peeling it off her wrists. Amy rubbed her wrists to help the circulation.

'Thank you,' she said.

The man looked at her and his eyes turned cold again.

'I don't make mistakes,' he said.

He suddenly picked Amy up by the waist and threw her over the side of the bridge. The forty-foot drop to the concrete below was fatal but didn't kill Amy instantly. She struggled for breath and tried to move to no avail. Her back was broken, and she couldn't see out of one eye, the impact to her head severe. She lived for a few minutes, struggling the entire time to get up and to try and walk back to her sleeping daughter. She hoped that Trevor would be back home soon to take them both away. To take them to the sandy beach that she'd dreamt about.

A passing motorist called the police who found her lifeless body an hour later.

The inquest that took place six weeks later. The police investigation found no evidence of foul play. There was no sign of forced entry into the house, no sign of any struggle, just a couple of drops of blood that could have been there for some while. The report suggested that pressures of being a mum whose partner was not present to assist with the baby brought on a mental breakdown that led to her committing suicide by jumping off the nearby bridge. Trevor and Amy's parents argued that this was not something that Amy would do, that she was a strong-willed woman who wanted nothing more than to bring up their daughter.

The inquest gave an open verdict, that there was insufficient evidence for any other verdict. The coroner explained that despite the police investigation and report, there was no evidence that Amy had any mental health issues nor that that there were any previous records of self-harming or suicide attempts. He also said that despite Trevor's insistence that there was foul play involved, there was no evidence to suggest that there was.

Amy March's death was reported in the local papers as a suspected suicide, despite the open verdict. Very few people sent sympathy cards or gave support to Trevor or Amy's parents, such was the stigma attached to suicide at this time. Trevor, distraught as he was, took Kendra to his parents who gladly took her in and raised her. He sold their dream house and moved further away, initially plunging into his work as an undercover operative in the British Army that took him to many dark, dangerous, and uncertain situations, before realising that his life had now changed immeasurably, and that the army life was not for him any longer. He resigned soon after.

The killers of his beloved Amy were never brought to justice for their heinous crime.

ACKNOWLEDGMENTS

My ongoing thanks to you, the reader, for continuing on this wonderful journey with me. I hope that you are still enjoying these books as much as I am writing them and especially in developing the characters within.

I'd like to thank Alastair Allen for his assistance with the armed support unit information, and Andrew 'Sam' Salmon for his detailed insight into the workings of the SBS and Three Commando Brigade.

Finally, a few words for my loved ones without who I would not be able to continue this journey, thank you for the love and support that drives me to put the words down each and every day.

Thank you, to you all.
TH

ABOUT THE AUTHOR

Theo Harris is an emerging author of crime action novels. He was born in London, raised in London, and became a cop in London.

Having served as a police officer in the Metropolitan Police service for thirty years, he witnessed and experienced the underbelly of a capital city that you are never supposed to see.

Theo was a specialist officer for twenty-seven of the thirty years and went on to work in departments that dealt with serious crimes of all types. His experience, knowledge and connections within the organisation have helped him with his storytelling, with a style of writing that readers can associate with.

Theo has many stories to tell, starting with the 'Summary Justice' series featuring DC Kendra March, and will follow with many more innovative, interesting, and fast-paced stories for many years to come.

For more information about upcoming books please visit theoharris.co.uk.

ALSO BY THEO HARRIS

DC Kendra March: The 'Summary Justice' series

***

Think you have gotten away with it? Think again!

Printed in Great Britain
by Amazon